FATE IS A WITCH

FREAKY FLORIDA BOOK 3

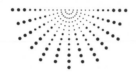

WARD PARKER

MAD MANGROVE MEDIA

CYBER-EEL

I t was not every day that a moray eel wriggled out of her laptop computer screen. Missy Mindle had never experienced a computer virus quite like this.

First, her page of internet search results about retirement planning for witches was taken over by a video of an underwater coral reef. In the video, a moray eel popped out of a hole in the reef and opened its jaws aggressively. As annoyed as she was at the attack on her computer, she was impressed by the high definition of the video, by how three-dimensional it appeared.

The eel had swum out of its hole toward her. It was brilliant green with blue, hazy eyes. Its body was fat and long, more like a fish than a snake. As it swam toward the camera, it opened its jaws revealing sharp teeth in an impossibly wide, open mouth. It was mean-looking, a pure predator. Missy backed away from the screen involuntarily.

She wondered if she were the victim of an illiterate hacker who created a fishing instead of a phishing attack.

But then things got serious and the impossible happened. The eel's snout poked through the plane of the screen. Internet World was intruding into Missy World.

She screamed as the head and the beginning of its body passed through the screen. Its head landed on her keyboard with a *clack*. Tiny drops of water rolled off onto the surface of her kitchen island.

As the eel slithered through it, the screen didn't break. It was as if it were made of gel that held the seawater back but allowed the eel through. And it passed through quickly.

She jumped up, knocking her stool over, as the eel snaked its way onto the keyboard and her kitchen island. It kept coming, more than three feet of it, writhing on the island, snapping its jaws at her.

She was so shocked, all she could do was back away while staring at the monstrosity that shouldn't exist.

The moray eel's entire length was now draped over her kitchen island. Her two gray tabby cats appeared in the kitchen doorway, curious about the intruder. Brenda stared, wide-eyed. Bubba tensed, preparing to leap onto the island.

"Bubba, no!"

The eel fixed its bluish eyes upon her and lunged.

She staggered backwards as the eel's fat body landed on the floor with a wet slap. It squirmed forward, snapping at her feet.

The cats disappeared from the kitchen in a microsecond.

Missy slipped outside the kitchen, opened the pantry door and grabbed a broom, swinging it, hitting the eel and pushing it backwards. It sank its teeth into the lower handle of the broom and wrapped its slimly body around the broom head.

Fighting off panic, she reminded herself that the eel was a marine creature, and out of the water it should be starving for oxygen any moment now.

The eel didn't get the memo. It kept coming at her, following her into the dining room.

"Get your freaking saltwater and slime off my hardwood floors," she said as she whacked it again with the broom. "Do you realize how much it cost to refinish them?"

The broom was less effective now in knocking back the eel. In fact, the eel seemed larger than before, the resistance of its weight against the broom was greater.

Yes, the thing was growing, she realized. And though its gills were quivering, it didn't appear to be getting anywhere close to asphyxiation.

She needed a better weapon. As she ran into her laundry room and opened the interior door to her garage, the clatter of wooden furniture knocked about came from the dining room behind her.

The dining room furniture included antiques. Now she was becoming just as angry as frightened.

She glanced around her one-car garage that had no room for a car. The collection of junk was dimly illuminated by the early-morning sun streaming in the single window. She didn't own a gun. Or a sword. Or a spear. The only weapon she immediately thought of was the shovel hanging from hooks on the wall beside her. She grabbed it and raced back to the dining room.

Only to find the table knocked on its side, half her chairs broken into kindling wood, and the glass door of her hutch shattered.

Then the eel writhed out from behind the keeled-over table.

The creature had grown large enough to swallow a large dog whole. Its head had to be three feet tall. As it moved away from the destroyed dining room set, its body kept coming: six feet, eight feet, ten.

It bared its carving-knife-size teeth at her and snapped its jaws, sending saltwater spraying.

"Okay, I see a shovel is not going to do the trick," she said aloud.

It was time for her magick. The eel was obviously created by some form of sorcery, so the only way to destroy it was through a spell of her own. The problem was, it can be difficult to cast a spell when you're panicked and running from room to room trying to avoid being eaten by a hellish creature straight out of a nightmare.

Further into her forties than she'd prefer to admit, Missy had finally come into her own as a witch. What used to be a hobby was now a vocation. What used to be hidden, undeveloped talents were now burgeoning powers. But she still had much to learn. Namely, how to fight an aquatic monster that had escaped from her laptop screen.

And was now sliming its way over the hardwood floors into the hallway, blocking her access into the living areas of the house. Her escape routes were either the bedrooms or the garage. Knowing that the cats would be under the bed in her bedroom, she led the creature away from them and bolted for the garage. Once inside, she slammed the door to the laundry room behind her, pulled her keys from her pocket, and locked the door. Not that eels can open doorknobs, but it just felt better to do it.

Now it was time to fight back. It was too late for a protection spell, because the creature was already in her house. Killing with magick was against her morals, so her best bet was a repelling spell. She had one that was great for mosquitoes, but an eel-monster was going to require a lot more juice.

But it occurred to her that repelling it from the house would involve broken doors, windows, or worse. And once it was outside, what then? She couldn't have a gigantic monster eel flopping around until it died on her front lawn. What would the neighbors say?

When you're involved with the world of the supernatural, discretion was the first law. Having to hire someone to bring in a dump truck and front-end loader to dispose of an eel carcass weighing hundreds of pounds was not discrete. Or, if the creature simply refused to die of asphyxiation, having it slither through her Florida neighborhood devouring pets and slow joggers was even less discrete.

She needed a different spell.

The door and entire wall shook as the creature flung itself at it trying to get to her. The rake and other yard tools fell to the garage floor.

Yes, she needed a different spell, and fast.

Calm down and concentrate, she told herself. There had to be a better solution. It was hard to concentrate, though, while the wall was shaking, and the door threatened to come off its hinges from body blows by a creature that shouldn't exist.

That's right, it shouldn't exist.

It was conjured into existence by a witch, wizard, mage, or some type of sorcerer. It was constructed with magic—she believed it was earth and sea magick of the sort she practiced and not black magic. Therefore, magick should be able to deconstruct it. A living creature would not be killed; a spell would simply be cancelled.

Right? A real eel hadn't been transformed into this morphing monster. After all, it came into her home via the internet.

Yet, it wasn't a pure phantasm. The wall shook again and sounded like it might give way soon. The conjurer who created it must be supremely skilled and powerful to give the eel actual mass. But maybe a less talented magician like herself could nevertheless find the right thread to pull to enable this creation to unravel.

Over the noise of the banging against the wall and the pounding of her heart, she willed herself into a meditative state. Grasping with her left hand a charm she kept in her pocket, she used its low-level power to relax and ignite her spell-casting abilities. Once her pulse and breathing slowed, her mood stabilized, and her mind cleared, she felt confident in her powers.

She formed a mental image of the eel. Her senses had sent data that tricked the mind into concluding that the creature was real and made of flesh, just as the brain turns twenty-four frames of video per second into real, moving imagery.

The conjuration also fed upon her belief that it was real, drawing power from that, and manipulating matter on the atomic level. This power could create sound and impact the molecules that made up the objects in her home.

It was artificial, but it could break things. And it could kill her.

As she zoomed into her mental image of the eel, using her imagination and transcendent magickal vision to see the eel as if using a microscope, she found the secret. The eel was not made up of living cells. No, it was constructed out of pixels and each of these was merely data—the ones and zeroes of computer code.

So her spirit reached out to the earth below her feet, to the magnetic energy deep within its core from pole to pole. She drew upon this energy, sipping upon it as if from a thermal spring. She amassed this electromagnetic energy inside her until her body hummed and her ears sang with it. She felt full to bursting.

And then she directed this mighty force against the elaborate apparition on the other side of the wall.

With her magick vision, she saw what happened. The electromagnetic energy hit the eel like a wave of water and instantly dissolved it, erasing the computer code and the billions of pixels it had created. It destroyed the eel as suddenly and easily as a magnet next to your wallet wipes your credit cards clean.

Good thing morays aren't electric eels, she thought.

The house was silent. She unlocked the door which now hung precariously from its hinges and peered into the laundry room. The washer and dryer had been knocked into odd positions. There were huge dents in the drywall on the garage-side wall.

There wasn't a single trace of water or slime anywhere.

She went into the house. Still no sign of water, although a couple of spots on the hardwood floors showed slight water damage. The dining room was a wreck. Her antique furniture had been broken and splintered like a bomb had gone off. That was not an illusion.

Her kitchen floor was dry and free of slime. Her laptop had been pushed to the very edge of the island, but it was open with the screensaver showing the word-of-the-day floating around the screen.

The word-of-the-day was "kudos."

Somehow, she felt it was directed to her.

She approached the laptop. She was a bit frightened of it now. Her trusty machine had delivered a monster into her life.

She touched a key to wake it up and typed in her password.

The video of the underwater coral reef still played. Various fishes, from clownfish to Bermuda chub, swam about. An invasive lionfish with its long barbs passed by. The soft corals and sea fans swayed gently in the current.

Her gaze was fixed upon the crevice in the reef from which the eel had emerged. She didn't want to see it again. She didn't want anything to come out of that hole. But she couldn't tear her eyes away from it or shut down her computer.

The camera began to slowly zoom into the reef, moving closer to the opening. She didn't want to see what was in there, but couldn't tear her eyes away.

No, it wasn't zooming. The camera was actually moving through the water, approaching the hole. Now it was entering it, into darkness.

The screen went black.

An image appeared on the periphery on the screen. The camera was moving out of the blackness. She realized it was moving away from the black pupil of an eyeball. Now she saw the grayish-blue iris and the white sclera. The eyelid blinked with long eyelashes. As more of the person's face was slowly revealed, it was clear that it was a woman's face. The camera pulled back farther.

It was her face. She was looking at her own face. It wasn't video footage, it was live.

Even though she had long ago covered the laptop camera with black tape.

Her face registered the shock she felt. Before the screen went black.

What am I going to do about those wrinkles around my eyes? she wondered.

Missy picked up the stool she had knocked over earlier and sat down, closing the laptop lid. Would she ever be able to trust her computer again? She gave the loud sigh of someone who was absolutely drained. Not only was the fear-induced adrenaline gone, not only was her mind exhausted from her mental calisthenics, but her body was a quivering mess after all the earth energy it had absorbed and then expelled into the eel.

Bubba jumped onto the kitchen island, sniffing the counter. He looked at her questioningly. His sister explored the floor below.

"It's gone," she said. "It wasn't even real to begin with, but I don't feel like trying to explain that to you."

She was the one who needed answers. Who conjured this creature? Though it wasn't of the material world, it certainly had an impact on the material world and could easily have killed her. And why was she the intended victim?

She remembered seeing "kudos" on her word-of-the-day screensaver. She wondered if that was just the screensaver's normal random choice of a word, or if it was a message to her. She wouldn't be surprised if it was, since the magician had obviously gained control of her computer.

Why would this person try to kill her and then congratulate her for escaping? Was this some kind of perverted test?

Whatever the answers, she feared she would be attacked again. She was almost certain of it.

2

ABRA CADAVER

Sergeant Ty Montgomery's motorcycle led the funeral procession the four miles from the church to the cemetery. At each intersection he would turn on his flashing lights and stop traffic while the fourteen cars, headlights on, passed through. Then he'd hop back on his bike and speed to the front of the motorcade.

One of the vehicles in the procession was weaving. Not dangerously, but enough to indicate the driver was intoxicated. It was a rusted-out, red Chevy pickup with a Confederate flag fluttering from a pole installed in the bed of the truck.

Montgomery was a kind-hearted soul and intended to look the other way. His main duty was to lead the procession and keep the cars together. He didn't want to ruin the funeral by arresting a mourner. He understood that some people turn to alcohol when grieving. As long as the truck stayed in its lane, he would allow it to get to the cemetery.

However, while he was stopping traffic in the intersection of Jellyfish Beach Boulevard and Pine Lane, the pickup truck almost clipped his bike when it drove by. He rolled it out of the way at the last moment. A few seconds later, three empty cans of cheap beer flew out of the cab and landed on the road.

Okay, Montgomery thought, I'm going to arrest this idiot as soon as the funeral is over.

The procession arrived at the cemetery without further incident, and Montgomery guided the vehicles through the gate and onto the perimeter road. He parked his motorcycle and leaned against a gatepost to watch the service. The gravesite was only about fifty feet away.

The three occupants of the pickup truck, three bearded Caucasian men who appeared to be brothers, climbed unsteadily from the cab. They wore ill-fitting powder-blue tuxes that must have been from their high-school proms years ago. His concern grew when he saw them stagger over to the rear of the hearse to join the pallbearers gathering there.

This could be a problem, Montgomery thought.

And sure enough, the three inebriated men lined up on one side of the end of the hearse. Supervised by the funeral director, they each grabbed a handle of the casket as it was eased out of the vehicle. There was no wheeled cart to roll the casket to the grave. This was going to be old-school, carry-the-box.

Montgomery clenched his jaws and actually said a prayer on behalf of the deceased's family, imploring God to prevent from happening what Montgomery was envisioning.

At first, the six pallbearers moved in a straight and steady manner toward the open grave. Then, one of the drunken brothers stumbled slightly, but the other pallbearers corrected the lurch, and all was well again.

Next, the casket began drifting off course. The three brothers were leaning into the casket, steering it toward the tent and the people seated on rows of folding chairs, until the sober pallbearers on the other side of the casket managed to push back and correct course toward their destination: the low platform positioned at graveside.

Someone shouted. And then the brother in front tripped and went down. The second brother tripped over the first one's prone body and fell. Then the third brother, unable to support his side of the casket all by himself, went down as well.

And what Montgomery had feared came to pass: The casket tipped, dropped, and landed on its side, amid the horrified gasps and cries of the crowd. The lid snapped open and the deceased occupant popped out onto the ground.

Except it wasn't the deceased. It was a couple of bags of cement mix. Otherwise, the casket was empty.

It would seem the funeral home had some explaining to do.

MATT ROSEN, staff writer at *The Jellyfish Beach Journal*, often covered Florida Man stories. The funeral debacle was a colorful example of one of these, combined with a greater crime the likes of which was classic Sunshine State: the bizarre theft of a body and possible fraud.

It was Florida Man times ten.

Matt had previously covered vandalism at a cemetery in Miami where grave robbers stole bones to be used in black magic. And he'd reported a story about a crematorium that secretly sold bodies to be used by a college's embalming class. But he'd never reported on a case of a dead body being switched, after the wake and before the burial, with dead weight.

The question, of course, was where did the body go? He inquired with the state regulatory body, the Division of

Funeral, Cemetery, and Consumer Services. They had nothing to tell him. The Florida Department of Law Enforcement, FDLE, was leading the criminal investigation but so far refused to answer any of Matt's questions.

Matt did learn from the local police that the body missing from the funeral, the owner of a bowling alley, had died in a freak bowling-ball avalanche. Understandably, he had had a closed-casket wake. This fact opened the possibility that the body hadn't been embalmed, meaning it had greater value on the black market. Searching South-Florida news sites, Matt learned this was not the first incident of missing bodies in recent months.

The funeral director and manager of the Jellyfish Beach Memorial Funeral Home was Izzy Perez. He sat at his desk across from Matt, and behaved as if he were as much a victim as the family of the missing dead guy.

"With all the changes in the funeral industry, reputation is still critical," the skinny man with a shaved head and tiny goatee said. "This could be a big blow to us. That's why I humbly ask you to be fair in your reporting."

"Of course," Matt said.

"I was bought out by a conglomerate four years ago and they keep pressuring me to produce more revenues. Business is normally great in Florida. You know, 'God's waiting room.' But how can I help it if people live healthier lives today?"

"They say that life expectancies are decreasing lately," Matt said. "Look at the bright side."

"True, but our parent company has already factored that into our revenue goals." The man quivered with nervousness. "I had to refund the bereaved family. Let's hope they don't sue us anyway."

"So what do you think happened to the body?" Matt asked.

"Could it have been an accident—like it was sent to cremation by mistake and an employee tried to cover that up?"

"That's really unlikely with the system we have. I suspect my embalmer, Joe Molloi. I think Joe is up to something. I've put him on probation."

"I assume the bad act would be selling the body."

"Obviously."

"To whom?"

"Even with people donating their bodies to science, there's still a market for black-market cadavers that eventually end up at medical schools for dissection. But the big thing nowadays is the biotech industry. They use a lot of human tissue."

"Really?"

"Absolutely. Artificial skin grafts, blood vessels, and bone replacements. If they're fresh enough, heart valves, tendons, ligaments, and more, can be transplanted. The possibilities are limitless. And so are the cases of abuse."

"Wow," Matt said. "I didn't know real human flesh was in such demand."

"It's rather disturbing. If you sold all the component parts of a body, you could probably get over a hundred grand. But before you get any ideas, you can't sell your own body. Tissue banks sell it."

"And where to they get it?"

"Ah, that's the rub. They need donations. And the demand is far greater than the supply of donated tissue."

"Do you think your employee, Mr. Molloi, sold the body to a biotech firm?"

"Not directly. Probably through some middlemen. But I can't fire him until he gets charged by the police or FDLE."

"Thank you for your frankness," Matt said. "Has this happened before?

Perez hesitated. "Not that I know of."

Not that you're willing to admit, Matt thought.

"I'm a bit surprised you brought up the idea of selling bodies," he said.

"Losing the body through incompetence, even if it was just one guy's fault, makes the whole company look bad. But you can't blame the company for one guy's secret criminality."

"Is there anyone else working here who could be responsible?"

"I'm looking at everyone," Perez said. "But Joe Molloi was the embalmer and handled the body from intake through transferring it to the hearse."

"Can I speak with him?" Matt asked.

"No. Sorry."

"Why does he still work here?"

"Corporate insists we follow due process. And, just so you know, even if I end up firing him, he can't talk to you. Corporate makes everyone sign a non-disclosure agreement."

Matt was disappointed. But what could he do?

"Okay," he said, standing up. "Thank you for your time."

"Please quote me in your story saying that missing corpses are exceptionally rare."

"You bet."

When Matt left the funeral director's office, a door opened at the end of the hall. A young man with a beard stared at him and nodded before closing the door. What was that all about?

When Matt reached his car in the lot behind the building, he found a note stuck beneath a windshield wiper like a parking ticket.

I know where the body went, it read, followed by a phone number.

3

TOO HOT, TOO COLD, JUST WRONG

odern Florida, teeming-with-seniors, would not exist without air conditioning. The hardy pioneers who settled the state didn't even have electric fans but somehow survived. The increasing flow of vacationers and retirees who came to the state in the first half of the Twentieth Century did have electric fans, but they wisely chose to avoid coming here during the hotter months. Once air conditioning became common in the 1960s and '70s, the stream of people coming to Florida turned into a flood.

Yet modern conveniences are fickle things. Missy's air conditioner picked a rare winter heat wave to bite the dust.

A new condenser, a new air handler, and thousands of dollars later, Missy had a brand-new HVAC system months ahead of the brutally hot summer to come. Not that she could afford it.

Of course, the next day was a typical winter day of temperatures in the low-seventies and she didn't need the AC. She sat in the living room of her small house, with the system off and the windows open, using her bank's app to assess the damage to her checking account.

Her witchcraft didn't provide any income. Her real job as a home-health nurse for vampires, werewolves, and other creatures didn't provide a whole heck of a lot either. Retired, elderly supernaturals were notoriously cheap, especially vampires. This was despite how wealthy some vampires were after having centuries for their savings to compound. So they negotiated low rates with their care provider, Acceptance Home Care, resulting in a low salary for Missy. Which was why she also had a part-time job at the Jellyfish Beach Mystical Mart and Botánica.

She signed off from the banking app. It looked like some extra shifts at the botánica were in the cards.

The air conditioner kicked on.

She was positive she had turned it off. She went to the thermostat on the wall between the living room and the dining room. It was indeed set on "off." She jiggled the switch to "cool" and back to "off."

Still, the air handler hummed in its hallway closet, and cool air poured from the vents in each room. She looked out a window at the side yard and the condenser's fan was spinning happily.

She would have to set up an appointment for a repairman to come out again. This had better not cost anything. They must have done something wrong during the installation.

Boy, that air is cranked really cold, she thought. She rubbed her arms as goosebumps formed. She fiddled with the thermostat again with no effect. Finally, she went into the garage and turned off the circuit breaker for the HVAC system.

But when she returned inside, the AC was still pumping out cold air.

She was perplexed. Until she sensed the energy of magick in the air flowing from the vents. Someone else's magick. It was a cold spell. Get it?

She couldn't believe she was being attacked again so soon after the cyber-eel. And the attack escalated quickly. The air flowing from the vents increased in amount and velocity until the house was filled with a loud moaning that reminded Missy of a hurricane. The crashing of aluminum on hardwood flooring came from the hallway when a vent popped off.

She recited a quick, simple spell while she grasped the power charm in her pocket. It was just enough to neutralize the HVAC system. The air handler went silent. The fan in the condenser outside stopped spinning.

But the cold air kept rushing out through the vents, even stronger now.

She closed her eyes and studied the magick in the blowing air. Sure enough, it had nothing to do with the air conditioner. It was a gale summoned from Antarctica, from air chilled in pockets of the deepest sections of ice. It was so infused with magick that it almost had a life of its own.

The temperature fell even farther. The air was bitingly cold now. It felt like she was on the top of a mountain during a winter storm. She began to worry when frost appeared on the flanges of the nearest vent.

She needed to bring the cats to safety out on the porch and begin casting a counterattack spell. Now.

The sliding-glass door to the porch was closed and locked. She was sure she had left it open to enjoy the nice day. When had it closed? She flicked the lever open and pulled on the handle.

The door wouldn't open. She struggled with it fruitlessly. Her heart began to race.

She tried the front door. It, too, would not budge. Then, the outside door in the kitchen. No luck. She raced through the laundry room into the garage. The overhead door wouldn't open with either the motor or when she pulled on it manually.

Time to check the windows, though she suspected how that was going to turn out. Sure enough, running from room throughout the entire house, she couldn't open a single window.

Her home was on magick lockdown.

The temperature kept dropping and her shivering was not just from fear. Every breath she took caused a cloud of vapor. She went into her bedroom to find a heavy coat. But her closet door wouldn't open. Neither would her dresser drawers. Of course.

She was about to yank her comforter off her bed when she noticed two lumps beneath it. Her cats, Brenda and Bubba. Hopefully, they were faring better than she was. She went to the guest bedroom to grab that comforter, but the door to the room, which was always open when no one was staying there, was closed. And locked.

This spell was getting very personal. It was just between her assailant and her. May the best magick win.

She put on a sweater she found on the floor of the laundry room (please don't judge her on her housekeeping). But her fingers and toes were going numb. She felt lethargic and was having difficulty concentrating. She worried, is this the beginning of hypothermia?

She made her way to the kitchen, past air vents that were blasting frigid air white with frost. The cup of tea she had left by the kitchen sink had a thick coating of ice. The natural light was dimmer in here with the windowpanes iced over.

Shivering, she quickly drew a magick circle on the floor

with chalk and knelt inside it, her body scrunched into a ball for warmth. She was cold to her very bones. All she could think of was heat. As she put herself into a meditative state, she reached out for the energy of the sun, but it was waning as the afternoon grew later.

She sent psychic feelers seeking additional sources of warmth and energy, probing deep into the earth. And then she realized where she needed to drill, the hottest place on earth: the planet's molten core.

Here the blend of iron, nickel, and other elements had a temperature of thousands of degrees. And here, the earth's magnetic field was generated. The core held almost limitless amounts of power that could be harnessed by Missy's magick and by other forms of magic. But it was dangerous. Even the most experienced witch could not dip into it directly, just as you can't walk into a nuclear reactor to plug in your battery charger.

Besides, she had never done this before. The power she normally harvested from the earth was from ley lines, thermal springs, and other sources close to the surface of the planet. Her near panic, and her muddled thinking as hypothermia set in, caused her to act impulsively and seek the hottest thing she could imagine.

Her probes were many miles above the core when the surge of energy hit her. It rushed into her so quickly it was frightening. Instantly, her body warmed, from the center of her stomach spreading outward through her torso, legs, arms, fingers and toes. Her head was feverish, and her ears flushed with heat. The floor nearly burned her knees and feet as she knelt upon the tiles.

She opened her eyes. A glow of light emanated from her skin. *That* was a first.

The frost on the windowpanes melted and the room grew brighter. Her breath no longer produced vapor. The entire kitchen became warm and the cold air rushing from the vents billowed with vapor as it hit the heat rising from the floor. She sensed the warmth spreading throughout the house.

The Antarctic gale slowed and then stopped altogether.

Her crazy magick's quest for heat had worked.

Or had it worked too well?

Trepidation crept into her heart. It was a post-traumatic response, she realized, as memories invaded her from being tortured by the evil, ancient god Moloch last year. He had demanded she betray a juvenile dragon she had been nursing back to health. Moloch wanted her to sacrifice the dragon to the god in the manner that children were killed on the altar for him thousands of years ago. He wanted to steal the dragon's power of magick.

But she had resisted, and Moloch tortured her with non-physical fire to make her suffer the agony of witches in the darker chapters of human history. She received no actual damage to her body, but the sensation of burning was real. Afterwards, she had hoped she would have no lasting psychological damage.

Yet as the heat she had summoned from the earth's core engulfed her and her home, her trauma was reawakened.

She noticed a prickling sensation from the foreign magick that had invaded her home. It was up to no good, as if her warmth spell had caused it to react. Someone or something was watching her, she was certain.

Suddenly, the link broke between her mind, her magick, and the earth energy. Her head snapped backwards and then she collapsed on the kitchen floor.

The heat seeped away. But the cold air didn't return. The house was a normal temperature, maybe a little warmer.

She got to her feet, a little unsteadily. All was calm inside her home, but she couldn't relax. She still had anxiety from her memories of burning. And she knew, just knew, that the invading magick was not finished with her.

The first thing she did was check if the house was still locked down. She reached for the kitchen door that led to the backyard. She touched the doorknob—

And flames engulfed the hardware.

She jerked her hand away and looked at it. There was no pain and her skin didn't appear to be burned. She touched the metal knob with her index finger. A yellow flame with blue at its center wrapped around the knob as if it came from a butane lighter. The door's white paint at the base of the knob bubbled and turned brown. She pulled her finger away and the fire was gone.

The fire was coming from *her*.

She couldn't believe it. Fire really freaked her out since her trauma, and now she was a source of it?

The attacker's magick—or maybe it *was* black magic—must have traced the source of her heat infusion, severed her connection with it, and then tapped into the inner-core earth energy itself. It was attacking her now with her own weapon.

Absentmindedly, she rubbed her hands on her thighs and her jeans caught on fire. She dropped to the floor and rolled until the flames were smothered. She had stopped it before her skin was burned, but her jeans were lightly scorched and there were small holes on both legs.

So the fire only came from her hands and only when she touched something. What was she going to do about this?

She went to the sink. Fire erupted when she pushed the

faucet handle and vanished when she withdrew her hand. She placed both hands in the stream of water. Nothing happened. Okay, she thought, at least my hands can't burn water.

When she picked up one of the utensils that lay unwashed in the sink (please don't judge her on her housekeeping), flames covered the fork. She held it under the flowing water. The water put out the fire, but only where the water landed on the steel. Fire still ignited on the rest of the surface that her hand touched. She dropped the fork and the fire went out.

Light clicking of nails on the tiles announced the entrance of Bubba who had finally left the bedroom after the frigid gale had ceased.

"Bubba, stay away," she said in a stern voice.

It didn't matter. He walked right up to her and rubbed against her leg and meowed. He wanted a treat. She spoiled her cats horribly and it only empowered them to demand she raise the bar in spoiling. Bubba expected to be rewarded with a treat for merely entering a room.

Without thinking, she reached for the packet of crunchy treats on the counter. It erupted in flames. She put it out with the sprayer hose from the sink, flames encircling the sprayer head in her hand. The odor of burnt plastic, grains, and "tantalizing tuna" filled the room.

Bubba had retreated a few feet away when the fire broke out. He gave her a puzzled stare and meowed. He still expected a treat, and always would, regardless of whatever magick or black-magic spell she was cursed by.

"Bubba, I can't feed you right now. Finish your breakfast," she said, pointing with her foot to the bowl of half-eaten wet food on the floor next to the island.

Bubba chirruped with frustration and left the kitchen with

his tail twitching. Even witches can't get their cats to be reasonable.

So what was she going to do? Without being able to touch anything she was helpless. She couldn't even go to the bathroom, unless she could remove her jeans in the running shower without burning them. She shuttered at the more technical steps of the peeing procedure. Toilet paper was definitely not an option.

And forget about eating anything. She certainly couldn't go food shopping.

A tiny, high-pitched insect buzzing entered her right ear. She chuckled.

"Oh, yes. Yes. Come here. Let me see you. Come to Missy."

The mosquito came into view in front of her face. Her hand darted toward it.

The mosquito exploded in flames.

That was one of the most satisfying moments of the week, she thought.

Still, she had to get out of this predicament. Like with the other attacks, it was too late to use a protection spell. She couldn't hold the charm she kept in her pocket that boosted her power when casting spells. She scratched her head as she pondered her next move.

Big mistake. Burning pain flared on her scalp and singed-hair smoke filled her nose. She jumped to the sink and stuck her head beneath the faucet. The pain went away. She didn't have the stomach to look in a mirror at the damage she had done. Fortunately, she never spent much money on hairstyling.

Back to strategizing, she tried to simplify the problem as she paced back and forth across the kitchen, afraid to touch anything. She was infected by fire, and this infection was possibly powered by the ephemeral connection she had made with the core of the earth, hijacked by her magical opponent. Fire was a basic element of her magick, as was water which, of course, extinguishes fire.

The solution must somehow involve water.

The human body is up to sixty percent water. Florida is surrounded by water, is dotted with lakes, and has a high water table. Could the vast elemental energy of all this water cancel whatever spell was infusing her with fire?

She knelt within the magick circle that was still on the floor from her last spell. It needed to be closed again. The piece of chalk caught on fire but lasted just long enough for her to fill in the small gap created when she broke the circle after she was attacked.

She closed her eyes, chanted a combination of words that put her into a trance-like state, and directed her powers inward. She watched her blood coursing through her arteries, veins, and capillaries. Her focus zoomed in deeply to the cellular level. She immersed herself in the fluids that comprised her body and were influenced by the moon like the ocean tides.

Then she sent probes to the freshwater canal across the street, diving through its water to the bottom and then underground to the limestone marl that stretches across Florida. Her consciousness travelled through the pockets of groundwater, passed beneath the beaches and then out into the Atlantic. Not far offshore was the mighty Gulf Stream pushing northward. It was full of natural energy, energy that connected with the saltwater that filled the miles-deep trenches and stretched across two thirds of the planet.

The power of the earth's water wasn't concentrated like its molten core. It was dispersed but stronger in its totality. It was time to tap into that power.

She clasped her hands together and a giant ball of fire

appeared between her palms. An equilibrium was tipped. A catalyst was set in motion.

And then the life-giving water of the earth flooded her, drowning her consciousness, engulfing her being, saturating her soul.

She woke up lying on her back on the floor. It was dark outside.

And she had to pee really, really badly.

As she stood up, she carefully touched the handle of a cabinet. Nothing happened. There were no flames. She touched the counter. Nothing. She touched the roll of paper towels. Even the paper didn't combust.

It was over.

Then she noticed something odd. On the floor tile, just outside of the magick circle, were smudges of black ash, as if a finger covered in ash had written on the floor.

It was an A-plus symbol. Like she had been graded for her spell casting.

After she went to the bathroom, she caught a glimpse of herself in the mirror. She was disturbed by what she saw, and it wasn't because of her burned hair.

"Oh my," Missy said aloud. "I look bloated. Am I retaining water?"

4
POUNDS OF FLESH

"So did Izzy try to blame me?" asked the man who answered the number Matt called from the note on his windshield. The man identified himself as Joe Molloi, the funeral home's embalmer.

"He said he suspects you," Matt said.

"That coward. He knows it wasn't me, but he wants to throw you off track. If he really thought it was me, he would have fired me. He's hoping the whole investigation will dry up and go away and he doesn't want to have to find a new embalmer and cosmetician."

"Then who was responsible? Do you know?"

"I don't know who physically took the body," Molloi said. "Mr. Blatt—that was the deceased—wasn't embalmed. His family wanted a green burial. That's really trendy nowadays. So I just cleaned him up, did minimal restoration, dressed him in a suit, and put him in the casket. It was a closed-casket wake, on account of what the bowling balls did to his head, so no need for makeup. Afterwards, he went back into the fridge. He must have been taken later that night or early in the morning before the burial."

"You said you don't know who physically took the body," Matt said. "But do you know who was responsible for that?"

"A flesh broker."

"A what?

"Well, that's my own term. I mean a broker who buys and sells human body parts for the biotech industry. I found some printed-out emails on Izzy's desk. . ."

Molloi went silent.

"You still there?" Matt asked.

"Yeah. Look, I don't feel comfortable talking over the phone. I'm sure I'm being surveilled. Meet me at Flounder Park at six tonight. Okay?"

"Yes, thanks. I'll be on one of the benches closest to the water," Matt said before ending the call.

At this time of year, it was already dark at 6:00 p.m., but that must have been the earliest Joe Molloi could make it due to his work schedule. The park was empty, so Matt had no problem finding a seat on the bench with the nicest view.

The park was on the shore of the Intracoastal Waterway, the water highway of connected canals and lagoons that stretched north and south along Florida's east coast, separating the mainland from the barrier islands on the ocean. It offered a route of protected water so boats didn't have to travel in the ocean, but it also connected with all the inlets to allow ocean access.

Tonight, there was no wind and the water was flat. A southward current from the incoming tide could only be discerned by the eddies formed behind the pilings of the park's small dock. Reflected light from the condo buildings on the opposite shore, about half a football field away, were like paintbrush streaks across the glassy water. About a mile to the south, headlights crawled across the Jellyfish Beach Boulevard bridge.

A *plunk* came from the water near the dock of a large fish feeding. Matt wished he had his fishing rod with him. Otherwise, it was silent and relaxing with the faint smell of saltwater and newly mown grass. He sat up straight on the bench, afraid he was going to nod off, even though it was early.

A beam of light swung across a palm tree to his left and he craned his neck to see a car pulling into the empty parking lot past the playground on the far side of the park. The headlights turned off. He hoped it was Molloi. The man was ten minutes late.

There was movement in the shadows behind the playground. Soon a figure emerged from the darkness, walking with the squish-squish steps of soft-soled work shoes along the asphalt path that bisected the park to the waterfront. It was a man, but the lighting on the path was too poor and the man was too far away to be recognized.

Matt was just about to turn away when a dark shape raced through the jungle gym in the playground. It ran toward the man, leaped in the air, and tackled him from the side, knocking him off the path and through a hedge.

A shriek pierced the night, sending chills down Matt's spine.

Growls, grunts, and the crashing of bodies in the shrubbery prodded Matt to his feet. He ran toward the attack even though his common sense told him to stay away.

Sounds of tearing fabric and flesh were followed by screams. More growls. Then a howl of agony ending in the wet rattling of expiring breath.

Matt stopped suddenly when he saw a pair of yellow eyes

looking at him from behind the shrubbery. Then the head of the attacker ducked down and the sounds of rending flesh continued.

Matt ran. It was too late for heroics. He was certain the victim was past saving. And Matt didn't have any weapons. What was he supposed to do to stop the attacker? Wrestle with it? It must be a wolf or bear. Which made no sense in Jellyfish Beach. Maybe it was a coyote, but were they big and strong enough to bring down an adult man?

Or, it could be a werewolf. Matt had recently learned that werewolves do, in fact, exist. His friend, Missy, had some as her nursing patients. A drug-dealing werewolf had almost killed Matt when he was investigating some murders.

If the attacker was a werewolf, it was even more important to get as far from here as fast as possible.

Matt couldn't get to his car, because it was in the parking lot near where the victim—he assumed it was Molloi—had parked. About a block from the park, he stopped running and called 911.

"A man is being attacked by a wild animal," he spoke quickly, panting, "in Flounder Park. Jellyfish Beach."

"Okay, please slow down. What kind of an animal?"

"Something large, like a wolf."

"Could it be a dog?"

"Could be, but listen, this man was being torn to pieces. He needs help now. I couldn't intervene."

"The police and an ambulance are on the way. We just need to know if the personnel's safety is at risk."

"If the creature is still around, hell yes."

After Matt hung up, he walked down a couple of blocks of residential streets until he reached the relative safety of a well-lit commercial street. Now that his panic had lessened, he wondered what Molloi had planned to tell him. He was probably going to explain about the flesh broker and reveal what he had read in the printed emails.

He wondered if Molloi had the email print-outs with him when he came to the park. Matt regretted running away like a frightened rabbit. Maybe he should have stayed near the attack scene until the animal had left and then searched the dead man's clothes.

No, that sounded pretty dumb and dangerous. But, still, he jogged back to the park. Sirens and flashing lights approached. Two police cars were followed not long afterwards by a firetruck and ambulance, turning east and passing him.

When he returned to the park, the fire-rescue vehicles were in the parking lot and the police cars were pulled up on two edges of the property. A third one arrived. The park was bathed in pulsing red and blue light.

He entered the path that led to the scene of the attack. A police officer shone his flashlight on the ground behind the hedge. But most of the first responders were in the playground. As Matt approached it, he followed their flashlights. The beams roved along the bars of the jungle gym.

An eviscerated body was draped at the pinnacle of the arc of monkey bars bridging the structure. Flesh-stripped limbs dangled below it.

Matt's stomach turned over. But he noticed the cop that had been behind the hedge had come to the playground to gawk at the gory remains on display. Matt moved into the shadows and went around the hedge, approaching it from the other side.

There, at the base of a gumbo limbo tree, was the slaughtering ground. Very little light penetrated from the nearest streetlight, but it was easy enough to notice the grass was torn up and the mulch beneath the hedge was scattered. Blood soaked the ground and spattered the trunk of the tree as well as the leaves of the hedge a few feet away. Shreds of clothing were scattered about. One shoe lay next to the tree but the other wasn't around.

There were no body parts in sight, just blood. Lots of it.

Further along the hedge, maybe ten feet from the epicenter of the killing, was a brownish lump on the ground. At first it looked like a small animal. Matt approached it. It was the scrunched-up remains of a pair of khakis.

Matt glanced around to make sure no police officers were nearby. He gently probed the cloth with his shoe. He felt something stiffer than cloth but still pliant to the touch. Paper?

He girded himself and reached down, feeling in the wet fabric for a pocket opening. He found it. Inside were tightly folded papers. He yanked them out, stuffed them in his back pocket, and quickly moved away from the area and onto the paved pathway leading to the playground.

The officers and paramedics still stood staring at the husk of a body atop the monkey bars.

Matt recognized one of the police officers from his work covering crime stories.

"Hey Paul," Matt said. "I'm the one who called it in."

Paul turned and acknowledged him. His face was pale despite the colors of the strobe lights.

"The dispatcher said it was a wolf or dog," the officer said. He sounded nauseous. "An animal wouldn't have thrown the body up here."

"What kind of human would?" Unless they were trying to send a message, Matt thought.

"The abdominal cavity is completely empty," a paramedic said. "And I don't see organs lying around anywhere."

"Were they eaten?" the cop asked in a low voice.

"Maybe they were stolen," Matt said. "To be sold. You've heard of the people who were drugged and had a kidney stolen."

"But the people weren't just slaughtered."

"You guys can stop the speculating now," said a flat voice behind Matt. "It's a waste of your valuable time."

Detective Affird had arrived. He worked most of the murder cases in Jellyfish Beach. And he was a thorn in the side of Matt's friend, Missy, because he was a rare cop who suspected that supernatural creatures existed. And some of those creatures, the elderly ones, were Missy's home-health nursing patients.

"Did anyone I.D. the victim?" Affird asked. He was tall and gaunt, always wearing sunglasses even at night.

The officer named Paul answered, "We found his wallet on the other side of that hedge there, where the attack occurred. His name is Joseph Molloi."

"He works at a funeral home," Matt said. "He was supposed to meet me here tonight."

Affird looked down at him. "Great, Rosen. Just the reporter I want pestering me every day."

"You never return my calls. Ever."

"Because you're a pain in the butt. So why was the victim meeting you? And did you witness the attack?"

"If you ever answered my calls, I wouldn't be such a pain in the butt. But anyway, here's what happened."

Matt gave a detailed account of what he had witnessed tonight. The figure he had seen tackling Molloi had appeared human-like to him, but he admitted that he had seen it only when it was leaping at Molloi and it was too dark to make out much.

"Why was he meeting you here?" Affird asked.

"I was afraid you'd ask that."

"Well?" Affird's frown deepened.

Matt explained the body-snatching story and that Molloi wanted to clear his name and provide evidence against his employer.

"That's an FDLE case," Affird said. "The state guys don't like reporters poking around in their work."

"Yeah, I know, but—"

"The Jellyfish Beach Police Department should have been involved in this case. There should be a joint task force. The FDLE can be a bunch of arrogant jerks."

Desperate to gain an ally, Matt said, "You're absolutely right, detective. They haven't responded to any of my questions."

Affird looked down at him, inscrutable behind his dark glasses. "So you're a pain in the butt to them, too?"

"Yes, I am. Will you talk to me after you receive the forensics report on Molloi?"

"Maybe. Or maybe not. Depends on the mood I'm in."

That was the best Matt could hope for. He hung around the crime scene a little while after the forensics team showed up, waiting to see if they discovered any organs lying around. It seemed like too much of a coincidence that Molloi wasn't merely killed but also had his organs stolen. Matt could believe that Molloi was killed to silence him, but not that his organs were harvested at the same time by a flesh broker. And what kind of flesh broker could slaughter a human like this?

Finally, he was shooed away by a cop he didn't know. He got in his car, becoming sickened when the blood on his hand was revealed by the interior light.

He was relieved neither Affird nor the officers had noticed the blood. Tampering with a crime scene was a felony, as was stealing evidence. Matt quickly came up with the rationalization that Molloi had probably intended to give the papers to him.

Okay, so what if that would never hold up in court?

He drove to *The Jellyfish Beach Journal*, parked, and used his electronic pass to get into the building. After twenty minutes of scrubbing his hands in the bathroom, he went to his desk in the sparsely populated newsroom. Finally, he removed the papers from his pocket and opened them.

The blood-flecked sheets of white paper were, in fact, the printed emails Molloi had mentioned. There were three pages, each with one email. The email headers showed the recipient was Izzy Perez, the funeral director. The sender was Omar Johnson, from a personal account. There was no trace of a company name. Why in the world did Perez print them out?

The most recent email was a threat. It stated that although $25,000 had been paid in advance to Perez, "the promised goods have not been delivered." Serious repercussions were threatened, but exactly what they might be was not specified. The dollar amount was highlighted on the paper by a yellow marker.

The next page was an earlier email. It spelled out specifications required of cadavers that this Omar Johnson wanted. They ranged from, "Time elapsed since death shall be no more than seven days," to, "No embalming fluids or other preservative chemicals shall be used." There were several additional lines that were more technical or, frankly, disgusting, including instructions about bodily fluids, washing of the bodies, and removal of hair. He hadn't realized prepping bodies to be harvested for the biotech industry was so complicated.

Maybe Perez had printed that email to serve as a checklist when inspecting Molloi's work, because he had actually made check marks in pencil beside each specification.

The last email consisted of only an address and the instruction to use the freight entrance in the rear. This must be where the corpses were to be delivered. Matt looked up the address on the internet. He gasped.

The address was the Jellyfish Beach water utility office and treatment plant.

Why was a flesh broker working out of a city utility? It made no sense. It also freaked him out when he pictured corpses delivered to the same place that treated his drinking water. He made a mental note to pick up some bottled water at the grocery store.

Maybe it was a dumb move, but he decided to send an email to Omar Johnson. He entered the address on the printout and typed a simple request. He said he was doing a story on successful local businesspeople and would love to be able to call Mr. Johnson to ask a few questions. The email would probably be ignored, but hopefully Omar's ego would get the best of him and he'd reply. Matt clicked "send."

Almost instantly, a "delivery failure" notification popped up. The email had bounced.

When he left the building, a full moon was rising above the nearby buildings. He wondered if Molloi was, in fact, killed by a werewolf. And was it a random attack, or was it meant to stop him from being a whistleblower?

Matt was certain it was the latter.

5
WOMEN OF WISDOM

The Jellyfish Beach Mystical Mart and Botánica was usually busy early in the morning on weekdays. Working folks wanted to get their occult shopping done before work. A brisk business was done in oils or powders to help in business deals, tame difficult bosses, inflame a romantic interest in coworkers, assure safe travels, or ward off the guy who steals your leftovers from the lunchroom.

Witches, on the other hand, tended to shop in the late afternoons, which was when Missy worked her part-time shifts three days a week. Missy suspected that the afternoon witch traffic could be explained by last-minute runs for new ingredients for failed potions, the way normal folks ran to the hardware store when they realized they had the wrong-size screws.

Missy opened the door with its tinkling bell and pushed through a cloud of incense right after the morning rush petered out. She was anxious to consult with the store's owner, Luisa, a Santeria priestess who was both a friend and spiritual advisor.

"Good morning, Missy," Luisa said, looking up from her laptop as she sat behind the counter. She was a tall African-Cuban in her forties with high cheekbones and striking brown eyes. "*Chica*, are you retaining water?"

"Funny you ask," Missy replied. "But that's the least of my problems."

She looked around to make sure the store was empty of customers, and told Luisa about her travails. First had come the attack of the cyber-eel, then the Antarctic gale, followed immediately by the spell that turned her into a fire-starter.

"Why is this happening to me?" she asked, realizing her voice was filled with self-pity.

"Wow," Luisa said. "That is powerful stuff. Does it feel like earth magick or black magic?"

"Earth magick, although it's trying to harm me. Or kill me. The evil intent would indicate black magic. So I'm really confused."

Missy practiced magick, the benign art of harnessing power from within oneself, from the earth and universe, and from external supernatural forces. To the few people she discussed the subject with, she stressed the difference between magick and black magic, which was sorcery performed for malign intentions and ends, often involving demons. And then there was plain old magic—the performance art of tricks and illusions that were really not magical at all.

"But your magick defeated it?" Luisa asked.

Missy nodded.

"Did you try a spell to find out who's doing it?"

"No. I've been a little busy. Trying to survive and all that. And, to be honest, I don't think I'd be able to find out."

"I can't help you there, *amiga*. But there is something interesting about these attacks."

"Interesting is not the word I would use."

"You were attacked by a creature from the sea, by freezing wind, and by fire. Water, air, fire—three of the five elemental energies of magick," Luisa said.

Missy thought about it. "Is that just a coincidence? If not, what's the purpose?"

Luisa shrugged.

"Maybe you're trying to read too much into it," Missy said.

"Maybe you're not seeing the big picture. Maybe it's about more than someone trying to kill you."

"*More* than trying to kill me? Trying to kill me is quite enough, thank you."

"Maybe there's a bigger meaning to it."

"But why? What's the point? And who is doing this?"

"Maybe these attacks are tests," Luisa said. "Trying to see if you have the power and knowledge to beat them."

Missy remembered the word "kudos" on her screensaver after the cyber-eel was destroyed and the "A+" smudged on her kitchen floor. She recounted these details to Luisa.

"See," Luisa said.

"I still can't imagine why they would be doing this. If it's an evil magician who thinks I'm a rival, why test me? Why not kill me as quickly as possible?"

"It could be someone trying to recruit you."

"For what?" Missy was getting frustrated. "I assume it's someone wiser and more powerful than I am. Then what would they need me for?"

"How would I know? I'm not a *bruja*. But who says all witches work alone like you do? Maybe they need you for some extra manpower. I mean, witch-power."

"Who on earth would need that?"

"Who says it has to be someone on earth?"

"Oh my," Missy said, "you're not making me feel any better."

You see, Missy had had contact with beings that did not reside on the earth. One of which was the evil, ancient god that had tortured her. He had made his way to the In-Between, a land of limbo for departed souls that hadn't reached Heaven or Hell, a place where certain living creatures (like dragons) who knew how to get there could take refuge. The evil god also appeared on earth, but he was defeated and was hopefully stuck back in Hell for a long time.

There was also the matter of Missy's deceased parents. They died when she was too young to remember them. Her father's cousin and his wife adopted her. She didn't know until after her adoptive father's funeral that he was related to her real dad.

That's also when she found out that both her birth parents had been witches, and that they had been murdered, possibly because of their witchcraft. That's all her adoptive parents could tell her. At least she finally understood then why they had always discouraged her from having any interest in witches, even banning books about the craft.

Luisa's throwaway line about someone not on earth might be more accurate than she realized.

ON THE WAY home after her patient visits, Missy stopped by the shop that did her dry-cleaning, sewing, and alterations. It was just down the road from the two communities where her vampire and werewolf patients lived. There weren't many businesses on A1A. The north-south state highway that runs along the beaches of Florida's east coast was mainly residential, interspersed with beach parks and inlets. But there were occasional clusters of restaurants and retail in towns along the way.

Such was Three Sisters Sewing and Alterations. It was next to a deli across from one of the last remaining beachfront trailer parks in Florida. It was a cramped and dingy shop, but it was so conveniently located for Missy. And the shop always seemed to be open, no matter what time she stopped by.

As usual, Greek folk music was playing from an unseen sound system. A customer stood at the counter, an elderly man who was mostly bald except for regularly spaced hair plugs like early plantings in a cornfield. One of the sisters, Atropos, was running the clickety-clackety conveyor belt that moved hundreds of dry-cleaned garments hanging in clear-plastic wraps from wire hangers with numbers taped to them. Atropos stopped the machine, removed a group of garments, and hung them from a hook next to the counter.

"Forty-six ninety-nine," she said with her Greek accent made rough from chain-smoking. She was short and stout, older than her customer, and kept her hair wrapped in a scarf.

"You're gonna drive me to the poorhouse, I tell ya," the man said, plucking bills from his wallet.

He paid, received change, and grabbed his clothing.

"See you again next week," he said as he turned to leave.

"No you won't," said Atropos.

The man stopped. "Huh? You going out of town?"

"No, I'll be here. But you won't." She gave him a big smile.

He laughed nervously, assuming it was a joke he didn't get, and walked past Missy on his way out of the shop.

"That wasn't very nice," Missy said to Atropos.

"I was just telling the truth."

"Humans don't always want to hear the truth. Especially that kind of truth."

Atropos and her sisters, Clotho and Lachesis, were the Moirai, also known as the Fates. They were the Ancient Greek goddesses who controlled your destiny and your number of days upon this earth. In the legends, Clotho wove the cloth of your life, Lachesis determined its length, and Atropos snipped it off with her scissors. Nowadays they plied their trade in this sewing and dry-cleaning business. They had migrated to the U.S. decades ago, and like so many senior citizens, ended up in Florida. They lived together in the nearby trailer park.

Of course, when Missy first patronized the store, she had no idea the owners were goddesses. That fact was not on the store's sign or on their business cards. But as a witch she was ultra-sensitive to supernatural energies and immediately sensed that the three sisters were brimming with power. Even though they hadn't been worshipped in a couple thousand years, they still had the goods.

They also sensed that Missy was not a normal human and had some powers of her own. On her second visit to the store to pick up her dry cleaning, Lachesis admitted that they were the Fates. She nagged Missy about remarrying. She, of course, knew if and when Missy would do so but refused to tell her.

So when Atropos told the customer with the hair plugs he wasn't coming back, she knew of what she spoke. Her scissors were soon to give his life the final snip.

"What can I do for you tonight, my little flower?" Atropos asked. "Are you picking up?"

"Dropping these off," Missy said, handing her a folded pair of jeans. "They got some burn damage. Can you cover the holes with pretty patches with patterns?"

"Ah, something tells me this was the result of a curse," Atropos said, unfolding the jeans.

"Sort of." Missy didn't want to explain.

Atropos pulled a red bandana with a paisley pattern from a drawer.

"How about this?" she asked.

"Yes! I love that."

"Ready next Tuesday." Atropos said, brandishing a pair of scissors.

Missy nodded. And winced at the scissors.

6

I ATE SOMEONE BAD LAST NIGHT

H arry Roarke woke up on a rooftop. He was naked and covered with blood. This was not as disturbing to him as you might imagine. Most people in this predicament were guilty of getting extremely intoxicated and then killing someone, or something, or multiple combinations thereof, before passing out. They woke up in horror to a life forever changed for the worse.

But not Harry. He was accustomed to bloody mornings bereft of memories. Harry was a werewolf. When he was younger, after he was infected by the werewolf virus when attacked in the New Jersey Pine Barrens, he would regularly transform into his monster state and create all sorts of havoc. It was sort of like a young man who partied too hard and too regularly.

Now that he was in his sixties and retired, he only transformed when required to by nature: each month on the full moon. And he tried not to roam around killing things these days. It was too risky. It could lead to him being arrested and found out as a werewolf, resulting in a possible summary execution by the cops. It could also expose the other werewolves living in his oceanfront retirement community to public discovery.

Instead, during his monthly transformations into a bipedal wolf, he spent his energy and lupine aggression carving waves with the Werewolf Surfing Club. It was the perfect excuse for coed nude surfing and no humans were killed.

So what happened last night? Why was he on this rooftop?

His stomach gurgled and he felt like he was going to be sick. He must have eaten something too rich or spicy. His stomach just wasn't what it used to be.

Had it been a rich or spicy human he ate? The thought made him queasier.

The morning sun was getting stronger and he feared a sunburn on his naked body. All of his wolf fur had fallen off and littered the asphalt roof around him. He groaned and stood up, his muscles aching. God, what had he been up to last night? It had been years since he last experienced amnesia after going wolf.

As he surveyed his surroundings, his heart sank. He was on a very, very large roof. And around it were other very large roofs, some a bit higher and others lower.

He was on top of the shopping mall. Of all the freaking places to wake up naked smeared with blood, it had to be here?

He didn't know what time it was, but the sun was higher in the sky than he would have liked. The immense parking lot surrounding the mall was already filling with cars. He didn't see his clothes on this roof or the others within his line of sight, so they were probably miles away.

He had to get the heck out of here before he was arrested.

But how, exactly, does a naked guy escape a crowded mall in daytime?

Two buildings away was the parking garage. If he remembered correctly, there were thick bushes at the far end where the garage was close to the access road. And just across the road were more trees where he could hide until night fell when it would be safer to make it home.

He had to go for it before he roasted alive on the hot roof, was caught by a maintenance worker, or both.

Running gingerly on his sensitive bare feet, he traversed the roof he was on, made the short jump to the lower, adjoining roof, and made it across that structure. He had one more section of roof to cross before he reached the parking garage. There, he would go down the stairwell, hopefully alone, hide in the bushes until there was no traffic, and dash across the access road to safety in the small woods on the other side.

The glitch in his plan became obvious when he reached the last section of roof before the parking garage. A large skylight was in the way. There was no way to get around it to the garage roof.

The ornate complex of windowpanes was probably forty feet long, but only, maybe six feet wide. On his side of it was a raised section of roof covering ventilation ducts. With the added elevation, he just might be able to jump over the skylight.

In werewolf form, the leap would be a breeze. But he was a sixty-eight-year-old dude with a large gut. He still had good upper-body strength, but below the waist he was hardly a gymnast. Could he jump far enough?

If he thought about it too long, he would chicken out. So he climbed atop the raised section, took off running, and sprang with everything he had.

He sailed gracefully over the glass.

Until his momentum slowed.

Then stalled.

Barely two feet from safety his feet hit the glass and broke through. And then his butt. And then all of him was dropping in a shower of broken glass into a bright courtyard with seating and a fountain down below.

The ancient man reading a newspaper didn't even appear startled when Harry slammed down on the sofa next to him. Harry landed butt-first in a perfect sitting position. And if it weren't for the tremendous impact and the shards of glass falling everywhere, you would think that the naked man had simply sat down on the sofa to rest his feet.

"Waiting for your wife, too?" the old man asked over the top of his newspaper. "I have no patience for shopping. No way am I going to follow her around from store to store, carrying her bags and smiling sweetly."

"Same here, buddy," Harry said.

HARRY SOMEHOW MADE it out of the mall, wearing a tablecloth liberated from Crate and Barrel as a skirt. He had only minor injuries from his fall—a couple of bruises and small cuts. He even successfully crossed through the bottom level of the parking garage. But hiding in the bushes next to the access road proved to be a bad idea. He would have thought a well-maintained property like this would not have any fire ant colonies. But he ended up choosing a hiding spot near an ant mound. And the ants quickly found him.

As the excruciating bites spread over his legs and his private parts, he ran screaming across the access road toward a pond on the other side, nearly getting creamed by a delivery van. He was standing in the middle of the shallow pond, swatting the tenacious fire ants, when the security guards found him and fished him out.

Believe it or not, Harry was blessed by good fortune. The water washed away most of the blood from whatever creature he had eaten the previous night. And the security guards, who worked for a contractor that underpaid and undertrained its workers, didn't feel it was necessary to get the police involved.

Harry cooperated and cracked a bunch of jokes. He made up an unlikely story about his religious practice of worshipping the moon goddess on the full moon, a ritual that involved nudity. He had been in a religious trance and didn't realize he was trespassing when he climbed to the roof of the mall. And he was so tired he fell asleep up there until well past dawn.

The security guards were a nineteen-year-old in his first job and a sixty-six-year-old who had returned to the workforce after running out of retirement money. They both wanted to get through each day with a minimum of hassles. And they actually believed Harry. Not about the moon ceremony, but that he wasn't a criminal. He was simply yet another naked Florida Man caught doing something stupid. So they let him go, after he signed a waver stating that he would not sue the mall for having a skylight that didn't bear his weight.

HARRY'S WIFE Cynthia picked him up at the mall. She paid for the tablecloth that he had stolen to cover his nakedness and gave him some clothes he put on in the security office. When they got in her car, she gave him a stern, disapproving look. She wore a Grateful Dead T-shirt and had her long, gray hair in a ponytail. She wouldn't let him avoid her eyes.

"I can't believe you weren't arrested."

"Me too. Guess I'm lucky."

"What got into you last night? We were all waiting for you on the beach to go surfing. The conditions were excellent."

"The full moon was a supermoon. You know how those affect me. I couldn't stop myself."

"What did you do?"

"I think I ate someone last night. And I feel horrible."

"Oh boy. Who was it?"

"I don't remember. I was having a deep-wolf episode. I can't remember anything. I'm not even sure it was a human, but with the indigestion I have this morning, I'm afraid it was."

"Could it have been a dog?"

"No hair in my mouth."

"Oh boy. Let's hope this all blows over."

Late that afternoon, back in their oceanfront condo in the Seaweed Manor community, Harry and Cynthia were napping. Cynthia growled, which woke him up. She whined, growled again, and twitched her feet.

She must be dreaming about chasing prey, he thought. He wondered if it was human prey.

Loud knocking at the front door woke her up. And that was when Harry's good fortune ran out.

He answered the door in his boxer shorts and T-shirt to find two police officers and a detective in plain clothes and sunglasses standing there.

"Harry Roarke?" the detective asked.

"Yeah?"

"You need to come with us to the station. We have some questions for you."

"About what?"

"You're a person of interest concerning an incident last night."

Harry's stomach dropped. It felt like he was falling through the skylight again.

"What if I don't want to go?" he asked.

"Then we'll have to arrest you," the detective said. "It's a lot more pleasant if you come willingly." He smirked.

"Cynthia!" Harry shouted. "Bring me my pants and call Paul Leclerc."

Paul was a criminal attorney who was a werewolf. Harry had used his services in the past to get him out of some scrapes more minor than this. The lawyer was also retained by the vampires next door in Squid Tower, since they needed representation by someone who understood supernatural creatures and, unlike a vampire, could attend court proceedings in the daytime.

He really wished he could remember what he had done last night. And if he had really eaten someone.

WHEN HARRY ROARKE'S attorney entered the conference room at the police station, he wore an expression that was not reassuring. Paul Leclerc was short, fat, and balding. But his most unfortunate attribute was his graying ponytail that he insisted on wearing. He wore it despite the fact the hair on the rest of his head was guilty of failure to appear and the fact he was a sixty-four-year-old attorney. Werewolves have a preoccupation with hair, Harry knew, but a ponytail? Didn't judges have a problem with that?

"Thanks for coming, Paul," Harry said.

"Of course." Leclerc awkwardly shook Harry's hand which

was handcuffed to his other in front of his body. "Did they question you?"

"They tried to. I said I wasn't talking until you got here. What do they have on me?"

"They won't tell me yet. All I know is that someone was murdered in Flounder Park last night and then you show up at the mall this morning naked and covered with blood."

"The blood could have been mine. I got some cuts when I fell through the skylight."

"Tell me the truth," Leclerc said, taking the chair next to him and leaning close to his client. "Be careful what you say. The room is probably bugged."

"I don't remember anything. It was a supermoon, you know." Harry whispered. He glanced nervously around the room. "Those supermoons really get to me. After I shifted, everything was a blur. I did eat something, but I have no idea what it was."

The door opened and the detective who had arrested him entered, still wearing shades.

"Detective Affird," Leclerc said, rising and shaking Affird's hand.

"Mr. Leclerc. I haven't seen you in a long time."

"And that's a good thing. So, what evidence do you have against my client?"

"All in due time," Affird said, sitting down across the table from them. "Your client claims to have no memory of last night."

"That's true," Harry said. "I blacked out. Partied a little too heavily." He laughed awkwardly.

"Maybe you should work a little harder at remembering," Affird said.

Harry shrugged. "I'm sorry. I'll try."

"I'll be frank," Affird said looking at Leclerc. "You take on a lot of clients who are odd—that's the only way I can put it. Especially the residents where your client lives and those in the condos next door."

"They're just a bunch of retirees. Full-time residents and snowbirds."

"I have to be careful of how I put this, but I've gotten clues here and there that the residents have peculiarities not found in normal senior citizens."

"Detective, this is Florida," Leclerc said. "Everyone is peculiar."

"I think you know what I'm talking about. And the more I learn about these . . . people . . . the more I become certain that I don't want them in my community because of public safety concerns."

"That's—"

"I don't want to hear it," Affird said, standing. "Before I came in here, I spoke to the district attorney. Your client is charged with the murder of Joseph Molloi."

Harry gasped.

"With what evidence?" Leclerc asked

"You'll find out during discovery."

Before he knew it, Harry was brought outside and put in the back of a police van with thick mesh wire covering the windows. His stomach clenched twenty minutes later when the van pulled up to the gate of the county jail. The same dark and distressing thoughts ran through his mind that most just-arrested defendants have. But he also had one very unique, pressing concern:

The next full moon was in four weeks. If he were still in jail when he shifted into werewolf form, people may die. Including him.

7

MAN OR MONSTER?

Missy performed her patient home visits at night. Since most of her patients were elderly vampires, that made perfect sense. Her employer, Acceptance Home Care, had assigned her to Squid Tower, a fifty-five-plus, active-adult vampire retirement community.

People who were already elderly when they were turned into vampires were destined to spend eternity as elderly vampires. And, as anyone who is elderly knows, winter sucks. So old vampires tended to move to Florida and Arizona just like their human counterparts. Since they couldn't go to human doctors, they depended upon home-health nurses like Missy for their basic healthcare and screenings.

The community right next door to Squid Tower was Seaweed Manor, two buildings filled with elderly werewolves. Missy had patients there as well, whom she visited in the late afternoons and early evenings. She did avoid Seaweed Manor during full moons.

Missy arrived there just before sunset on the day after the

full moon. She had only two appointments. The first was with a woman in her late eighties. Werewolves were not immortal like vampires, and as they aged, they generally shifted into their wolf-like forms less regularly. The transformation took a toll on older bodies, so they usually limited their shifting to only during full moons when it was biologically necessary.

Her first patient, Josie, was different. Despite being eighty-seven, she said she shifted once a week with the retirees who made up the Werewolf Women's Club.

"It's good that you're so active," Missy said, wrapping the cuff around the woman's tiny arm to take her blood pressure.

"Oh, yes, the club is quite a handful," Josie said. She was petite with short white hair and an impish grin. "We do regular fundraisers for charity. And every Thursday night, we shift and hunt as a pack in the rural land west of town."

"One twenty over seventy. Great numbers," Missy said, unwrapping the cuffs. "Um, what exactly do you hunt?"

"Single men." When she saw Missy's alarmed expression, she added, "No, just possums, raccoons, rabbits. Wild hogs and deer when we're really hungry."

"Be careful. Make sure the police don't catch you," Missy said.

"Of course, of course. I didn't get to this age by being stupid."

After Josie's exam was completed, Missy went to the other building of Seaweed Manor for her next appointment. Cynthia Roarke answered the door with red, swollen eyes.

"Hi, Cynthia," Missy said. "I'm here for Harry's appointment. Is something wrong?"

"The police took Harry away," Cynthia said as new tears streamed down her face.

"Oh my. They arrested him?"

"They said they wanted to question him about some incident last night. That was hours ago, and I haven't heard from him. I called a lawyer who said he would go straight to the police department, but he hasn't called me either."

"You guys were here surfing during the full moon, right?"

Cynthia hesitated. Then began crying harder as she shook her head.

"Harry ran off. It was a supermoon last night and those have a big effect on him. He says he doesn't remember where he went or what he did."

Missy tried to console her as best she could for as long as was appropriate.

"Please let me know if there's anything I can do for you," Missy said as she left. "I'm sure it's all a big misunderstanding with the police."

As soon as she got to her car, she checked the local news headlines on her phone. She hadn't had the chance to read the paper, watch TV, or even go online today.

There it was—the lead headline:

"Jellyfish Beach man murdered in savage Flounder Park attack."

Her friend, Matt Rosen, had written the story. She quickly scanned it before calling him.

"Why didn't you call me about this attack?" she said.

"Hello to you, too. I've been fine, thanks. And you?"

Matt had feelings toward her. She had a bit of an attraction for him, too. He was in his forties, tall and cute in a bookish way, with dark, curly hair and a trimmed beard. But she never allowed that to get in the way of their professional relationship. Which happened to involve supernatural creatures.

"This is serious," Missy said. "Did a werewolf kill that man in Flounder Park?"

"I don't know. It was really nasty. I couldn't mention it in the article, but there was hardly anything left of this guy except for his skin and skeleton. I mean, all his flesh and organs were missing. Either it was all eaten, or it was taken away."

"I wish you had told me about this, Matt. One of my werewolf patients has been taken in by the police."

"Sorry," he said. "But first of all, it's unclear if it was done by a werewolf. And, in any case, it's not as if you're the keeper of all werewolves."

"You know I have several as patients." She couldn't keep the anger from her voice. "Their welfare is very important to me."

"Look, Missy, I was there. The victim was a whistleblower. He was supposed to meet with me to give me information about crimes he knew about. My first assumption was that he was killed to silence him. Does this werewolf patient have anything to do with funeral homes or the biotech industry?"

"No. He's a retiree who likes to surf."

"I heard the attack as it took place. It was horrible. But I didn't hear anything that specifically sounded like a wolf. It didn't even occur to me that it could have been a werewolf until I noticed the full moon rising."

"Okay. I'm sorry I lost my temper. I'm just worried about Harry."

"I could have been killed last night, too," Matt said. He seemed to be trying to elicit some sympathy from her.

It didn't work. "We have to meet so you can tell me more details about this," Missy said. "And I'm going to need your help in clearing Harry. Assuming he didn't do it, that is."

"Sure. When do you get off work?"

"Now. I was supposed to be seeing Harry right now."

"Finally we can get together at a normal socializing time,

instead of early breakfasts," he said. "Meet me in half an hour at The Ripped Tide. You know where that is?"

"Yeah, I do. That bar is nasty."

"It's not that bad. But the important thing is that there won't be any undertakers or biotech brokers there to see us. I'll meet you there."

THE RIPPED TIDE was on the edge of what was considered "downtown" in tiny Jellyfish Beach: a half a dozen blocks of two- and three-story buildings built in the early 1900s with stores and restaurants as well as some professional offices. As you headed west toward the railroad tracks, rents were lower and the establishments a little more iffy. Right next to the tracks, standing alone, was the iffiest place of all, The Ripped Tide.

The building had been a feed and seed store in the early days of Jellyfish Beach when pineapple and vegetable farming were the mainstay industries. It had had several other existences before it devolved into a dive bar frequented by bikers, surfers, and just about anyone else who wanted cheap drinks. Missy heard that they served a great burger, but on the few occasions she'd ventured inside, she couldn't muster the courage to touch any food served by this establishment.

Missy parked in the lot behind the building. It was dirt and gravel and had always been. Apparently, asphalt was too high class for this joint.

Matt was waiting at a table for two, drinking a bottle of some obscure craft beer. She was glad the table was near the entrance, in case they had to make a quick escape when a brawl broke out.

Matt stood and pulled out a chair for her. "What are you drinking?"

She couldn't stomach the thought of consuming a drink served in the glassware here, so she pointed to his beer. He went to the bar and returned shortly with a beer for her and a glass.

"Thanks, but I'll skip the glass," she said. "Are there no servers here for the tables?"

"Jane was supposed to work tonight, but she had to shoot her boyfriend. She'll probably be back in tomorrow."

"Nice," she said. "Now let's get straight to the matter at hand."

"Okay. It all started when a guy was getting buried at the municipal cemetery. There was a little accident with the pallbearers, and it turns out the casket didn't have a body in it."

"They dropped the casket?"

"Yeah. They were drunk."

"Of course."

"Anyway, I learned that there's a big business in human flesh," Matt explained. "Biotech firms need it for skin grafts, heart valves, and stuff like that, but it's not easy to get ahold of. People aren't allowed to sell their own bodies. They have to donate them. And this isn't the same thing as specific organ donation. Body brokers, or flesh brokers as my source called them, supply the biotech firms. From the little bit of research I've done so far, I'd say that some of these body brokers are sketchy characters."

"So the body missing from the funeral was sold to a body broker?" Missy asked.

"That's the working theory. The funeral director was pointing the finger at his embalmer, but stopping short of outright accusing him. The embalmer, Joe Molloi, left me a note to call him, which I did. But he felt nervous talking on the phone, so we agreed to meet in Flounder Park."

"Oh my," Missy winced at the thought of what happened to the embalmer.

"The most obvious conclusion is that someone killed Molloi to silence him. But who? Someone with the funeral home? A body broker?"

"A werewolf?"

"Right," Matt said. "My first thought was that a wild animal attacked him. But it happened in the bushes and the remains were tossed on top of the monkey bars of the playground. No animal would do that. When I realized the flesh and organs were gone, I wondered if a body broker took them. But that seems really far-fetched that you would harvest the flesh right there in a park at night in unsterile conditions. Then I thought the missing flesh was meant to send a warning to others not to cross this body broker. But, of course, it was a full moon."

"If a werewolf did it, wouldn't that be a huge coincidence?"

"Yeah. Unless the werewolf was a hitman for someone in the body business," Matt said. "Which sounds totally crazy to me, but I didn't even know that werewolves actually existed until fairly recently."

"Tell me who you think did this? I want to help Harry Rourke."

"I'm not sure I should mention this, but I did acquire printouts of emails that Molloi meant to give to me."

"You took them off his body?" Missy asked, horrified.

"No. I took them from his pants, which were at least thirty feet away from his body."

Missy shuddered.

"The emails were between the funeral director and someone I assume is a body broker. They were instructions on how to prepare and deliver bodies. And it sounds like the funeral director was behind in producing the bodies he'd already been paid for."

"You're going to give these emails to the police, right?" Missy asked.

Matt was silent.

"*Right?*"

"I already told them that Molloi was a whistleblower and the story behind it."

"Those emails are important evidence. You need to share them."

"If I can figure out how to do it without incriminating myself for taking them."

"Drop them in the mail."

"The police know that I was the only unofficial person at the crime scene."

"Tell them you have reason to believe there are incriminating emails in the funeral director's account. They can get a warrant to search it."

"What if he deleted them?"

"The police will still be able to find them. Do it, Matt."

"Okay. But we're still leaving one huge question unanswered. Why did it look like a werewolf killed Molloi? Unless a werewolf really did kill him."

"As long as it wasn't Harry Rourke," Missy said.

"Are you sure it wasn't?"

"No," she said, feeling deflated. "His wife said he was on the prowl last night, but didn't remember anything. I just know that Harry's human-hunting days are long behind him."

Matt gave her a skeptical look that was making her mad.

"Just follow up on the body broker," she said. "That's your best lead so far."

But then an idea came to her.

"Can you show me the spot in the park where it happened?" she asked.

"Yeah, but why?"

"I want to try a little magick."

THEY DROVE SEPARATELY the short distance to the park on the Intracoastal Waterway. The gate to the parking lot was closed and locked, but Missy didn't see any yellow crime-scene tape in the park, so she parked on the side of the road nearby. Matt pulled in behind her.

"Normally they don't close this gate," Matt said. "But I'm surprised the tape is gone. I guess they're done with all the forensics work."

Missy didn't answer. She was already receding into her spiritual center in preparation for her spell. Negative energy from the violence was still present, like invisible fog clinging to the ground.

"Let's move our cars a block or two away," Matt said. "I've done my fair share of trespassing in my line of work, and I can guarantee that when the nearby residents see two junky cars outside of the closed park, someone is going to call the police. And no offense about your car."

"I have no shame driving a junk heap," Missy replied.

After they moved their cars, they returned to the park, walking casually like a couple out for a stroll. Except for the parking lot, the park wasn't fenced off, so Missy and Matt entered in the least-visible spot, through a cluster of palm trees.

Now she had to relax and clear her mind all over again. Thanks, Matt.

"Before I begin, show me the spot where the killing took place," she said.

Matt motioned to her to follow him down an asphalt path cutting diagonally through the park toward the water. Right before they reached the playground, he pointed to a hedge that looked as if it had been damaged.

"Right behind here," he said, pointing to the base of a gumbo limbo tree. "What, exactly, are you going to do?"

"I'm going to try a spell. I haven't used it before for this specific purpose, but it might help. I think I might be able to tell if a werewolf, in wolf form, was here recently. I won't be able to identify a specific individual, but there should be traces of its supernatural energy lingering here."

"How can I help?"

"Make yourself scarce."

He complied, walking to the waterfront and sitting on a bench.

She pushed through the hedge to the circle of mulch beneath the tree. It looked as if a lot of water had been sprayed here. Probably to send the blood deeper into the soil where it wouldn't be a biohazard, she figured.

There was no way she would kneel on this ground. But she didn't really need to. She grasped the trunk of the tree in both hands. It was about ten inches in diameter, with the wispy, peeling bark gumbo limbos were known for.

The tree witnessed what had happened here. Its roots had drawn in water laced with blood and other bodily fluids. Its leaves had soaked in chemicals released into the air by the violence that occurred.

She recited the words of the spell while reaching deep within her being for the power that resided there—the power of the earth and that which had been born within her. A warmth spread from her solar plexus and out through her arms. Her hands tingled as she touched the tree.

Trees are more sentient than humans could ever imagine. But their language is so unlike that of humans and other animals that we can't even begin to comprehend it.

Unless, of course, we use a little earth magick.

Her head filled with song. Nothing that human ears would recognize as music, but that's what it was. The vibrations that trees and plants use for communicating. It hummed inside her head and through her arteries and veins. It was simple and soft, eternal and true. It was a language that preceded humans and would outlast them, even if only simple lichens survive on the planet that we ultimately destroy.

It was a universal language that transcends genus and species.

And Missy understood it and heard what the tree had observed last night.

But she needed more information. She sent psychic probes around her, seeking the various types of energy residing here. There were the usual forms of natural life. And suddenly, she sensed it—something beyond nature, beyond the natural.

Supernatural energy, faint and fading. She zeroed in on it and focused every bit of her mind and powers upon it. She cranked up the spell to interpret what it was. And after a few minutes, she knew.

A werewolf had not been here. A supernatural creature had, in fact, killed the embalmer, but it wasn't a werewolf. She didn't know what it was, whether it was another kind of shifter or any other sort of creature. It was evil and permeated with death, but it was entirely unfamiliar to her.

She was relieved to know that Harry Roarke was not the murderer. But she couldn't go to the police and tell them that she cast a spell and communed with nature, concluding that Roarke was innocent. She would have to find out what kind of creature, exactly, had committed the crime.

Just what Jellyfish Beach needed, she thought. A new kind of monster roaming around.

"WHAT DO you mean you don't know what kind of creature killed him?" Matt asked.

"That's what I mean. I don't know. But at least we can conclude it wasn't a human assassin working for a body broker or biotech firm."

"But could it be a monster working for them?"

"I guess," Missy said. "Who knows?" She was tired from casting the spell and had no energy for further speculation. She sat next to Matt on the bench overlooking the water and just wanted to zone out and stare at the moonlight reflected on the gentle current.

"I keep remembering the sounds when it was killing him. I agree it couldn't have been human. And now it makes sense that it didn't sound like a wolf. But what the hell *was* it? It's really clear to me now: This monster was devouring him. It wasn't harvesting his parts. It was chewing and swallowing them. Sorry, does that freak you out?"

"Not any more than I'm already freaked out."

"Speaking of which," Matt said, "maybe it's not a good idea for us to hang out here. This monster could come back."

"I don't sense any evil nearby right now. But you're probably right about risking our safety. Let's get going."

"Can I buy you a late dinner?" Matt asked.

"There's nothing open now except some fast-food places and that hideous bar."

"I could cook you something. My place isn't far."

"Are you serious?" she asked as they walked to their cars. "We're at a murder scene and there's a monster of some sort out there, and all you can think of is putting the moves on me?"

He stopped in his tracks. Oh boy, she thought, she had insulted him.

"I thought we were friends working together on this. I was just offering you some food. Is food really so bad?"

"I'm sorry, Matt," she said. "You didn't deserve that. But, to be honest, food does sound kind of bad right now. We just left the scene where a guy was eaten."

"You're right. I've lost my appetite."

8

SUPPORT YOUR LOCAL JOURNALISTS

Matt and Missy agreed that their only lead at the moment was the emails Omar Johnson had sent to the funeral director. Matt asked Missy to try finding the sender with a spell, but she said she couldn't find someone using only a name. She needed more details or physical objects associated with the person.

So that left journalism, which meant lots of tedious work and dead ends. The only magic involved was the feeling he had on the rare occasions he stumbled across a scoop. That didn't appear likely sitting here in the newsroom on a Tuesday.

There were many Omar Johnsons popping up on his internet search. When Matt searched for "Omar Johnson body broker," he came up empty. What a surprise. Searches of property taxes and public records also came up empty. Next, he searched the archives of *The Jellyfish Beach Journal* for any stories mentioning the man. All he found was an obituary for an Omar Johnson who died in 2012. A photo showed the seventy-two-year-old corporate attorney sporting a giant handlebar mustache. He, alas, could not be the body broker Matt sought.

Before he clicked away from the story, Matt's eye caught at the bottom a mention that services would be held at the Jellyfish Beach Memorial Funeral Home. Interesting coincidence.

There were several biotech firms in Florida, and he plunged into their websites. Some didn't appear to use biological materials at all and created synthetic imitations instead. Others did use human biological materials (although their product descriptions avoided the word "human"), such as ground-up bone or highly sterilized, dehydrated skin tissue. All the materials sounded so far removed from the humans from whom they had come.

Emails and phone calls to the companies ran into the roadblocks of confidential, proprietary information. One public relations person admitted that they acquired their bio-materials from "sources overseas."

He quickly realized that contacting the companies was a waste of time.

A memory came to him. He dug though his lower desk drawer and found the folder holding notes from his story a few years back about the bodies fraudulently diverted from a crematory to a local medical school for dissection. There was no body broker involved in this story, only a corrupt school administrator and a venal delivery truck driver. The driver had gone on the record for the story, cooperated with prosecutors, and received a light sentence. It couldn't hurt to give him a try.

Clarence Pipwitch was a jovial man who didn't seem to harbor any ill will toward Matt.

"Oh yeah, man, I remember you," he said. "Your stories made me look like less of a dirtbag than the TV news did."

"Yeah, we're all just working stiffs. Wait, bad choice of words. Anyway, how are you doing nowadays?"

Pipwitch described adjusting to life after prison and then finding a successful new career as a state legislator, though he admitted it was not a step up on the morality scale. After some more small talk, Matt jumped right to the point.

"Back when you worked for the crematory, did anyone else besides the medical school offer to buy bodies?" he asked.

Silence. Matt was afraid that Pipwitch was going to hang up on him.

"Like who?" he finally responded in a low voice.

"Like maybe a body broker for the biotech industry," Matt said.

More silence. "There was this guy once. Really creepy, hanging around the back of the facility. He wanted a lot of bodies. I figured it had to be something to do with the medical industry, but he didn't mention a company or give me a business card."

"What was his name?" Matt asked.

"He didn't say. And something about him gave me the willies, so I never took him up on his offer. Later, after I began my, er, arrangement with the medical school, this guy showed up at my house. He said he knew about my arrangement and would pay me double what the medical school was paying. But he said it in a threatening way, like he was a mobster, and hinted that I'd better not refuse. I told him I would do it, after I delivered the rest of the bodies for the fall semester. Then I was arrested and that was the end of the story."

"What did this man look like?"

"You know, it's hard to say. First time I saw him, he was dark-skinned, wiry, but he stayed in the shadows so I couldn't get a good look at him. The second time, I didn't recognize him until I realized what he was talking about. He looked different, bigger. But he stayed in the shadows again."

"You only saw him at night?" Matt asked.

"Yeah. Both times."

"And he was definitely human?"

Pipwitch laughed nervously. "Of course. What else would he be?" He didn't seem as strong in his conviction as he should be.

"Any clue of how I can find this guy?"

"Nope," Pipwitch said. "If he wants to, he'll find you. And I really don't think you'll want him to."

Matt thanked him and said goodbye. He immediately called Missy and filled her in.

"The shadowy guy sounds too shadowy," Missy said. "I wish we had a lead on how to find him."

"Nothing we can do on that right now except talk to Izzy Perez, the funeral director where the victim worked. My guess is that either the broker is the murderer or arranged for someone to do it."

"Remember, whoever or whatever did it was supernatural."

"It doesn't matter," Matt said, frustrated by the complications. "Perez is involved somehow. You saw the emails telling him how to deliver the bodies. He might even be the supernatural creature. If not, he can at least lead us to the body broker. It's time to play hardball."

"Let me go with you," Missy said.

"Why?"

"When a hardhead says he wants to play hardball, it's a recipe for failure. I'll try to mitigate that."

MATT AND MISSY arrived at the Jellyfish Beach Memorial Funeral Home when it opened in the morning. They told the receptionist that they were a grieving couple with a mother who died in a freak food-processor accident. They apologized for not having an appointment.

"I'll tell our funeral director, Mr. Perez, you're here," the receptionist said, calling his extension. She was young and heavily tattooed, a little out of place in a conservative business like this. "He's not answering. I'll try again in a bit. He has a lot on his plate today."

Missy performed a credible act of crying and blowing her nose. The ruse of being potential customers would fail as soon as Perez recognized Matt, but at least Perez would be caught off-guard and less ready to obfuscate.

They sat down in some nicely upholstered chairs in the wood-paneled drawing room and waited. And waited.

"Will a pot roast be okay for dinner tonight, Sweetie?" Missy asked.

"Where is he?" Matt asked in a hoarse whisper.

The receptionist glanced at him. "Let me go check on Mr. Perez."

She got up, opened the door to a hallway and closed it behind her.

"Yeah, I'm a little antsy," Matt said. "The police no doubt questioned him after the murder, so he's more likely to try avoiding answering questions again."

"We can play good-cop, bad-cop," Missy said. "I'll be the—"

The receptionist screamed in horror from behind the door.

"Bad cop?" Missy whispered.

They bolted to the closed door and Matt led the way down the hall to Perez's office.

The receptionist stood behind the desk. She screamed when Matt entered the room. And again when Missy followed.

"He was fine an hour ago," the receptionist said before sobbing.

Matt peered around the desk at what remained of Perez.

"Yeah, it's not like he came down with the flu," he said.

Perez was in approximately the same condition as Molloi had ended up. Basically, like an orange that had been consumed, leaving nothing but the seeds and peel. In this case, he was not as scattered as Molloi's remains had been. His skin was laid out like an upside-down animal-skin rug. His rib cage was snapped open and his skull cracked like a walnut.

There were no organs and precious little tissue remaining, except for some sinewy stuff clinging to the skin.

The receptionist screamed one last time and then threw up on her boss' chair.

"Can you call 911, please?" Missy asked, carefully leading the young woman from the room.

"Well, at least we can rule out Perez as a suspect," Matt said when Missy returned. "We've got that going for us."

"Except now we don't have anyone to help us find the broker." Missy studied the remains behind the desk. "I don't know what kind of shifter did this. It doesn't look like the work of a mammal predator like a lion or bear."

"Then what was it?"

"I have no idea."

"You're the expert on monsters," Matt said.

"My patients are vampires and werewolves. And the occasional elf or troll. And a few ogres. Oh, and the fae couple from New Jersey. But that's it. I'm no expert. I have no idea what else is out there."

"I didn't even believe in vampires and werewolves until recently. And witches, no offense."

"You're not alone," Missy said. "I've always had an interest in the occult, but I'm always learning more. Magick and the supernatural are filled with wonders so vast that humans will never stop discovering new things. It's just like the scientific world, but plays by different rules. Most humans simply refuse to accept those rules, so the occult stays hidden for them. Those of us with open minds get to enjoy the wonders."

"That," Matt said, pointing to the mess on the floor that used to be Izzy Perez, "is not a wonder."

"No. It's a defiling of nature. And you don't need to be supernatural to do such a horrible act. In this case, the crime happened to be committed by a supernatural creature. Let me read the energy here before the police show up."

Matt stayed quiet while Missy pulled a small pouch out of her pocket with her left hand. She closed her eyes and held both arms out. Her lips moved as she chanted something silently.

Even Matt, the least magical person he knew, sensed something electric in the air.

A few minutes later, car doors slammed outside. The police had arrived. Matt parted the blinds. The paramedics were here, too, though there was nothing for them to do.

"Let's get out of here and let them get to work," Matt said. "Did you find anything with your . . . whatever you were doing?"

"I sensed something similar to the first murder. I think the same creature did this."

In the front room, he and Missy were questioned by an officer until Affird showed up. He greeted Matt with a smirk and studied Missy through his dark shades.

"We've met before," Affird said.

"Missy Mindle," she said. "Home-health nurse."

"Oh yes, it was during the murders near Squid Tower."

Affird seemed to struggle with a memory. Missy had told Matt about Affird being mesmerized by a vampire to forget the detective's attempt to stake one of them. Missy stopped him with her magick before the memories were wiped clean.

Affird turned his attention to Matt.

"Funny how you keep turning up at my crime scenes."

"Funny isn't the word I'd use. But you know why I'm here. I'm reporting on the body snatching. I think Perez was the one selling bodies to a broker. Do you have any leads on the buyer?"

"I'm the one who gets to ask questions," Affird said. "Did you witness what happened today?"

"No. We showed up afterwards. The receptionist didn't know he'd been killed, which means she didn't hear anything. It must have happened before she arrived for work."

"Harry Roarke is innocent," Missy blurted out. "The body broker did it."

"What do you know about body brokers?" Affird asked.

"What I learned from him," Missy said pointing to Matt.

"What do *you* know?" Affird asked Matt.

"Well, not any more than you do, than what the average person can look up on the internet."

That remark angered Affird. "Something tells me you use more than the internet for your information."

"What can I say?" Matt shrugged. "I ask a lot of questions. So do you. It's a job requirement, last I checked."

"After the last murder, this case no longer belongs to the FDLE," Affird said. "It's a joint task force now, with the Jellyfish Beach P.D. as the lead agency. Do you understand what that means?"

"That you're happier now?"

"It means that I'm going to come down on you like a ton of bricks if you withhold information from me. Do you understand?"

"I understand freedom of the press."

"Don't make me laugh," Affird said.

9

FLESH PEDDLING

Jellyfish Beach was among the top-rated cities in Florida for municipal water quality. At least that's what it said on the sign outside the water utility office. There was even a fountain where people could fill water bottles for free. Matt was inside the office under the pretense of paying his water bill (two weeks before it was due) in order to have an excuse for being on the property. Missy wandered the parking lot doing reconnaissance, normal-human style as well as using magick.

There was absolutely nothing about the facility that suggested it was the place you would send human corpses, despite Omar Johnson's email saying so. There were no signs saying, "Corpse delivery in back," and no hearses parked anywhere. It was rather ironic, she noted, that the city-owned cemetery was just on the other side of a busy street from the utility.

The complex consisted of an office building facing the street with the water treatment plant behind it and a large water tower that could be seen from miles around, even by boaters on the ocean. She couldn't get inside the actual plant, but wandered around the out-buildings knowing she was probably trespassing. There was a large pumping station with unseen machinery that hummed loudly. Various sheds and storage buildings nearby required a key card to enter.

There were lots of things on the property, and they were all owned by the city water utility. Nothing indicated a separate company operated here. Why would corpses be delivered here?

She wondered if the email to Izzy Perez giving this address came from an employee or contractor here. Perhaps someone with access to the property used it as a place to transfer the bodies for shipment elsewhere.

The plant purified the fresh water pumped from the surficial aquifer, the table of water in sand and gravel closest to the surface. The wells the city used varied from fifty to 250 feet in depth. Florida has a lot of water in its aquifers in a complex honeycomb of porous limestone and other rock that spreads deep beneath the land. Down there were countless caves, sinkholes, and springs.

All that water deep below ground contained natural energies that skilled witches and sorcerers could use in spells and wonderworking.

While Matt was in the utility office, Missy roamed the parking lot in a semi-trance state, mentally probing beneath the ground with her ability to sense energy. She searched for concentrations of power. And she found plenty of it among the many channels of water beneath her. There were deep wells and a huge network of pipes, both main and subsidiary, snaking out from here to all parts of the city like roots spreading from a giant tree.

There were also tunnels for servicing the pipes. She sure

wouldn't want to go down there, she thought. There was something that disturbed her nearby, traces of negative energy of some sort. The traces were too faint to identify.

Matt came out of the office and headed for his car. She met him there.

"I didn't see any evidence of another company or any reason why corpses would come here," Missy said. "I think it's an employee with a side job who takes the corpses elsewhere."

"That makes sense. Did you find anything with your magick?"

"No." She started to say more, but hesitated.

"What?"

"I felt some negative energy, way down below," she pointed to the ground. "But it was very faint. I can't tell whether it's natural or has something to do with evil."

"Is it anything like what you felt at the crime scenes?"

"It feels similar, but I can't tell for sure. It's only a trace."

As Matt drove out of the parking lot, Missy asked, "What's next."

"We find out if Omar Johnson works for the water utility department."

"Shouldn't you ask in the office here?

"Nah, that's just the customer-service office," he said. "They would never answer such a question. We're going to City Hall. I've got a lot of sources there. Going all the way to the top."

WELL, that was a waste of time, Missy thought. Matt's sources "all the way to the top" wouldn't speak with him. The city manager told him to ask the administrator of water and sewer services who was offsite at the moment. They waited on a bench next to a vending machine that was punched and kicked by dozens of irate people when it didn't dispense their drinks.

When the administrator finally returned to City Hall, they followed him into his office where he sat down at his desk, made a few keystrokes, and announced there was no Omar Johnson on the payroll of Jellyfish Beach in any capacity.

"So now what do we do?" Missy asked as they left the building.

Matt sighed. "All I can think of is checking with other funeral homes to see if they've been approached by Omar looking for bodies to buy. Of course, if they are currently doing business with Omar, they won't tell us."

Their next stop was the Horowitz Family Funeral Home.

"Frankly, I'm offended you would even ask me such a thing," said Ben Horowitz, rising from his chair indicating he was done with them.

"Have the police spoken to you?"

"Yes. They asked me the same question."

"Were you offended then?" Matt asked.

"Mr. Horowitz, we never thought you were involved with Omar Johnson," Missy said. "We just need to know if he approached you or your employees. Or if you've heard about your competitors dealing with him."

"Unscrupulous body brokers sometimes target funeral homes and crematoriums. And we tell them to go walk off a pier. We all have reputations to protect."

"Which of your competitors have the worst reputations?" Matt asked.

"Between you and me, I wouldn't bring my worst enemy to the Jellyfish Beach Memorial Funeral Home."

Missy and Matt exchanged glances.

"Anyone else?" Matt asked.

"Dean's Discount Undertakers." Horowitz visibly shuddered. "They should have gone out of business years ago."

As they got into Matt's car, he said, "Do me a favor: If I die, tell my family to bury me in their backyard themselves."

DEAN'S DISCOUNT Undertakers was in a seedy part of town among auto parts stores, pawn shops, and cheap motels. It occupied a building that appeared to have been a fast-food restaurant in a previous life. A van from the county coroner was at the drive-through window, the driver leaning out and consulting with someone at the window. Posters covered the other windows and touted specially discounted funeral packages.

"They're like combo meals," Missy said.

The restaurant part of the building had been converted into a viewing chapel and the former ordering counter was now the sales area, with cutaway coffin samples mounted on a recently installed wall behind it. The embalming and body prepping was probably done in the back where the fryers used to be. Hopefully, the refrigerator was big enough to hold bodies instead of burger patties.

A sign on a stand announced that franchise opportunities were available.

"I do think they're onto something here," Matt said, pointing at the sign. "We're talking major growth potential."

"How can I help you folks?" a short, heavyset woman with a Southern accent asked. "We have a no-down-payment special but only if you sign today."

"That's very tempting, but we're currently not in the market," Missy said.

"Pre-planning your death-care needs is the smart way to go," the woman said.

"I'm Matt Rosen with The Jellyfish Beach Journal. And this is Missy Mindle. Can we ask you a few questions?"

Her eyes narrowed with suspicion. "Are you doing a muck-raking story about overcharging customers?"

"No, we—"

"Or about stealing jewelry from the deceased?"

"Absolutely not. We're—"

"Or about violating health and safety standards?"

"No. Let me—"

"Or about the environmental hazards we create?"

"No. That's not—"

"Or about selling bodies?"

"Um, yes, actually. About selling bodies."

"Really?"

"We're not going to name any businesses. What we really need is how to locate a body broker who's working in the area. That's all."

"I'll be frank with you. This is my last week here. I just got a job offer today from the Jellyfish Beach Memorial Funeral Home. So I don't mind telling you that the embalmer here is buried in debt. Pardon the pun. He went to one of those fly-by-night private trade schools and has tons of student-loans. Plus he has a gambling habit. If there's anyone who's making nice with body brokers, it would be him."

"Is he back there?" Missy asked, pointing where the kitchen used to be.

"We don't let him come up front."

"Let me talk to him," Missy said to Matt.

"Sure, you're less threatening than me."

"I was thinking less obnoxious. Ma'am, can you introduce me to him?"

The salesperson led Missy through a flimsy door into the back area. A steel table with drains in it stood in the center of the cramped space. A smaller table on wheels holding surgical instruments was beside it. The original stainless-steel refrigerator remained, as Missy had theorized. But looking at it, she realized the bodies would probably have to be stored standing upright in order to fit. There was a sink, several cabinets, and piles of boxes in the corner.

And sitting on a stool, playing a game on his laptop, was a young man who looked like a troll. He was overweight, had an overabundance of long, frizzy hair, and wore scrubs and an apron that were stained by bodily fluids that presumably weren't his.

"Jack. This lady is Missy. She has some questions about the body broker you deal with."

Missy was shocked by the woman's frankness. So was Jack.

"I-I-I don't. . ."

"Get over it, Jack. She just needs the guy's name. She's not going to incriminate anyone."

Through his unruly hair, Jack's eyes stared wide-eyed at them.

"Hello Jack, nice meeting you," Missy said. "I just need the broker's name and a way to contact him."

"His name is Omar Johnson. And I don't contact him. He just kind of shows up," Jack said. He had a light, squeaky voice. "Always at night."

"What does he look like?"

"It's kind of funny, but I've never gotten a good look at him. He kind of hides in the shadows. From the little I've seen of him, I do think he has a mustache, though."

"Does he take the bodies, or do you have to deliver them?"

"Wait, I don't—"

"Skip the crap, Jack," the saleswoman said. "Tell her the truth. You know that I put in my notice here, so you'll never have to deal with me again. But if you don't spill the beans, I'll tell Dean and get your butt fired."

"I delivered the bodies to the water treatment plant. Just two bodies. And I did it only one time."

"Who took possession of them?" Missy asked. "What did they do with them?"

"I don't know. Mr. Johnson told me to stay in the hearse while his helpers unloaded it. I tried to watch in the mirrors, but I only saw one person removing the bodies one at a time. And he didn't use a gurney, he carried each body over his shoulder. Isn't that crazy?"

"Where did he take them?" Missy asked.

"Somewhere in the grounds of the plant. I didn't see."

"Okay, thank you for your help. By the way, we think he's murdering his suppliers. So you might want to avoid him from now on."

Jack's eyes widened even more, beyond what the human eye should be capable of.

10

THE MUSTACHE OF EVIL

Missy's internal clock was completely thrown off. Serving her vampire patients required her to work at night and sleep during the day. She could bend those rules slightly, since she woke up in the afternoons long before sunset when the vampires did, and she usually finished her appointments and went to bed hours before dawn. She basically had the schedule of a college student on vacation.

Today, however, really messed her up. When Matt drove her home, it was mid-afternoon, not long before the hour when she normally rose. She was exhausted. But she had cats to feed, bills to pay, clothes to wash, and other chores.

Night had fallen and she was still awake. She poured a glass of Chianti Classico and took it to the porch where she sipped it in the darkness, trying to relax. Bubba and Brenda perched on the armrests of her chair while she listened to the insects, tree frogs, and other sounds of the night.

Suddenly, the cats launched themselves at the screen. They

did that when small lizards were on it, or a stray cat was on the other side, and she always worried that one day they'd break through. This time, after some serious sniffing of the air, they took off running through the open sliding-glass door into the house.

And the insects and tree frogs went quiet.

Something was out there. Something bad.

She froze in her chair and listened. There was nothing. No twigs snapped; no shoes scuffed the patio pavers outside. Palm fronds rustled in a faint breeze, but that was it. The only other sound she heard was the pounding of her heart.

"Good evening," a male voice said outside the screen door leading from the porch to the patio.

She jumped and stopped herself from screaming. Then rose from the chair silently.

"Who's there?" she asked in a hostile voice.

"It's me, Omar Johnson."

"I'm calling 911," Missy said. Too bad her phone was charging inside on the kitchen counter. If she moved toward the kitchen, she would be dangerously close to the screen door.

"No need," the deep, whispery voice said. He had an unrecognizable foreign accent. "I only want to ask why you are searching for me."

"A friend of mine is in jail for a murder he didn't commit. I want to help him."

"You think I am the murderer? Why is that?"

"I have no idea. How did you find out who I am and where I live?"

The latch of the aluminum screen door was locked, but he opened it with ease and stepped up into the porch. He stood there in the light spilling out from the kitchen, tall and broad-shouldered in a well-tailored dark suit and gold tie. He had caramel-colored skin, a full head of white hair, a broad nose, and a giant, white, handlebar mustache. His clothing and posture spoke of wealth and refinement.

Then he smiled and revealed yellow teeth with sharp points. And a faint stench of rotting flesh surrounded him.

This man, or creature, was not a vampire, Missy knew in her gut. She had no idea what he was, but her scalp tingled from a field of supernatural energy emanating from him. He was definitely not a regular human. After she focused on him for a few seconds his aura appeared, black and swirling like ink rising in a glass of water.

There was menace in his eyes.

She quickly shielded herself with a protection spell, like yanking a curtain across a window. It was minimal protection, but she began adding power to it.

He smirked. "You're a witch? I should have known. I sensed something the moment I arrived on your property."

"What do you want?" she asked as she fortified her spell.

"I want you and that reporter to stay out of my business. You've seen what I do to those who cross me."

"Yes. Are you harvesting their organs? Or just eating them?"

He lunged, crossing the porch in a blink.

The impact when he hit her shield knocked her backwards into the chair. He strained against the spell, pushing with his chest and scratching with his hands, trying to reach her with the claws that had sprung from his fingers.

Her bubble of safety ended only four feet away, so he was close enough to display his raw, animal hunger. He was a force of pure need, of insatiable wanting. His eyes were no longer intelligent, they were bestial. And what he wanted to devour, Missy knew, was her.

She had no idea how long her spell would hold, especially

with her fear threatening to overpower her. So she went on the defensive.

Gathering more energy from the earth below her, the air around her, and the magick charm she clutched in her left hand, she chanted a brief spell. The energy coalesced within her, a ball of heat inside her stomach.

And then she sent a bolt of power into the shield, crackling like electricity around the outside of her shield. It hit Omar Johnson like a bolt of lightning.

He grunted and flew backwards, crashing through the porch screen, and landing on a low schefflera tree.

"You will regret that, witch," he said, getting to his feet. He brushed dirt from his suit and resumed his air of dignity. "Stay out of my business. Next time I come for you, you'll be dead before you know it's me."

He walked away. At the edge of her yard, in the light from the setting half-moon, he changed in a subtle way. His refined bearing disappeared, and he slumped, almost as if he were drunk. He assumed an ape-like posture and raced toward the fence, propelled by his hands as well as his legs. He vaulted over the fence and was gone.

Missy's expelled breath made a loud hiss. She went inside and locked the slider. She considered calling the police, then decided it would be a waste of time. The creature that called itself Omar Johnson wouldn't be wandering the streets where the police could find him.

Where he would be instead was the question.

MISSY WAS HAVING difficulty paying attention while the vampires read aloud their short stories. It was the weekly writing workshop she taught for the undead seniors at Squid Tower, where she performed many of her patient visits. The gig provided a little extra cash and while its purpose was to keep the seniors' minds active, it also gave her insight into those minds.

Some pretty freaky insights.

"The princess feasted on the blood of her human lover," Gladys read aloud. "She was dangerously close to draining him and ending his life. If he died, she could bring him back with her own blood and turn him into a vampire. Then, they could spend eternity together."

"Don't do it!" Doris interjected.

"Yeah, the vampire children you create are nothing but a burden. Forever," Sol grumbled.

"This is not one of those make-your-own-adventure stories where you can choose the ending," Gladys said. "I already wrote what happens."

"You write so well that I'm swept up into the drama and forget that it's a story," Doris said.

"And it wasn't one of your usual sex scenes, so I was actually listening for a change," Sol said. "But I mean it, create a vampire and you create a gaping maw of need that is never satisfied."

The vampires in the class were in their sixties, seventies, and eighties. In body age. In actual age, they were each over 100 years old and their human children had passed on. A couple of them had a few centuries under their belts. Sol was 450 years old. All had seen grandchildren and great-grandchildren grow, age, and die. Marjorie had two grandchildren who had been turned into vampires (not by her) when they were still cute children, and they had been visiting her for the holidays since she moved to Florida in the 1970s.

Marjorie was an exception. When most of the vampires

spoke about children, they referred not to the children they had when human but rather the vampires they had created. That occurs when they drink their prey's blood excessively causing death by exsanguination. A vampire can revive the victim by putting their own blood into his or her mouth and then inducing them to feed upon their killer.

The victim then begins a new existence as a vampire, one who is totally helpless at first and dependent on his or her maker for sustenance and education about the world of vampires. They have to master the complex world of hunting, mesmerizing, and feeding upon prey. They have to know the dangers of sunlight, how to heal wounds, how to avoid detection by humans, and other vampire secrets. Even after doing so, they remain emotionally attached to their makers. Their makers retain a strong, almost magical pull upon them. It's a true parent-child relationship that lasts for eternity.

"And they still ask for money," Doris said. "I say to my son, 'You're a 120-year-old and you haven't learned how to manage your money?' And he keeps signing up for more credit cards. Why do they send applications to a 120-year-old with a horrible credit score?"

"Don't get me started," Sol said. "My son has been creating vampires of his own. Every time he feeds on a pretty girl, he turns her. Now he has a basement full of dependents he can't afford so he expects me to help. His generation never learned to save and invest money. He used to run around with Edgar Allan Poe and all they did was drink and write poetry."

"What kind of supernatural creature eats human corpses?" Missy asked.

The room went silent as the vampires looked at her as if she had lost her mind.

"Aren't we supposed to be talking about creative writing?" Gladys asked.

"Sorry, I'm kind of preoccupied right now," Missy said. "So, this creature will eat live people but also has no problem eating corpses that have been dead a while."

"Are there zombies in Florida?" Doris asked. "You'd think there would be with all the voodoo going on down in Miami."

"Don't get me started on Miami," Sol said. "That traffic! I've spent more than a few human lifetimes stuck on I-95."

"And the prices down there, can you believe it?" Doris asked. "I know a vampire who lives in a retirement community in Aventura and her HOA fee is *four times* what ours is."

"Missy," Bill said. He'd been uncharacteristically silent tonight. "If you want a real answer to your question, you should ask Agnes. She knows more than this whole group combined about monsters."

"Can I finish reading my story now?" Gladys asked plaintively.

AGNES GEBERICH WAS the president of the HOA and a youthful 1,500 years old. She was born to a noble family of the Visigoth people and was turned into a vampire while the declining Roman Empire still existed. Aside from her HOA board position, she served as the unofficial leader of the vampires of Squid Tower. Ninety-something years old in body age, she got around with the help of a quad cane, but could still throw a spear with deadly accuracy. Not that this ability was needed very often in a condominium tower full of senior citizens in Jellyfish Beach, Florida. But it did come in handy once when she killed a couple of young vampire punks with spears made of sharpened rebar bought at a home-improvement store.

"In ancient times, there were many more supernatural creatures wandering the earth than today," she said to Missy as they sat on wooden benches overlooking the beach at the end of the community's dune crossover. "There were monsters the likes of which the world has long forgotten."

"I'm not surprised," Missy said. "I've also learned about many from the New World, from the Caribbean and South and Central America that show up in Florida. But I don't think this is one of them."

"If I had to guess," Agnes said, "I would say the creature is a ghoul."

"I've heard the term 'ghoulish,' but I don't really know what a ghoul is."

"They originated in what we once called Arabia. They are demonic creatures that rob graves and eat corpses. Some of them can shape-shift into a human form to lure people to an out-of-the-way place where they attack and eat them."

This sounded eerily like Omar Johnson and his body brokering.

"Ghouls migrated from Arabia, attracted by mass-casualty events in other parts of the world," Agnes continued. "I've seen them in Europe after great battles when corpses were left to lie on the battlefield. After night fell, the ghouls would crawl out of tunnels and roam among the fallen, devouring corpses and the few wounded soldiers left alive. Whenever the Black Death spread, ghouls were not far behind. Apparently, they didn't mind eating bodies that had died of the plague. The European armies fighting in the crusades wrote about them. Even in modern times there have been reports of ghouls, picking corpses clean in the no-man's land between the trenches in World War One or following the German army as it retreated from Russia in the Second World War."

Missy explained her and Matt's investigation of the body snatching and Omar Johnson.

"I'm surprised ghouls are here in America," Missy said. "We haven't had great wars like in Europe."

"Don't forget the American Civil War. That's when the first reports of ghouls in this country began. They migrated here from Mexico, Peru, and other lands where the Spanish Conquistadors killed thousands and spread diseases that killed countless more. There were tales of ghouls after battles in the Western frontiers."

"Why would they be in Florida?" Missy asked.

"For one very simple reason: The elderly come to Florida in droves. Those who don't exist forever, like we vampires, will pass away here. That's a lot of corpses every year."

"So the ghouls are just another example of the parasites, like financial scammers, that come here to exploit the old people."

"A good way to put it," Agnes said.

"How do you kill a ghoul?"

"I don't know for sure. I've never come face to face with one. In the legends, a single blow with a sword will do it. But a second blow will bring them back to life. However, this Omar Johnson you describe sounds like a more powerful ghoul, since he can shape-shift. It might be harder to kill him."

"Right now, he's the only ghoul that has threatened my life."

"If you need my help," Agnes said, taking Missy's hands into her cold vampire palms, "don't hesitate to ask."

When Missy got home, she waited until it wasn't too early in the morning before she called Matt. She told him about Omar Johnson's visit and what Agnes had told her about ghouls.

"Here I am once again, learning about another supernatural creature that's not supposed to exist, yet does in Jellyfish Beach," he said.

"I thought you'd be used to it by now."

"I seem to still have the ability to be gobsmacked. So, tell me what our friend Omar looks like."

She described the tall, dapper fellow and his striking mustache.

"Wait a second," he said. The clicking of a computer keyboard came from his end. "So a large, white, handlebar mustache?"

"Yes."

"Full head of white hair, parted on the side?"

"Yep."

"I'm sending you a link with a photo. Tell me if it looks like him."

A few seconds later, Matt's email arrived, and she clicked on the link. A page from the Jellyfish Beach Journal archives came up. She was surprised to see that it was an obituary.

Because the Omar Johnson in the photo, who passed away in 2012, was the same Omar who showed up on her porch the previous night.

"It's the same guy," she said in a low voice.

"Maybe he faked his death?"

"No. I did some research after I spoke with Agnes. The ghouls who can shape-shift often take on the appearance of a person they ate."

"Jeez," Matt said. "So after Mr. Johnson was brought to the

funeral home—which, you'll notice, was Izzy Perez's place—he ended up as supper for this ghoul. I wonder why it keeps using his likeness after all these years?"

"The mustache," Missy said, "what ghoul would not want a mustache like that?"

11

SINKHOLE

It was Tuesday, just after sunset, and time for work. Missy packed her tote bag with fresh medical supplies and got ready to leave. She had four patient visits scheduled, routine vampire health-screenings (if you accept that giving vampires medical exams was something you could call routine).

But she sensed supernatural energy pouring in from somewhere.

Uh-oh, she thought, is this another magick test?

The energy was alarmingly strong now. But she didn't know what or where was the source.

An odd, low rumbling came from the front of the house. Then a loud pop. She stuck her head out the front door. In the light from the moon and her front-porch lamp, it was readily apparent that a long, jagged crack had split her concrete drive-way. While she was watching, another, wider fissure snaked across the driveway beneath her car.

"Hey!" She called to whoever or whatever was causing the magick. "I just had that driveway resurfaced. It was expensive."

More rumbling noises came from beneath the ground.

Then came a sharp jolt and vibrations like an earthquake. She held on to the doorframe, but the tremor was brief. A loud crack hit her ears. It sounded like a truck hit her house, but she saw nothing of the sort.

Until a giant hole in her driveway and lawn opened and her car disappeared into it. The hole appeared deep. From where she was standing, she couldn't see the bottom of it. Down there in the darkness was her ancient Toyota with 250,000 miles on it and water damage in the interior. A trade-in value of about $140, gone.

Sinkholes were common in Florida. In fact, there are more here than any other state. They're caused when pockets form in the porous limestone beneath the state and the roof of the pocket collapses. They were rare in the Jellyfish Beach area, however. This fact confirmed Missy's guess that it was caused by magick.

If it were true that these attacks against her were based on the five elements, she'd already been through water, air, and fire. Presumably, this one represented earth.

And if the attacks were actually tests of her powers and abilities, what was she supposed to do here? Use her magick to lift her car out of the hole? What if she'd rather just take the loss?

A *BAM* followed by thunderous rumbling startled her. Then a huge section of her lawn disappeared. The hole was now twice as large, and it threatened to take her house down with it. So the answer to her question was: Stop the freaking sinkhole!

This was all new to her. She'd never created a spell to stop something from caving in. She forced herself to think quickly. The most obvious route would be to shore up the roof of the pocket in the limestone, the way you'd try to stop a mine shaft from collapsing. The problem was, she didn't have any large timbers lying around to prop up the roof.

Well, she did have a fifteen-year-old Toyota that was already in the hole. Her main concern was the ground collapsing beneath her house. If she could wedge the car under the roof of the underground limestone pocket as close as possible to the house, that should stop the collapsing. Hopefully the pocket didn't extend all the way under her house. In that case, her abode was a goner.

Her secondary concern was how the heck was she going to move her car? Missy had always possessed the rudimentary power of telekinesis, the ability to move matter with her mind. She had this ability before she even learned about the magick in her blood. Stopping her phone from dropping to the ground or transporting a plate from the table to the sink with her mind alone was not a big deal. Combining her telekinetic abilities with her magick could accomplish much, much more.

But move a car like a four-by-four piece of wood?

Faint rumbling came from the earth. She'd better hurry. She moved outside, as close to the hole as she dared to stand, and immediately began to form a spell. Drawing upon all the powers within her and from the earth beneath her feet, she focused everything she had on her mental image of the car.

She had an image of it lying on rocks, tilted to the side. She envisioned it rising slightly so that it no longer rested on the rocks. She forced power through her extremities toward the car —her telekinetic powers plus an added boost from the magick. She heaved the car up with her mind. She sensed its great weight, and she felt it lifting. Then she moved it toward her and the house.

The hole was giant and there was room for the car, hovering about the bottom, to drift toward her until it was nearly beneath her. Suddenly there was resistance. The car had reached the edge of the hole. Now came the even trickier part.

She tilted the car so it stood vertically, hood up, trunk down. And then yanked it toward her until it wedged itself between the floor of the sinkhole and the limestone roof. She pulled it, the whine of scraping metal escaping from the hole, until the car shuddered to a stop. It could go no further. Hopefully, it would keep the ground from collapsing anymore.

"Wow," Missy said aloud. She'd never moved such a large object before, especially not manipulating its position like that. Had she passed the test?

The creatures crawling out of the sinkhole would indicate a big, fat "no."

It was like rats crawling out of a well, but in this case the creatures were humanoid. No, scratch that. Dozens of them pouring out of the hole, then shuffling on all fours across her lawn. She ran back into the house and slammed the front door just before bodies thudded against it.

She couldn't stop herself from screaming.

The creatures were ghouls, she was sure of it. She didn't study them carefully before fleeing, but what she had seen were pale, gray-fleshed, naked beings. They were skinny and bony and had long claws on their hands and feet, thin tufts of hair on their heads and upper bodies, as well as a small patch on the bottom of their pelvic areas. Their gigantic mouths hung open, revealing sharp, discolored teeth. Their noses were merely twin holes above their ravenous mouths.

Their eyes were giant, dark pupils surrounded by yellow. Hungry, merciless eyes that had all fixed upon her the moment they each pulled themselves out of the hole.

They weren't human, but there was something humanoid

about them. That made the sight of them even more repulsive and disturbing.

The door thudded again and again as they threw themselves at it. She worried that it wouldn't hold.

One of them crashed against the living room window. It clung to it like a tree frog, pressing its face against the glass. Its pointy tongue slurped the window as if could smell and taste Missy through it.

Thank God she had installed impact windows so she didn't have to install shutters every time a hurricane threatened. The ghoul didn't break through, but the window was still cracked. The monster continued pressing against the window, staring at her hungrily.

This magick test was costing her a lot of money, from her car to the landscaping and window damage. But no time to regret that now.

She had to get rid of these ghouls. Not just for her own sake but before they began eating her neighbors. The night was still early enough that dog-walkers would be passing by her house, not to mention curiosity seekers looking at the sinkhole. They could all end up as ghoul food unless she did something fast. All it would take would be for one dog to be devoured and she would be persona non grata in this neighborhood.

The first thing she did was cast a protection spell in order to seal the house shut and prevent the ghouls from entering. As when Omar threatened her, she had to cast this spell quickly. But now she had time to add power to it and make it self-sustaining enough to allow her to focus her attention on other matters.

Next, she needed a warding spell to try to repel the ghouls. This spell was a bit more labor-intensive. For her, spell casting was usually an elaborate ritual involving drawing a magick circle on her floor and a lot of other time-consuming steps. But she didn't have that luxury tonight. So she began by grasping her power charm in her left hand, the most direct channel to her heart, and by reciting a general invocation in Old English meant to guard against invaders and evil spirits.

At the same time, she marshaled all the energy she could absorb from the earth, air, and deep within herself. She needed to create a giant surge of power like when she had fought off Omar Johnson. But this time, the power had to be massively greater.

She recited the invocation again and again. Its words sparked some magick, but mostly they helped her focus her mind and spirit while she amassed the energies. And it was difficult to do so while the front door shuddered from repeated blows.

When she felt the pressure and heat in her solar plexus grow to the point of being painful, she launched the spell. A wave of exhaustion spread over her along with a feeling of emptiness.

The ghoul dropped from the window and scurried toward the sinkhole. The beating upon her front door ceased. She looked through the spiderweb of cracks in the window. The porch light had been destroyed by the ghouls, but the moonlight illuminated the chaotic scene of ghouls scrambling to return to the hole while new ones attempted to climb out.

It was like the chaos when ants pouring out of their mound collided with those trying to return. Only this wasn't ants but naked ghouls scurrying about on all fours in her front yard.

She needed a neutron bomb-like spell to wipe them out like insecticide sprayed on the ant mound. But she didn't have that kind of power or knowledge to create the spell. Moreover, the thought of killing her enemies en masse bothered her. That was an evil black-magic act which went contrary to the rules of her white magick.

And the number of ghouls below the earth could be inexhaustible. Whatever she did to stop them tonight would only be a temporary fix.

A small flash of light came from the house at the far end of her street. It was the front door of the Vansetti's house opening and closing. Old Man Vansetti was taking Fifi out for her evening walk, heading toward Missy's house. Both were about to become dead meat fought over by scores of ghouls.

Dead meat. That gave her a weird idea for a spell that didn't involve blasting anyone. It wouldn't even require as much power as her last two spells had. However, she had never created one like this before.

A spell that worked not by raw force, but by raw smell.

A stink bomb spell that smelled like rotting flesh. The most wonderful odor in the world if you were a ghoul.

This would not be a mass hypnosis of the ghouls. Nor would she create molecules of stink out of thin air. No, she would need to create the illusion of a cloud of stink. A virtual stink.

Not having sampled the smell of rotting humans before, she had to use her imagination. So she focused on olfactory memories of the smell of rotting fish on the beach, or the reek of spoiled meat and shellfish in the dumpster behind the tourist seafood restaurants along highway A1A. Or the recent occasion when she came across the dead armadillo on her street.

There was a unique smell to rotting flesh and it normally triggered the gag instinct in humans. Evolution did that for us so we wouldn't eat meat that made us sick. But the smell does the opposite in vultures and, she was betting, in ghouls.

So she focused on this olfactory memory and directed layers of power into it, giving it substance and staying power. She cranked up the odor level until she smelled it in her own living room. She bundled it in a tight package of power. Then she mentally lobbed it into the sinkhole like a hand grenade and directed it to burrow as deep into the earth as possible.

A final jolt of power activated it.

The ghouls stopped where they were and moved their heads about, opened their giant mouths even wider, and sniffed hungrily. Then, as if answering the dinner bell, they raced into the sinkhole, bowling over the others who were climbing out. Or should she call it the stinkhole?

In less than a minute, her property was free of ghouls.

Old Man Vansetti appeared in front of her house and stopped, staring at the sinkhole in shock. His white Pomeranian yapped furiously, trying to get to the hole. Fifi caught the scent of the creatures in there, though her master had no idea. The old man took pictures with his phone and then dragged his dog away. Missy remained inside until he left, because she didn't want to be engaged in conversation. She didn't trust that a stray ghoul wouldn't pop out of the hole.

Once he was gone, she stuck her head out of the door and sniffed. She didn't smell anything bad. The cloud must have travelled deep into the limestone fissures beneath the earth. And hopefully the ghouls would stay down there and not come back up this hole.

It looked as if she had passed the fourth test of her magick. With Water, Air, Fire, and Earth under her belt, that left Spirit. When would that come?

In the meantime, she had to call her lawn guy and tell him not to show up tomorrow because there was no lawn left to mow. And she had to find a way to get to work since her car was now underneath what was left of the missing lawn.

She had passed this magick test, but boy was it expensive.

12

YOUR OWN WORST CRITIC

Two hours and two cancelled appointments later, Missy stood in front of her house, next to the fluttering yellow caution tape she had tied around stakes at the edge of the yawning sinkhole.

The freakishly odd thing was that the sinkhole was gone. She'd walked out the front door and blinked in disbelief when she saw her lawn had returned to normal, except for a slight depression where the hole had been. Her neighbor Old Man Vansetti also blinked in disbelief from the street with Fifi straining at her leash.

Wasn't this past Vansetti's bedtime?

"What happened to the hole," Vansetti asked.

"Oh, it's there. You're just looking at a temporary covering of AstroTurf. It's purely aesthetic, so don't let Fifi walk on it. I didn't want to depress everyone else's home values."

Old Man Vansetti blinked some more and then pulled Fifi back to his house. He looked back once at her. He clearly thought she was nuts.

She waited for the ride-share car to arrive to take her to her remaining appointments. Her auto insurance company had been arguing that they didn't cover sinkholes, so they wouldn't pay for a rental car. She planned to inquire if her home insurance policy had any coverage, but in the meantime she was carless.

The sinkhole had magically been covered over, but the power that did it forgot to get her car out beforehand.

The ride-share app said Bill in a Kia was going to show up. Instead, a brown station wagon rattled slowly down her street with flickering headlights and stopped beside her. The car looked like one her adoptive family had owned when she was a child. The driver stepped out, a pale, skinny guy in blue overalls and a greasy comb-over.

"Ready to go, Missy?" he asked.

"You're not the driver who is supposed to pick me up."

"Oh, yes I am. I've always been. We best be going now. We have a long trip."

"I'm going to Squid Tower on the beach. It's like five miles away. I'm a nurse. I have patient appointments tonight."

"Oh, no. I'm taking you to the In-Between. This has been commanded."

That's when Missy realized something was seriously wrong. She finally sensed the magick. Was this the fifth test?"

"Sorry, I'm not going to the—"

Suddenly, she was in the backseat of the car and they were driving not down her street at night but across a narrow bridge over an endless sea in daylight. She looked ahead and behind and there were no other cars. The bridge was an old stone structure, running not very high above the surface of the water. It reminded her of the original Seven Mile Bridge in the Florida Keys, however this one was not punctuated by any islands. It simply ran straight forever with no sight of land.

So they were going to the In-Between. Or maybe they were there already. She had been to the In-Between before. It was on a different plane of existence from earth, in an ill-defined point between Heaven and Hell like purgatory or limbo. It was a way station of sorts. Souls were stranded there before they could go to their ultimate destination. Creatures from different worlds and dimensions passed through there. A race of dragons used the In-Between as a hiding place when they were almost wiped out by humans in the days of yore. Demons from Hell and Angels from Heaven used it as a middle ground.

The In-Between was not a safe place for humans. She'd visited once via astral travel, which was only moderately dangerous. Another time she came physically, entering through a magical gateway that the dragons used. She had barely escaped with her life. So why was she forced to come here now?

"Hey," she tried to get the driver's attention. "Are we there yet?"

His eyes in the rearview mirror met hers. "Yes."

He stopped the car abruptly.

"We're here," he said.

"What are you talking about? We're on a bridge in the middle of an ocean."

"Oh we're here, all right. We've always been here."

Suddenly, she was standing on the bridge and the car was nowhere to be seen.

What was she supposed to do? she wondered. She could walk, but which way? There was no breeze at all, and the surface of the sea was as smooth as glass. No sun shone overhead; a dull gray light painted the entire landscape. The temperature was slightly cool, but not uncomfortable.

She stood for what felt like an eternity, but could have been only a couple of minutes since her sense of time didn't work here. She decided to walk. But which way? Her gut told her to go in the opposite direction than the one the car had been traveling. Ahead of her the road went perfectly straight as far as she could see until it disappeared at the horizon.

She walked at a steady pace. The concrete walls on either side of the road, and the road itself, were old-looking but they were not weathered. In fact, there didn't appear to be weather here. There were no seagull-droppings on the structure like you'd see if it had been on earth. It was sterile with no signs of mildew, insects, or any forms of life.

A figure appeared far in the distance. It could be someone dangerous, but she'd rather try her luck. So she continued walking toward it. Soon it became clear that the person was walking toward her.

As the distance between them diminished, the figure was recognizable as a woman. Before long, she made out that the woman was wearing blue nurse scrubs like herself. And had long, brunette hair, too.

Soon came a punch in her gut when she realized the woman walking toward her was her twin.

Missy, of course, was an only child. She knew this wasn't a twin sister she didn't know she had. The matching scrubs with the Acceptance Home Care I.D. badge made it clear that this woman was an apparition conjured by whomever was launching the magick attacks against her.

What was the apparition going to do? That unknown frightened her.

She slowed her pace, but the other Missy kept coming at a steady clip. They were close enough now that Other-Missy's facial expression could be read. It was twisted in disgust.

Missy stopped walking and waited as Other-Missy walked right up to her and got in her face.

"I should have let you walk all the way to me," Other-Missy said. "You look like you need to burn some calories."

"Who are you?" Missy asked.

"I'm your inner critic. Your nagging self-doubt. Your insecurities."

"Nice meeting you. But I feel like we've known each other for years."

"But you've never listened to me," Other-Missy said.

"I've listened to you too much. You've held me back in life."

"Held you back? You're the one who decided to throw away a promising career as an intensive-care nurse. You complained that you were burned out and over-stressed. You worried that you were losing your empathy toward patients. Boo-hoo. Poor little dear. Those were just excuses. You walked away from a good paycheck because you were weak.

"And you left it for what?" Other-Missy demanded with a sneer. "A low-paying job taking care of vampires and werewolves? Monsters that kill people. Monsters who don't even have proper health insurance!"

"My patients are senior citizens," Missy said. "They're mellow and cautious and don't kill people. Well, rarely."

Other-Missy snorted. "And you *still* haven't remarried? You're in your forties already. It's too late for you with your looks going and your personality souring. I suppose I shouldn't be surprised you couldn't find a new husband. After all, your lack of good judgement led you to marry a man who turned out to be gay. A man who cheated on you and became a vampire before he got himself staked. If I were you, I'd be reluctant to make another mistake like that."

"You *are* me. But you're really just my shadow," Missy said defiantly. "You don't have the courage to create an existence of your own. All you are capable of doing is to be a parasite and feed off my life, criticizing me after the fact for decisions I make in my *real* life."

Other-Missy slapped her in the face.

Missy froze, stunned. Then she slapped the apparition in its face. The sensation in her hand was just like slapping real flesh. It felt pretty good, actually. Other-Missy crouched, preparing to rumble with her better self.

"Why am I here?" Missy asked.

"To be tested. I represent the fifth element, Spirit."

"If this is a test of my magick powers, why was I brought to the In-Between. I can't access earth energies so my magick is really weak here."

"Exactly," Other-Missy replied. "The only powers you have are those you were born with and those you've developed over time.

"Who is testing me?"

"I don't know who or what conjured me. I only know that I am born of you. Everyone has the seeds of their own self-destruction inside of them. And I'm yours, girl."

Other-Missy sneered at her and a wave of depression swept through Missy, more severe than she had ever known. She felt silly and absurd in her quest to become a better witch. In fact, being a witch at all was a waste of time. It was a pretentious affectation to believe she had supernatural abilities and could use them to manipulate the material world. Or that she was more powerful than other humans. Or even deserved to be more powerful.

And she certainly didn't have what it took to gain greater

powers. She wasn't smart enough. Or strong enough. Or brave enough. She wasn't even a good enough person to wield white magick.

And what was the point of these powers anyway? It wasn't as if she were making the world a better place. She wasn't wiping out poverty with a spell, or ending ignorance and hatred with a bolt of power. She was fighting off ghouls who wouldn't have been trying to eat her if she weren't a pretend-witch to begin with.

Her assumption was wrong that the magick tests were meant to see how strong and knowledgeable she was. They were really meant to teach her how pointless and undesirable it all was.

She was a nurse. Not even a particularly good nurse. Just a nurse. She took blood and urine samples from monsters—creatures the rest of society didn't want to exist. Hers was a job anyone could do. If she disappeared forever no one would care or even remember who she'd been.

Her thoughts grew darker, her self-hatred more intense. She didn't deserve to live, and life wasn't worth living anyway. The pain from her depression was too much to bear.

Deep inside, she knew what was going on here. Some sort of magic was attacking her spirit, tearing it apart and depriving her of the will to even fight back. But knowing this was happening wasn't enough to help her stop it.

The urge to fling herself over the stone railing of the bridge and into the sea was intense. She didn't fear the agony of drowning.

She looked into the eyes of Other-Missy. She'd often seen her eyes in mirrors looking back at herself with disappointment or contempt. But the malevolence in Other-Missy's eyes was unnatural. Maybe it wasn't magick that was attacking her, but black magic. White magick shouldn't be used to make someone kill herself.

"Go ahead. Jump," Other-Missy said.

Missy looked down at the water. It was absolutely still and opaque, with no indication of how deep it was. She imagined no fish or other organisms were in it. It was pure and silent. A fitting grave. She hoped death would be quick.

A small part of her fought the urge by distracting her thoughts.

Missy stared at her doppelgänger and tried to assess the source of the magic that animated it. She had sufficient power inside her, even without earth magick, to probe what kind of magic was at work. Deep inside Other-Missy's eyes, there was no sign of evil. Whether black magic lurked inside, she couldn't tell.

If evil were in fact at work here, why not throw Other-Missy off the bridge instead of killing herself?

But her white magick was, at its core, a celebration of the wonders of the universe. It was about life and love, not death and hatred.

And she used it to probe Other-Missy. The magick that created the doppelgänger was not trying to kill her. It wasn't even trying to exploit her weaknesses.

It was searching for what love may remain in Missy's midlife heart. With no romantic interest, no children to dote upon, did her heart still have the capacity to love?

To love, most importantly, herself?

She studied Other-Missy. The eyes she studied looked back at hers and seemed vulnerable. They glanced away. They were actually pretty, in her humble opinion. Everyone had always said she had beautiful eyes with their dark, grayish shade of blue. The wrinkles in the corners of her eyes and around her mouth were signs of maturity and experience—not of her looks "going." The face showed a strong capacity for compassion and a deep reservoir of empathy.

This was a good person. A person deserving of life.

It was herself she was thinking about.

She realized self-doubt and criticism, along with insecurity, were inescapable. Being able to manipulate energies and move objects in the material world was a great power and privilege. It brought with it profound responsibilities. This, naturally, would make a witch question whether she had the ability and resolve to pull it all off. Whether she was even deserving of it.

Missy finally realized that if she were to achieve her full potential as a witch, she would have to acknowledge any self-doubt. And then cast it aside and fulfill the task at hand.

Her depression dissipated instantly, replaced by a sense of well-being. Other-Missy's eyes widened with surprise.

"You still could lose some weight," the doppelgänger said before vanishing.

Missy stood alone on the bridge. Now what? The only thing she could do was continue walking.

Before long, a rattling came from behind her. The brown station wagon approached. She stopped walking and it pulled up beside her. Without asking, she opened the door and sat in the back seat. The driver was the same skinny guy with the comb-over.

"Home, James," she said.

And seconds later, she was. It was night again. Before she exited the car, she tried to get an answer from the driver.

"Do you know what I'm supposed to do now?" she asked.

He kept his eyes facing the street. "Follow your destiny. What else would you do?"

Seconds after the station wagon disappeared down the street, the ride-share car arrived in front of her house. She checked her watch. No time had elapsed since the moment before she was taken to the In-Between.

13

JEANS THERAPY

Missy was overdue for picking up her jeans from the Fates. So after her vampire appointments at Squid Tower, she stopped by Three Sisters Sewing and Alterations. It was just before dawn and a normal tailor shop would never be open at this hour. Even the deli next door wasn't open yet. But, not surprisingly, bright light and the music of a bouzouki poured out of the shop.

"Good morning, little flower," Atropos said from behind the counter. "We've been waiting for you."

Missy leaned over the counter and gave her a hug. Atropos smelled of mothballs and cigarette smoke. Missy handed the grandmotherly goddess her claim check.

"We need to chat," Atropos said as she went to a rack in the rear of the store and returned with the jeans draped on a hanger. She held the garment up to show it to Missy. Clotho, Atropos' sister, had done a great job using the cloth from a red bandana as patches to cover the damage from the fire test when she had accidentally rubbed her thighs and set her pants on fire. The paisley pattern on the patches looked pretty cool.

"Nice job," Missy said.

"You don't see what I see. The story lies in the stitching."

"What do you mean?"

"The threads of your future life have changed," Atropos said, clucking with irony.

"I still don't understand. I know my genes can shape my future, but I didn't know my blue jeans could."

"You need to go across the street and talk to my sisters. Twelve Hemlock Drive." She handed the jeans to Missy. "They're expecting you."

"Uh, okay. How much do I owe you for the patches?"

"Nothing, my little flower. It's our gift to you."

Missy thanked her warmly. She decided to leave her rental car parked at the shop and walk to the mobile home. As she crossed A1A to the mobile home park, she had an ominous feeling. After the tests of the five elements, her ordeal should have been over. Apparently not.

The tightly packed mobile homes of the community formed a sea of aluminum. But if you could live right by the beach, who cares? The narrow streets ran perpendicular to the beach and she quickly found Hemlock Drive. The Fates' trailer was in the middle of the block. Lachesis sat on a folding chair on a wooden deck attached to the home. She wore a matching pink track suit with a flamingo made of sequins on her top. She was short and stocky like her sisters. In fact, they could almost pass for triplets.

An elderly man pedaled by on an adult tricycle with a large basket on the back. Greek and American flags fluttered from the basket. He wore a bathing suit and no shirt and had a tanned, bodybuilder's physique that looked twenty years younger than his face.

"Good evening, Hercules," Lachesis called to him.

He waved a muscular arm, but kept pedaling.

Could that be *the* Hercules? Missy wondered. She wouldn't be surprised if the Fates weren't the only mythological beings residing in Jellyfish Beach.

"Come in, young lady," Lachesis said. "We've been expecting you."

The Fates' trailer was a double-wide, but was tight inside with lots of old furniture that was too big for the space. Clotho sat in a recliner facing a large-screen TV watching an old Burt Reynolds movie while she knitted. She smiled and nodded at Missy without missing a stitch.

Lachesis went into the kitchen nook and returned with a cup of tea for Missy, then sat next to her on the couch.

"Did Atropos explain what was revealed when the patches were sewn upon your pants?"

"Not really. And I don't understand how something could be revealed. Clotho, you sewed the patches so couldn't you make the stitches mean what you wanted them to?"

"No, that's not how it works," Clotho said. "I sew, or weave, or knit with no agenda, and divine inspiration passes through me. Afterwards, the stitches can be interpreted for what they portend."

"Um, and what do they portend?" Missy asked.

"Your destiny has become clearer and more urgent," Lachesis said. "We have seen that you passed a series of tests, which actually shifted your destiny somewhat. Now you have a path ahead of you that leads to greatness."

Missy almost spit out her sip of tea. "Could you be a bit more specific? What sort of greatness?"

Lachesis and Clotho broke out laughing. They laughed long enough to be annoying.

"What's so funny?" Missy asked.

"Humans have pestered us for thousands of years to reveal their destinies," Lachesis said. "When we don't answer, they slaughter livestock and think they can divine the future from reading the entrails. Or by interpreting the patterns of flying birds. Or reading tea leaves. Tea leaves!" She snorted. "You mortals are so silly and vain."

"Can you blame us for wanting to know what's going to happen to us?"

"There's no point in knowing," Lachesis said. "My sisters and I will lead you to your destiny, and if you won't be led, we'll drag you kicking and screaming."

"We can tell her about her heritage," Clotho said.

"I was going to." She turned to Missy and her expression became more serious. "What I *can* tell you about what the stitching revealed is the strong pull of your birth parents upon your destiny. It was very minor before, but now it is dominating since you passed the tests."

"Did my parents have something to do with the tests? I don't know how, since they're dead."

"Even we don't know everything," Clotho said, and both sisters began laughing again.

Missy didn't know much about her birth parents' involvement as witches, since they passed away when she was a baby, and the mention of any form of magic was forbidden by her adoptive parents. She hadn't even known they were witches until her mom let it slip during her father's funeral.

"We suggest you talk to your mother and find out what you can," Lachesis said. "You can't ignore your destiny. If you don't embrace it, it will come find you."

"Thank you for the tea. And for what you were willing to tell me," Missy said as she headed for the door. "You wouldn't want to share tonight's winning Lotto numbers, would you?"

The sisters' laughter could still be heard when she reached the end of the street.

MISSY CALLED her mother when she got home. Her adoptive parents had moved to Tennessee when they retired, while Missy stayed in Florida. After her husband died, Mabel Mindle remained in their home.

"Hey, Mom, it's me."

"Hello, honey. Are you calling for money?"

"No! I haven't asked for a loan in years."

"Good. I'm glad you're finally becoming financially responsible. What do you need?"

"Maybe I'm calling just to say hello."

"I can tell from the tone of your voice," her mother said. "You need something."

"Okay, you're right. It's about Ted and Ophelia. I need to talk to you about them."

Her mother didn't answer for a while. "Why now?"

"You know that I've been practicing magick."

"Yes. And you know that I don't approve of it."

"Right, but I've had some stuff happen that I'm pretty sure is related to Ted and Ophelia. I need to find out how and why. Remember, you let it slip that Dad had saved some of their books and papers. Can I take a look at them?"

Her mother sighed. "I should have thrown them out when Mark died. There's still so much of his crap in the barn I don't even know where to begin."

"Mom, do you mind if I come for a short visit so I can look through the stuff?"

"Honey, you're welcome here anytime. You know that. And you have the right to see your birth parents' things. You should also know I think it's a bad idea to see those particular things."

"Thanks! See you on Saturday."

MABEL MINDLE LIVED in a former farmhouse outside of Franklin, Tennessee. The farm had been sold off to developers, but the home was on five acres and felt like real country. The rolling hills were blanketed with snow and Missy spent the afternoon in the kitchen chatting with her mother near the wood-burning, potbelly stove.

Mabel wasn't as tall as Missy and kept her hair short, but she had the same thin frame and grayish-blue eyes, so people were often fooled into thinking they were related by blood. They didn't have much else in common except for the "m" in their names. When Mark Mindle married Mabel, they thought it would be amusing to give their daughter, adopted as an infant, the nickname of Missy, which won out over her actual name of Elizabeth.

Personality-wise, they weren't alike at all. Mabel, a retired college professor, had the stern nature of an intellectual, while Missy was down-to-earth and a bit of a jokester. And the fact she was developing as a witch put more distance between the two women.

After her mother went to bed, Missy crossed the snowy lawn to the barn. The main floor was left unfinished, but the hayloft had been converted into an office for her father. A former marketing executive, he had a secret passion for reading about the occult. Maybe it was a common gene he shared with his cousin, Missy's birth father. So she wasn't surprised that he had collected the occult materials that Ted had owned.

She didn't realize how extensive the collection was until she looked in the office closet and saw dozens of boxes piled in the back with "Ted and Ophelia" written on them in marker. She didn't know where to begin or, even, what she was searching for. She had simply hoped that she would find something that would connect the magick attacks with her parents and explain their purpose in testing her.

The box on the top contained a wide range of books, including several titles by Aleister Crowley, Wicca spell books, and different editions of *The Key of Solomon*. Another box was filled with volumes on ancient Egyptian and Middle Eastern magic. A third was dedicated to African religions and magic.

Finally, she came across a carton with a different trove. Jade carvings of fertility goddesses, a Medieval painting on a plaque portraying Satan. Various knickknacks and souvenirs that seemed random. At the bottom was a wooden box, about the size of a cigar box but thicker. It was mahogany stained a dark shade with mystical sigils she didn't recognize carved along the sides. She pulled it out and placed it on her lap.

There was a tight seam running around the box indicating that the top was about an inch thick. It had recessed hinges on one side, but no sign of a latch on the other. She tried to open the lid and couldn't. There was no movement at all. If it weren't for the hinges, she would have guessed the seam was actually a groove and that the top didn't open.

As she handled the box, she felt the power of a locking spell. She closed her eyes and fell into a half trance. Probing with her mind, she assessed the locking spell, just as a thief would inspect the tumblers of a lock. Instantly, she knew it was extremely powerful. She put aside the thought of defeating it for now.

The box was polished to a brilliant shine except for its top which was covered with a haze. It was as if a coat of cloudy wax had been spread over it. Through it, some circles and lines could be faintly seen. She instinctively wiped it with her hand. That didn't help. She rubbed it for several minutes with the sleeve of her top, yet it remained cloudy. She felt an insistent need to see what was carved on that lid.

So she tried a clarifying spell. This was a versatile bit of magick that had come in handy for everything from clearing her muddled mind after waking up when tea wasn't doing the trick, to removing the smashed remains of love bugs from her windshield which otherwise is impossible without pulling over and washing them with a squeegee. Clever witches won't do their housecleaning without it.

She chanted a simple invocation while grasping her power charm, summoned energies from deep within and from the rolling hills around. Then she slowly waved her hand across the top of the box a couple of millimeters above its surface. After two passes the box top was as polished as its sides.

On it were grooves in the wood forming a pentagram, the five-pointed star that's the same shape as the star ratings we leave on websites. Only practitioners of black magic employ upside-down pentagrams which wasn't the case here, assuming the side of the lid with hinges was meant to be the top. On each of the five points were round, recessed discs. Mystics and witches often associated the five points of the pentagram with the five elements of magick.

And for her, each element represented an agonizing test that had seemed on the verge of killing her before she prevailed.

Was this design merely decorative and symbolic? She doubted it.

Her fingers traced the grooves and lingered on the recessed discs. Each one had the slightest give to it when she pushed, like it was a button.

Were the points a keypad that unlocked the box?

She spent several minutes pushing the buttons one by one in random order. Next, she tried different combinations of multiple buttons pushed at the same time. Nothing worked. The possible combinations and sequences of buttons boggled her mind. She had no clue how to figure this out.

After staring at the pentagram for a while, she got an idea.

There were no hard and fast rules, but generally the upper-left point of the pentagram represented Air. The upper-right one was Water. The lower left was Earth. And the lower right belonged to Fire. The point facing upwards at the very top symbolized Spirit.

What if the combination of this lock corresponded with the order of the magick tests she had endured?

The first one had been the Water test with the moray eel. So she firmly pushed the upper right disc. Next, had come the Arctic wind attack, so she pushed the upper-left button for Air, followed by the lower right button for Fire, when she had burned everything she touched. The sinkhole, and the ghouls that escaped from it, represented Earth, so she pushed the lower-left button next. The doppelgänger that undermined her sense of self and will to live was an attack on her Spirit. The last button she pressed was the one at the very top.

A loud click. Her pulse rocketed as the lid sprang open on its own.

Inside the box was a number-ten envelope sealed with wax. That was all. The paper was of quality stock, but had yellowed with age. The wax seal was embossed with a sigil of a dragon. She assumed the sigil was something she needed to learn about, so she gently pried it from the flap without damaging it before she opened the envelope.

A two-page letter was folded inside. It was less yellowed than the envelope She opened it. The message was written in old-fashioned calligraphy. It addressed her by her birth-name and read:

My dearest Elizabeth,

You are the light of my life, yet too young to remember me if I am taken from you, which now seems likely. If your mother and I are gone, you will be cared for by family and they will tell you all about us.

From the moment you were born, it was obvious that you had inherited the same magick I was born with. You wouldn't know this, but I achieved great power through my magick, and it is the reason that I will probably be killed.

You could have lived a normal life and ignored the magick inside you. But the fact you are reading this now means you have developed your magick to a dangerous degree and it triggered the spell I set up anticipating this.

You are reading this because you passed the tests I prearranged for you with that spell. Yes, they were cruel, but they were necessary. Your magick will attract dark forces like the ones surrounding me right now. You needed to be tested so you would be strong enough to face the challenges that lie ahead.

Visions of your future have come to me, of the terrible foes that you must defeat. Very soon, the lives of many innocent humans will depend upon you.

That is why I have two gifts for you to help you become even stronger. Neither can be left unguarded after I am gone. One you must seek and find. The other will come to you at a later time.

The first is a grimoire from which you will learn wondrous spells that will advance your power and abilities significantly, including remarkable healing spells for supernatural creatures as well as humans. It is a special edition of The Book of Saint Cyprian *with an addendum containing spells that use the magic of some of the native Florida nations before Spanish colonization wiped them out. Only one copy exists in the world.*

It was stolen from me, but I know it is still in the city of San Marcos. Even if the power it can bring you doesn't interest you, please find it before a dark sorcerer does.

The second gift is what I used for my seal, the Talisman of the Red Dragon. It will be delivered to you if and when you need it.

I apologize for these burdens you have inherited, and I wish you will see them more as gifts than burdens. Know that I will love you always, even from the Great Beyond.

Love and Godspeed,

Your father, Theodore Lawthorne.

Wow, Missy thought. Her mind was reeling. Who were all these humans she would need to save—and from what? It was a staggering concept.

She had been assigned an impossible quest. She didn't think she wanted to accept it.

But assuming she did, was she worthy of it?

14

BIRTHRIGHT

Missy did some quick internet searches for *The Book of Saint Cyprian* and they only made her confused. Apparently, there were several different grimoires by the same name, all falsely claiming to have been written by Saint Cyprian of Antioch in the third century, a pagan sorcerer who converted to Christianity. They were published during the seventeenth through the nineteenth centuries in Spanish and Portuguese during an era when mass-printed grimoires were hugely popular in the wake of the *Key of Solomon* and the *Grand Grimoire*.

The grimoires were like recipe books for spells, particularly for summoning demons. With the number of books sold at the time, one would think Europe would have been overrun by summoned demons, so Missy was pretty sure they didn't work. She'd borrowed some elements from various spell books herself, but her own grimoires contained proven spells passed down from true witches and none had instructions for summoning demons.

However, the grimoire her father's letter had mentioned sounded very different. It was a special edition of Saint Cyprian's book with an addendum of Native American magic. The spells in the book must have worked, or else her father wouldn't have sent her in search of it. There was no reference to this edition at all on the internet.

Ex-Father Marco Rivera-Hernandez might be able to tell her more. The defrocked priest she met through Luisa knew a great deal about demonology. Unfortunately, it wasn't enough to prevent becoming possessed by a demon himself during an exorcism gone wrong. She found his number and called.

"The Saint Cyprian lost edition?" he asked like an excited child. "I didn't think it truly existed. What a delightful surprise!"

"What can you tell me about it?" Missy asked. "I can't find any information."

"No one knows much about it except for rumors. Apparently, a wizard fleeing the Inquisition in Spain in the sixteen hundreds sailed to Havana. He soon discovered he wasn't welcome there, so he booked passage on a ship bound for San Marcos. The wizard, his name was Mateo, had an early version of the Saint Cyprian grimoire with him that he had brought from Spain. The ship wrecked just off the coast of Florida and the wizard was among a small group of survivors who made it to shore. They were captured by a community of indigenous people.

"All the Spaniards were eventually released," the ex-father continued, "but the wizard elected to live with the tribe for a few years, trading magic secrets with their shaman. He added the Native American spells to the blank pages at the back of the grimoire. He eventually made his way north to San Marcos where he died a mysterious death.

"That's when tales of the grimoire began to spread. The

spells contained in the addendum were said to do wondrous things, from healing to creating eternal youth. Supposedly there were even spells to heal supernatural entities. And I've never read about any black magic or spells that created harm in it. As you can imagine, the grimoire was considered a great prize. It changed hands several times until it disappeared when the British took possession of the city in the late seventeen hundreds."

"My father claimed he had the book before it was stolen from him."

"Did he live in San Marcos?"

"I don't know. It sounds like he did, at some point." Missy explained her parents died when she was a baby and she knew little about them. "How in the world am I supposed to find this book?"

"I'm sure it's locked away in someone's possession," ex-Father Marco said. "You'll have to use your magick."

"I don't know how to find an inanimate object, especially one I don't have a visual image of."

"Then ask all the stupid witches and wizards in San Marcos," said a voice that sounded like James Earl Jones. It was the demon who possessed the ex-father. The demon had a habit of taking over his host at random, embarrassing moments."

"Actually, you might be onto something, demon," Missy said.

Too bad there wasn't an online directory of witches and wizards that you could search by city.

Wait, she thought, I'd better check. You never know nowadays.

A few minutes later, she discovered there was in fact an online review site for Florida exorcists and spiritualists, but not witches and wizards. Okay, back to the drawing board.

ON THE MORNING of her flight home, Missy was drinking tea with Mabel in the kitchen, enjoying the heat of the potbelly stove.

"Did Ted and Ophelia live in San Marcos," Missy said.

Mabel seemed startled. "They did."

"Ted made a reference to it in some papers I found."

"From your tone, you believe that I've held back information from you," Mabel said. "I haven't."

"I spent my childhood not knowing I was adopted."

"That's the way it's supposed to be," Mabel said. "To form a true bond with your adoptive parents, you have to believe they're your only parents."

"I understand that. I don't blame you."

"When you were older, and asked some hard questions, we decided to tell you that you were adopted. We had to make sure you were mature enough to handle it."

Once she learned their names, Missy researched her birth parents as best she could. She learned nothing. Later, once the internet became prevalent, she searched again and still came up empty. Recently, on a whim, she tried the online genealogy services, but they were no help in tracing individuals who seemingly had left no public records.

After Mark's funeral, when Missy learned her parents had been murdered, she attempted another search using newspaper archives. She was certain the murders would have been at least mentioned in the press. But apparently, they hadn't been.

"But you waited until dad died to tell me that his cousin was my biological father. And that he and Ophelia were witches."

"It was for your own safety. I already told you that," Mabel said. "Look, I barely knew your parents. They came to my wedding, which was the only time I met your mother. After she and Ted divorced, Ted visited us a couple of times, but he didn't share much with me about his life. Mark kept in touch with him. He had a strange fascination with Ted and his magical stuff. That's why he accumulated some of Ted's belongings. And after they both died, we got you."

"Do you know why they divorced?"

"Something to do with magic, I assume. We also assumed their deaths were related to magic, too. That's why we discouraged you from becoming interested in witchcraft. Your father and I—the parents who raised you—wanted you to be safe from that world. It's dangerous."

"I know. But I'm afraid that world has found me," Missy said. "You can protect me from many things, but not my destiny."

"Destiny? Hogwash," Mabel said with true bitterness. "Your life is what you make it. A couple of sorcerers can't make their child become one, too, especially if they're not around to raise her."

"You always were and will always be my mom," Missy said, getting up and giving Mabel a hug. "But I was born with Ted's and Ophelia's genes. And I'm afraid they're shaping my destiny."

"Hogwash," Mabel said. And then she laughed.

THE NEWS-TIPS DESK forwarded Matt the email.

"I'm a prominent social media influencer with an exclusive video of a man being murdered in Jellyfish Beach. Call me if you're interested."

The "influencer" was named Dieter Dufusdunder. Matt looked him up. Dufusdunder made a point of presenting himself as a social media maven. He admitted he couldn't find any companies willing to sponsor him while he traveled around posting things, but he did make some money selling video footage and still photos. He posted tons of crap on YouTube and Instagram, and if anything went semi-viral, he got paid a little bit for it from one source or another.

Matt knew the type. The guy always taking selfies. The guy manipulating every social interaction, every vacation, every moment of his waking day to turn it into a photo shoot and then saturate the internet with the images and videos. Matt had the distinct impression that Dufusdunder hadn't been able to quit his day job yet.

"Did you tell the police about the video?" Matt asked the man over the phone.

"Yeah. I even sent it to them, but they never responded to me," Dufusdunder said. "I figured if they didn't want it, I'd sell it."

"Why did you come to us instead of the TV news?" Matt asked. "They can afford to pay you more than us for your video."

"They thought it was fake. Because it, like, appears to show a monster. I could probably sell it to one of those schlock cable programs, but people assume all those shows are fake."

"I believe you," Matt said. "I was there that night."

"Woah, dude, are you serious?"

"Yes. But I didn't see much when it was happening. And I didn't see you there. Tell me your version of the night."

"I was working, delivering pizzas, and there's this spot next to the park where I can take a nap—I mean, check my newsfeeds. I heard a scream and I went running toward it.

Guys like me, we don't run away from danger, we run *into* it, dude."

"Of course," Matt said.

"I have a video camera that's good in low-light conditions. And I saw—I swear on my grandmother's grave—I saw this monster ripping the stuffing out of some dude. I thought it was like a hyena or something. I got a little closer and zoomed in and it looked more like a naked person with a giant head and long arms with claws."

"Wow."

Dufusdunder took a long breath and continued. "Then it looked up at me and snarled. I practically pooped my pants. I ran behind the building with the bathrooms. But then I got enough nerve to sneak back to the scene. I saw the. . . whatever it was. I saw it throw what was left of the corpse on top of the monkey bars in the playground. And then—you're gonna think this is crazy—it walked behind a tree and transformed into a normal man. With clothes on. The dude just walked out of the park and then disappeared. Not like disappeared from view. He just vanished while I was looking at him."

"Did you get video of the man after the attack?" Matt asked.

"I sure did."

"Okay, I'm definitely interested. Upload the video to my Cloud account and I'll talk to my editor."

"How much can you pay me?"

"It's up to my editor. If he won't buy it from you, I will myself."

When he received the video, Matt was riveted. The footage was dark and grainy. It was jerky and unstable, as you would expect video shot by a frightened amateur to look.

But the video clearly captured the ghoul. Missy had texted him recently with a confusing statement about seeing ghouls in her yard, but she hadn't described them in detail. On video, the ghoul was horrifying. Matt couldn't imagine what it would be like to see them in person.

The only way Matt could describe it was an inbred creature from the bowels of the earth as imagined by H.P. Lovecraft. It was humanoid, but moved around the prone body of Molloi on all four of its long limbs. Its fingers and toes had long, curved nails that easily tore through the flesh and looked strong enough to burrow into the earth. As Dufusdunder said, it was naked, except for a patch of hair in the genital area.

When the ghoul looked up at the cameraman, Matt, too, almost pooped in his pants. The cadaverous face was long, with jaws that opened unnaturally wide. It had large teeth for breaking bones and needle-like fangs. The nose was simply two slits in the face. The eyes were sunken deep into the skull below a bulging forehead.

The eyes flickered yellow and stared at the camera with fury. And hunger. A hunger that would never be satisfied and arose from a corrupted soul of emptiness.

The camera jerked and swung downwards, showing the passing ground as Dufusdunder ran away. It resumed a stable view from the hiding place, but it was too distant to make out anything.

When Dufusdunder crept closer to the action, the images were still too confusing to make out. Until a large object went flying into the air. It looked like a giant animal pelt. When it landed, draped across the monkey bars, it was obvious that it was actually a human carcass, the one Matt had seen himself at the scene. He shuddered.

When the creature transformed into a human, Matt recognized the man, even in the dark, grainy footage, as Omar Johnson. The man from the obituary with the handlebar mustache.

The man whose appearance had been stolen by the monster that had eaten him.

And in seeing the instant, fluid nature of the transformation from naked ghoul to fully clothed human, Matt had a realization. The ghoul wasn't a standard shifter like a werewolf. Werewolves' bodies physically transform, and their clothing is either shed or ripped apart, a problem when they return to human form. However, this ghoul's clothing appeared out of thin air when the creature transformed.

Matt believed the ghoul hadn't shape-shifted physically. Taking on Omar Johnson's appearance was merely an illusion conjured by the ghoul.

That the ghoul had supernatural powers like that was disturbing. It meant the monster would be much harder to destroy.

Matt was also angry with Affird. The detective had claimed the surveillance cameras at Flounder Park didn't pick up enough detail of Molloi's murder to rule Roarke out or in. Matt had taken him for his word.

But Affird had never said anything about a video sent by a tipster.

Matt knew why: Affird wanted Roarke to be denied bail so he could keep him in jail through the full moon. Matt had been inside the condo of a werewolf drug dealer whom Affird summarily executed after the werewolf transformed back into human form. The condo was in Seaweed Manor, the community where Roarke lived.

Affird obviously assumed Roarke was a werewolf, and he had every intention of performing an extrajudicial execution of the shifter while he was locked in a cell at the county jail.

Matt had no allegiance to Roarke, but he was one of Missy's patients whom she cared deeply for. Plus they had entered an agreement about sharing information on supernatural creatures while preserving the anonymity and safety of the harmless ones. He couldn't just let this go.

So he called the defendant's attorney, Paul Leclerc. The lawyer was outraged by what Matt told him.

VAMPIRE ROAD TRIP

"Y ou can't find a city in America older than San Marcos, so the supernatural society there is very well-established and elaborate," Agnes said to Missy.

The vampire and human were sitting in the community lounge on the first floor of Squid Tower, illuminated by the dim light of a single lamp. Outside, the surf crashed with a soft roar mixed with the clopping sounds of pickleball matches on the nearby courts.

Agnes sipped a pint of whole blood (O-positive) from a clear plastic bag she had gotten from the Blood Bus delivery tonight. Missy tried not to watch. She was impressed, however, that Agnes used a straw of paper, instead of plastic. The straw was beginning to turn red.

"There is a guild of magic practitioners presided over by the Arch-Mage of San Marcos," Agnes went on. "Perhaps that is whom you should speak to."

"The problem I see," Missy said, speaking over the sound of Agnes' blood-slurping, "is why would any mage or witch help someone find a powerful grimoire when they would rather find it or keep it themselves? Especially since I'm from out of town and a relatively beginner witch. If anyone in the magic guild knows where the book is, they would have seized it by now. If they don't know where it is, they're of no use to me."

Agnes stood up with the aid of her quad cane to dispose of the now-empty blood bag.

"Let me do that for you," Missy said. She took the bag and tossed it into the trash can next to the kitchen area. As a nurse, handling the bag shouldn't have given her the willies, but the thought of what it had been used for did.

"Thank you, dear. Now tell me, how important to you is this grimoire?"

Missy had to pause to think. Acquiring the book was a command from a father she had never known. His reaching out to her long after his death made the book seem extra important.

But did she really need it? Improving her skills in magick had become a passion for her. They'd saved her life several times already and had come in handy in many other ways. Her next goal was to learn how to heal some of the ailments that her patients had that neither human medicine nor their innate supernatural powers could cure. Better, stronger magick could possibly achieve that. In fact, the grimoire's addendum supposedly contained spells to achieve precisely that.

Still, how much power did she need? She'd heard of many witches and wizards who became drunk with power for its own sake. Sometimes they turned evil and followed a path to their own destruction. She would never want that.

"I see my question has perplexed you," Agnes said.

"To be honest, I don't know enough about the book. But if it can help me heal, I would want it very much."

"Do you consider your late father its rightful owner? If so, that ownership would have passed to you."

"I don't have any proof that he owned it except his letter. I don't know if that's enough to convince anyone."

"If they don't want to be convinced, they won't be. I would not bother directly asking the Arch-Mage, the wizards, or the witches about the grimoire. They could always be relieved of the book without being asked," Agnes said with a mischievous smile.

"What are you proposing?"

"I know a few vampires in San Marcos. There has always been an active vampire community there since the earliest times. Vampires are drawn to older cities. The only reason there are so many of us in South Florida is we older vampires prefer the warmer weather down here. In fact, my friend came to San Marcos with the first group of settlers from Spain in 1565 under Menéndez."

"How can the vampires there help me?" Missy asked.

"Among the vampires in the city are a few infamous thieves who might be willing to provide their services."

"I can't afford to pay them anything," Missy said.

"Their payment would be in the form of the settling debts owed to my friend."

"Is your friend a loan shark?"

Agnes laughed. "No. He's the informal watchdog of the vampire community. He makes sure no one does anything to reveal the community to humans. San Marcos is an excellent city for hunting, with all the tourists that visit, but law enforcement wants to keep them safe so the economy doesn't get hurt. And my friend makes sure no vampire feeds on any of them to the point of death, so the vampire community doesn't get hurt.

The thieves owe him for allowing them to ply their trade, considering how much risk they create for the others."

"Ah, I see."

"We can travel together up to San Marcos," Agnes said.

"Thank you, but that's a very long drive. You don't need to put yourself through that."

Missy honestly didn't believe the 1,500-year-old would be comfortable on a long trip.

"I'm perfectly capable of sitting in a car for several hours," Agnes said, her eyes glowing red with annoyance.

"I'm very grateful. But why do you want to do this?"

"Because I'm rather fond of you, dear. And I'm intrigued by the possibility the grimoire has healing spells as you say."

Everyone thinks that vampires' supernatural healing abilities make them impervious to disease. It's not true. Yes, vampires can recover from wounds almost instantaneously. They're immune to many human diseases and ailments. And, of course, they exist forever if they don't starve or succumb to fire or the stake.

Nonetheless, Missy's vampire patients, all senior citizens, had the usual geriatric conditions when they were turned. Their newly attained powers heightened their senses, increased their strength and speed, and made them formidable predators. What the powers couldn't do was fully open plaque-clogged arteries, reverse spinal stenosis, and cure osteoarthritis. That's why they still needed medical care, although much less than if they had remained human.

There were also diseases unique to vampires. Though they were rare, they were beyond human medicine's capacity to cure. Missy had hopes that the special Florida addendum to *The Book of Saint Cyprian* might be the key to curing them.

"Thank you so much," Missy said. "How soon can you leave?"

"Whenever you wish. I have an eternity of free time on my hands."

And thus began the vampire road trip.

MISSY HAD THOUGHT the five-hour drive would be a great opportunity to bond further with Agnes. She hadn't counted on the backseat of her rental car being occupied by two additional vampires. Sol and Oleg were recruited by Agnes to be the "muscle" of the group. That guys in their seventies and sixties in body age, respectively, were considered muscle tells you what living in a Florida retirement community does to your perspective.

They left shortly after dusk, as Jellyfish Beach's version of rush hour was petering out. Once Missy merged onto I-95, she glanced in the rearview mirror at the "muscle." Sol, with his long nose, bat-like ears, and spectral face, looked like Nosferatu incongruously wearing a Red Sox cap and earbuds. He nodded his head to whatever music a 450-year-old would be into. Oleg, the baby of her passengers at only 300-some-odd years, stared out the window stoically. Passing headlights gleamed on the shaved head of the former cavalry officer under Catherine the Great.

This was the longest drive Missy had ever gone on with vampires. Unlike many seniors, Missy's passengers didn't have to stop frequently to use the restroom. Vampires don't pee very often, every other day at the most. They drink very little water and their metabolisms are exponentially slower than humans'. But that didn't mean the vampires were easy car-mates.

They constantly argued about the temperature settings. The rental car didn't have separate controls for the rear seat, so it was an unending battle. Agnes preferred warmer temperatures. The gentlemen in back wanted it cold. No matter who won out, the temperature was about ten degrees cooler than Missy could stand.

They had another annoying habit. Most vampires have a strong predatory instinct. Ridiculously strong. Missy discovered how strong when, along a rural stretch of the interstate, Oleg suddenly barked a command in his Russian accent that she pull over. With no idea what the problem was, she stopped in the break-down lane. Oleg leaped out of the car before it had stopped rolling and darted off into the forest of slash pines.

"What the heck was that all about?" Missy asked.

"There are some deer about a hundred yards into the woods," Agnes replied.

"You actually know that?"

"They make a lot of noise when they walk around in the brush," Agnes said. "And they have a very distinct scent."

"I told you guys I brought snacks so we wouldn't have to stop," Missy said. "There are plenty of blood bags in the cooler."

"It's instinctual, dear," Agnes said. "He can't help it."

Sol, stared in the direction Oleg had gone, but his own predatory instinct was apparently easier to overcome. He continued to bob his head to the beat of whatever was on his undead playlist.

Oleg emerged from the woods and sprinted over the grass to the car.

"Sorry about that," he said, wiping a few drops of blood from his chin with a napkin. "But it was refreshing."

"Is everyone all set?" Missy asked. "No more stops, I don't care what critters we pass."

"Yes, Missy," the vampires all replied.

SAN MARCOS WAS a city of contrasts. A massive fort with cannons poking from its coquina walls overlooking the bay—with rows of tour buses parked out front. Centuries-old stone buildings with overhanging second floors brought you back to the early Spanish colonial days—until a goofy tourist "trolley" passed by. Quaint Victorian homes with gingerbread details spoke of gentility—until loud groups of overfed visitors in T-shirts and fanny packs posed for selfies in front. Trendy, new retail shops stood shoulder-to-shoulder to stores that hadn't changed since the Civil Rights era, or, in some cases, since the Civil War.

Missy had wanted to stay in one of the many charming bed-and-breakfasts, but Agnes said the proprietors of those tended to be nosy. She instead selected a small motel in a less-desirable neighborhood where the vampires were guaranteed anonymity, even if they spent their days in their rooms.

They checked in around midnight. Missy went out to search for an open fast-food restaurant. The vampires went out to search for tourists. When she returned to her room with the greasy takeout bag, she had a surprise waiting for her.

A parrot was perched on the lamp beside the bed. It was a medium-sized light-gray bird with a red-tipped tail. Its face had a large white patch on each side surrounding each eye and extending to its dark-gray bill. She recognized the species as an African Grey.

"What are you doing here?" Missy asked.

"Waiting for you," the bird said in a sultry feminine voice. "Welcome to San Marcos, 'Florida's ancient city.' That's our official slogan. Kinda lame if you ask me." The parrot let out a whistle. "I'm Florence."

"Um, thank you, Florence. I'm Missy."

Missy had a friend who owned an African Grey. They were among the best parrots for talking. But none talked this intelligently.

"Why are you waiting for me?" Missy asked.

Florence shifted from one foot to another atop the lampshade, then dropped some poop on the telephone below.

"My owner wants to meet you."

"Who is that?"

"Bob McGuinn. He's the Arch-Mage of San Marcos and the rest of the county," the parrot said. "Flagler County, too, but that's only a transitional post."

Missy was alarmed. How did the Arch-Mage know she was in town?

As if reading her thoughts—and maybe it actually did—the parrot said, "He sensed your powers the moment you arrived in the city. He sent me to check you out. He monitors the activities of all the magicians, sort of like the Gaming Commission in Vegas."

"How did he know I'm staying at this motel?"

Florence whistled, then said, "Magic."

The parrot flew across the room to a guest chair near the door and perched on the top.

"Please come to the Pagan Surf Shop on the beach tomorrow morning at eight," it said. "It's near the pier. You can't miss it."

"Um, okay."

"Now please open the door for me."

"Sure, but then how did you get in here in the first place?"

Florence didn't answer. She cocked her head and squawked. Then deposited some poop on the chair.

After she let the bird fly outside, Missy tried to go to sleep. It was too early for her, due to her nocturnal schedule, but she needed some rest before her meeting in the morning. Although she was tired from the long drive, she had a hard time falling asleep. Especially when Sol returned to his room next door around 2:30 a.m. and spent the hours until dawn watching reruns of *I Love Lucy* on his TV with the sound cranked up.

16

THE ARCH-MAGE

Pagan Surf Shop was on the other side of the bay, on A1A, the two-lane beach highway. The store's name had led her to expect a funky-looking establishment, but the place was large and modern. It was packed with swim and surf wear, boogie boards, snorkeling accessories, and tons of T-shirts and souvenirs for the tourists. The rear section of the store was for dedicated surfers, with wetsuits and all styles of boards. Behind that, in the stockroom, was a workshop that did surfboard repairs.

The workshop was also the informal office of Bob McGuinn, owner of Pagan Surf Shop and Arch-Mage of San Marcos.

Bob led her into the room. He was a surfer dude in his early-sixties. He had a full head of long, blonde hair and a pleasant face with fat cheeks, and an ample beer belly. He was decked out in board shorts and a Hawaiian shirt. The only things out of the ordinary surfer look were his accessories: a cloth amulet on a leather cord around his neck, and a leather bracelet with a large, brass pentagram medallion.

Florence perched on a tall, wooden stand in the corner next to a workbench. She squawked a 'hello.'"

"Hi, Florence," Missy replied.

"Welcome to my place of toil. I'm Bob," he said, offering his hand which she shook. "This is my store, which started out forty-five years ago as nothing but a roadside stand. I'm also the head magic dude in San Marcos."

"Nice place," Missy said. "Can you get me a good deal on a pair of sunglasses."

"For sure, for sure."

"Thanks. So, how did you find out about me?"

Florence whistled. "I told you already," she said in her calm, soothing voice.

"You said he sensed my power arriving in town," Missy said to the bird. She turned to Bob. "But how did you know who I am and where I'm staying?"

"They didn't make me Arch-Mage for nothing," he said. "I've some pretty awesome spells for gathering intel."

"And he bribes hotel clerks," Florence said. Bob gave her a dirty look.

"Okay," Missy said. "What do you want to talk about? Do I have to pay a tax or something? I'm not in town as a witch, just a visitor."

"A witch visitor with three vampires tagging along?"

"They're friends. I'm their home-health nurse in Jellyfish Beach, and we've grown close."

"For sure. Everyone goes on road trips with old vampires. But why are you visiting San Marcos?" Bob asked, fixing her with frosty blue eyes beneath bushy, sun-bleached eyebrows.

"Antiques. There's good shopping here, right?"

"Dude, it's okay if you have, like, personal reasons you don't want to talk about. I know your parents once lived here."

"You do?"

"I knew them, sort of. Around the time you were born. I was just a broke surfer who learned a little magic as a hobby. I was crashing at this witch's house. I was her pool boy and boy toy. She taught me a few spells and introduced me to the magic scene. Your mom and dad were powerful, big time. But they caught the interest of a gang of black-magic sorcerers who put the squeeze on them, kinda like the Mafia extorting a local business. Stuff like that is why we all agreed to form a guild and put some rules into place."

Missy's head was spinning. "You told me how you knew I was in town, and who I was, but how did you know I'm the daughter of the couple you're talking about? I don't have their last name."

"I didn't know until you walked in here today and I felt your power. It's strong. And it's the same style and on the same frequency as your father's."

"That's amazing. I don't know what to say."

"Well, like, you can tell me why you came here."

"Okay, I admit I want to learn more about my parents. I was told very little about them while growing up, and now I feel my magick growing stronger, but I have no one to explain what's happening to me."

"Cool. Like I said, I didn't know them well, but I can introduce you to a dude who did. And I'm always happy to give advice." He smiled. It seemed genuine.

"Thank you. When do we start?"

"What's the tide now?" Bob asked Florence.

"High incoming," she squawked. "High tide is in two hours."

"Winds?"

"Out of the southeast. Ten to twenty miles an hour," the bird replied.

"Let's go talk to Wendall," Bob said. "I know exactly where to find him."

Bob led Missy to a parking area behind the store where an old, green Jeep with no doors sat on giant, fat tires. It had a surfboard rack on its roof. Bob got behind the wheel without any explanation as to where they were going. Missy climbed into the passenger seat, making sure her safety belt was secure. Florence flew from the shop and perched on Bob's shoulder. He started the jeep and drove down a residential street past his store and the parking lot where Missy's rental car was sitting. Then he pulled onto A1A and headed south.

It was a nice, sunny day and Missy could easily forget her burdens as they barreled down the coastal road, passing hotels on the beach, and then condominium complexes with expensive homes mixed in. On the west side of the road were residential streets with the occasional strip center containing restaurants and souvenir shops.

Abruptly, Bob hung a left and entered the sandy parking lot of a public beach. But he didn't park. He kept driving toward the beach and crossed a raised ramp over the dunes. And kept driving onto the beach.

Noticing Missy's surprised expression, he said, "Yeah, we can drive on some of the beaches up here. Our beaches aren't soft sand like down in Jellyfish Beach. Here, it's like Daytona Beach. When they first started auto racing over a hundred years ago, they raced on the beach long before the speedway was built. Nice, wide beaches with fine, hard-packed sand."

He drove slowly down the beach, far from any sunbathers, until there were no people except the occasional surf fisherman. An inlet was coming into view ahead. Bob slowed to a stop.

"Ah, there's my main man." He pointed to a surf fisherman who was standing right where the beach began its curve into the inlet.

He jumped out of the jeep and began walking toward the man, leather sandals flopping. Missy followed. Florence remained perched on Bob's right shoulder. The fisherman had four fishing rods twice his height in length standing upright in rod holders stuck in the sand. Taut fishing line extended perfectly straight from each rod to points far out in the surf. The man stood watching the rods carefully next to a wheeled cart that held a large cooler and a bait-cutting board. The man noticed them and wiped his hands on a rag.

"Bob!" he said with a smile. He was tall and skinny with a big, white beard. He was barefoot and wore swimming trunks, a khaki long-sleeved fishing shirt, and a wide-brimmed straw hat.

"I figured the pompano would be biting now and you'd be somewhere around here," Bob said. "Wendall, this is Missy Mindle. She practices the craft."

"I'd shake your hand, but I've got fish slime on mine," Wendall said.

"Hi Wendall, nice to meet you," Missy said, taking a step to miss the lip of the last wave creeping toward her shoes.

"What kind of magic do you practice?" he asked.

"It's hard to say. It's my own brand of magick—spelled with a 'k' at the end of the word. I began with Wicca, then expanded to additional stuff. I'm a bit of a traditional witch, a kitchen witch, and a hedge witch. It's all based on earth and sea magick and things I keep discovering within me."

Wendall gave another toothy grin. "You're an all-you-can-eat buffet of magic, it sounds like."

"And I like it all, from the sweet to the spicy," she said.

Wendall turned away to keep an eye on his rods. He probably had no idea why Bob had brought her out here.

"How's the bite?" Bob asked.

"I've almost reached my bag limit." Wendall opened his cooler. There were five pompano on ice, each a little more than a foot long. The flat, oval-shaped fish with forked tails were among the best-tasting fish you could find.

"Not bad," Bob said, "if you weren't a wizard."

"Don't give me that bunk. I wouldn't use magic for fishing. That's cheating." He looked around to see if anyone else was nearby. "I do use it to catch bait, though."

He gave them a wicked grin, bent over, made a complicated gesture with his left hand, and touched the sand near the edge of the surf. Dozens of sand fleas, also called mole crabs, burrowed out to the surface. He scooped up a handful of the half-inch long crustaceans and tossed them in a small bucket on his cart.

Bob laughed loudly. "Righteous, dude!"

"They're normally hard to find this time of year," Wendall explained. "I needed a little help."

One of Wendall's fishing rods jerked and its tip bent toward the horizon. Wendall yanked it out of its rod holder and reeled the line in. It took a long time. Finally, he dragged a large lead sinker and three empty hooks onto the sand.

"If I was using magic, this wouldn't have happened," he said. "I would have had a fish or two on."

Wendall put fresh sand fleas on the empty hooks, reached backwards with the long rod, ran forward a couple of steps, and with a huge exertion pitched the rod forward, casting the heavy sinker far out into the ocean.

There was an awkward silence, until Bob broke it.

"Missy is the Lawthornes' daughter," he said. "She practices magick like her father."

Wendall looked at her more intently than he had before.

"Wow," he said. "I'm surprised you're here. But I'm not surprised you practice the same kind of magic as your father. He spelled his with a 'k,' too."

"Why are you surprised I'm here?" Missy asked.

Wendall's face turned red. "I thought Ted's infant daughter was killed with him."

"She was rescued and given to Ted's cousin to raise," Bob said.

"What? I was almost killed?" Missy asked. The surf soaked her left shoe, but she didn't notice. "And who murdered my father?"

"No one knows for sure," Bob said. "The guild suspected the group of black-magic sorcerers who were harassing him. They allegedly wanted to steal his power. The guild drove them away after that."

They wanted to steal his power *and* his grimoire, Missy thought.

"Sorry for your loss," Wendall said. "Your father was a brilliant witch."

"What about my mother?"

"She is brilliant, too."

"*Is?* My mother was killed alongside my father."

"No. Your parents were divorced by then," Wendall said. "You father was caring for you and your mother wasn't killed with him. You didn't know that?"

"No," Missy said quietly.

"She was living in Orlando at the time. I don't know if she's still there. I don't know, honestly, if she's still alive."

"But I was an orphan when my parents adopted me."

"I'm sorry. I didn't realize you didn't know."

Missy was stunned. Was this yet another fact her adoptive parents had kept from her?

They parted on a friendly enough note with Wendall, and Bob drove her back to his store. When she was getting into her car, he asked how long she was staying in town.

"Just long enough to take in some touristy stuff. Why? Are you monitoring me?"

"Only if you get your magick on. It's my job to monitor that. Try to stay out of trouble, okay?" His stern expression broke into a huge, carefree grin.

OVER THE PHONE, Missy's mother quickly became defensive.

"I didn't know Ophelia was alive," Mabel said. "Is she still alive today?"

"I don't know," Missy said. "Where did you and dad get the notion she was killed with Ted?"

"Your father told me. He must not have known she was alive. I'm sure he wouldn't have lied to me about it."

"Who told him I was orphaned and to come and get me?"

"I always assumed it was the state."

"They would have tracked Ophelia down." A dark thought occurred to Missy. "Unless there was a protective order against her."

"That would explain it," Mabel said.

"Still, there's a lot that's odd here."

"I've told you all I know."

"I know, Mom. I know."

17

OLDEST VAMPIRES IN TOWN

T he oldest vampire in America's oldest city technically moved down to second place in age once Agnes arrived in town. Pedro Vasquez Rodrigo was nineteen in human years when he was the second mate on the flagship of Pedro Menéndez de Avilés when it sailed from Spain and landed in San Marcos in 1565.

However, Pedro happened to be a vampire who had been turned some sixty years prior to that, making him a total age of 79 when the settlement of San Marcos was founded. Add five centuries to that and the guy certainly deserved every senior-citizen discount he could get.

Agnes, born of a Visigoth family of generals who battled the Romans and other barbarian peoples, made him look like a toddler in comparison. The president of the Squid Tower HOA was turned into a vampire when she was around ninety (she claimed she was in her eighties, but everyone believed she was fudging it for vanity's sake). So when you saw the four-foot ninety-year-old in the same room as the tall, strapping, nineteen-year-old Pedro, you'd never guess they were both powerful leaders.

"I have already dispatched my spies and thieves," Pedro said to Missy and the vampires. He spoke with a pronounced Castilian lisp. "And one of them has a very good lead."

"Is the grimoire in the possession of a magician?" Agnes asked.

"A wealthy socialite who collects art and antiques," Pedro replied. "She regularly updates her security system with the latest state-of-the-art technology, but my thief defeats it time after time. He only takes single items, and does so rarely, but he keeps an up-to-date inventory of her collection and retrieves items of interest for his clients."

"Does he use supernatural abilities to defeat the alarm?" Oleg asked.

Pedro chuckled. "My thief is nothing more than your average vampire. His special ability is hairdressing. The socialite is his regular customer, and he mesmerizes her while he's doing her shampooing and gets her to give up her latest alarm password."

It was pleasantly cool that evening, so Missy and the four vampires sat on Pedro's terrace overlooking the marshes along the shore of the Intracoastal Waterway. His luxurious home was newer than she would have expected from a centuries-old vampire, but just because he was ancient didn't mean that he would prefer constant renovations.

It took some prompting by Agnes for Pedro to tell his guests his story. After a couple of decades in the King's service in early San Marcos, he retired with a small pension and made a living using his nautical skills by fishing and transporting freight. Over the centuries, his modest income grew into a fortune. When the tourism industry in San Marcos first boomed in the late nineteenth century, Pedro expanded his fleet of vessels and offered sightseeing expeditions. In the present day, he offered chartered sailing trips and sunset champagne cruises.

Behind the scenes, he ran his network of spies (he preferred calling them private investigators) and thieves. The moment he heard of any vampire—local or newcomer—endangering the vampire community by drawing police attention, that vampire would be driven from the city or staked.

When Pedro finished his tale, Missy asked, "Did you know a wizard named Mateo in the sixteen hundreds who came to town after being shipwrecked?"

Pedro placed his chin on his steepled fingers and closed his eyes. "That sounds familiar."

"He's the one who brought the grimoire to San Marcos," Missy said.

"Ah, I do recall him now."

"He was murdered. I guess by someone who stole the book."

"No," Pedro said. "He wasn't killed because of the book. He was killed *by* the book. I remember hearing that a spell he cast unleashed an entity that took his life."

"Oh, my. Is that what happened to my father?"

"I never met your father, but being in the supernatural community I knew about him. He was too powerful and experienced to allow something like that to happen to him. No, I believe he was murdered through common human treachery."

Missy began to understand more why her father had put her through the magick tests: to make sure she was strong enough to avoid Mateo's fate if she found the grimoire.

"The good news is, we can act tonight," Pedro said. "The socialite who allegedly has the book is attending a charity function. My thief is standing by. The best plan is for Ms. Mindle to come with me to the socialite's house to identify the book, so it can be returned to its place immediately if it's not the right one." He turned to Missy. "You won't need to come inside the house, but can wait outside."

"What about us?" Agnes asked. "We're here to protect Missy."

"That won't be necessary. It's too risky to have several individuals at the crime scene."

"Pedro," Agnes said, "I've known you forever—"

"Not forever. Our eternity has just begun."

"You know what I mean. I trust you, but not your vampire thief. And not any dark sorcerer who happens to show up."

"We will follow in the rental car and park a safe distance away," Oleg said.

"It's a wealthy neighborhood," Pedro said. "People notice strange cars parked on the street with someone inside it."

"Then we won't park," Oleg said. "We will drive around."

"Come, we don't have time for bickering," Pedro said. "We have to complete this before the charity function ends."

"What if she has security guards?" Missy asked.

"She has one, whom my thief will incapacitate. If anyone else is there, I'll take care of it. Let's go."

Pedro drove Missy in his luxury electric car while Oleg followed in the rental. She wasn't used to being with a vampire who wasn't a senior citizen. In fact, Pedro was much younger than her in body age. She could feel the energy humming in his undead body. It was both thrilling and a little scary.

She also felt uneasy about participating in a burglary. Even though *The Book of Saint Cyprian* had belonged to her father, the woman who possessed it now probably wasn't the one who stole it. She might not have even known it was stolen when she acquired it.

Missy reminded herself that she was the rightful heir of the book and that it would hopefully help her do good by treating illness. The deadly entity that killed Mateo was a twist in the tale that she couldn't make sense of.

Pedro drove across a tall bridge over the Intracoastal and then followed the road north through an area of expensive beachfront estates. He pulled into the dirt driveway of a construction lot beside a Mercedes convertible. He texted someone on his phone.

"Maurice is in position, ready to go in," he said. "Please wait here."

He got out of the car and shot away up the sidewalk so quickly, it was if he had teleported. Vampires could move incredibly fast, but her senior patients couldn't match that speed.

It seemed as if only a few minutes had passed and suddenly Pedro was back in the car. He had a large, leather-bound tome in his hands which he passed to her.

"I present you with *The Book of Saint Cyprian*."

She opened it and immediately sensed a problem. While old, the book didn't seem like it was from the seventeenth century. No one would call her a rare book expert, but based on the typeface, printing quality, and paper condition it appeared to be more likely from the nineteenth century. There was no printing date in the front, so she couldn't be sure. She opened the back cover and didn't find a hand-written addendum in the end pages. Randomly flipping through the book, past the instructions for cleaning ceremonial daggers and invocations for summoning demons, she didn't see any notations at all.

"This isn't it," she said, returning the book to Pedro.

He looked disappointed. "I feared as much. This seemed too easy."

He opened the door and disappeared again. Seconds later, he was back.

"Maurice returned it and left the home with the security system re-armed. The security guard is awakening from his trance. Maurice would have moved too quickly to be picked up by the security cameras. No one will ever know he was there."

"Great, but what do we do now?" Missy asked.

"It's back to the drawing board."

"No, really. How do we find an old book hidden in an old city filled with old stuff? It seems too daunting, even for your thieves."

"But I also have spies. Don't lose hope."

FLORIDA'S FIRST FLORIDA MAN

Missy awoke with a start in the dark motel room.

What was that noise she'd heard?

No intruder was in the room as far as she could tell. The heavy blackout shade blocked all but a tiny crack of sunlight, which was handy with her mostly keeping the nighttime hours of her vampire fellow travelers. Maybe a housekeeper outside made the noise.

Her watch said it was 8:10 a.m., way too early to get up, especially after the hours spent in a strategy session at the motel with Agnes and the others after the burglary dead end. Agnes had tried to game out logical plans for finding the grimoire, while Sol and Oleg had engaged in macho posturing, suggesting asinine adventures that would only result in dead bodies and no book.

After the vampires got bored with that, they went out hunting, leaving Agnes behind to sup on a bag of refrigerated whole blood while Missy ate takeout from a nearby seafood restaurant. She went to bed with indigestion and didn't sleep well. A few more hours in bed were what she needed.

She rolled over and tried to sleep. Just as she began to doze off, a loud *clunk* made her jump.

She turned on the bedside lamp. The small trash can next to the desk had been knocked into the TV console.

"Who's there?"

No one answered. She slipped from the bed, wearing her T-shirt and yoga pants, and checked the closet and the bathroom. They were empty of any intruder. She studied the trash can and tried to remember if she had knocked it over herself the previous night. Maybe the sound that had awakened her was an aural hallucination. She'd been awakened by those in the past and they had seemed so real.

Once her heart slowed down, she turned off the light, determined to give sleep one last try. Somehow, she managed to fall asleep.

In her dream, she was preparing to take a shower, but she was concerned that the water had been running for so long and here she was, still in bed.

Her eyes snapped open. The shower was running for real.

She grabbed the pepper spray that was always in her handbag and walked the few steps to the bathroom. The door was open, the light was off, and the shower was running at full strength with the curtain closed. A bit of steam floated out.

Taking a deep breath, she reached in, turned on the bathroom light, then yanked the shower curtain open.

The shower was empty. After the moment it took to register that fact, she turned off the water.

"Does this room have a freaking poltergeist?" she asked aloud to no one.

But someone answered.

"I'm not a freaking poltergeist. What does 'freaking' mean?" He had a Spanish accent, but it sounded as if he came from a different region of the country than Pedro.

She stepped out of the bathroom. Then suddenly yanked open the closet door.

This time it wasn't empty. A man stood there, just short enough to clear the hanger bar, wearing breeches and a frilly shirt from the colonial period.

He screamed in fright.

She screamed in fright.

He screamed louder.

So did she. They were now screaming in unison.

Someone banged on the wall. "Shut up in there!"

She and the man stopped screaming and regarded each other.

"Who are you?" she asked in a quavering voice.

"I am Don Mateo of Grenada."

"Wait, you're not the wizard who brought the grimoire to San Marcos, are you?"

"I am, indeed," he said with pride, bowing. He had a thick Spanish accent, but fortunately spoke English. He must have been a man of the world back when he was of the world.

"Aren't you dead?"

"I am indeed."

"Oh, my. You're a ghost."

"Took you a while to figure that out. Yes, I am a ghost, but not an ignorant poltergeist."

"But why are you here?"

"Ever since I died in a rather unfortunate accident that was completely no fault of mine."

"Something to do with an entity?"

His shoulders slumped. "You could say that. I had been drinking and was deep in my cups. I should not have been casting spells at all. But I wanted to impress a friend. I mispronounced the name of a benevolent spirit and ended up conjuring a demon instead who promptly tore me limb from limb. I would wager that my friend was quite impressed after all."

Missy realized that Mateo was one of the earliest examples of Florida Man, the usually drunk buffoon who does something idiotic that the rest of us find cruelly amusing.

"As I was saying," the ghost continued, "ever since my premature demise, my spirit has been bound to my grimoire. I do not understand why. Probably another mishap on my part. Instead of passing through the Pearly Gates, I am stuck here on earth haunting an old book."

"But why are you in my motel room?"

"Oh, that. My apologies for arriving without an invitation. Well, I was invited by someone other than you. Your father."

Missy was confused. "What do you mean?"

"Your father owned my grimoire for quite some time and we became friendly. Since I'm bound to the book, every temporary owner has had to deal with me. I can make their lives a nightmare, or I can be helpful. Your father and I were partners of a sort in his magick. He told me that one day you might prove your worthiness in owning my book and, if so, I agreed to be of service to you."

"Wow. That's very kind of you," Missy said. "Unfortunately, I don't have the book. And I have no idea who has it or where it is."

"You are closer to finding it than you realize. That is why I am paying you a visit."

"You'll tell me who owns it and where it is?"

"Technically, no one 'owns' it except for me," Mateo's ghost said.

"But you're dead."

"Well, yes, if you must bring that up again."

"You never answered my question," Missy said. "Who has possession of the grimoire?"

"I don't know. Whoever has control of it has kept the book hidden for many years. However, I can tell you where it is."

"Well?"

"Don't be so impatient," the ghost said petulantly. "There is an art to the big reveal."

"This is the twenty-first century when no one has patience for waiting."

"I see." He cleared his throat, even though a ghost would have no need to do so. "San Marcos is full of tourist attractions calling themselves the oldest this or the oldest that. My special edition of *The Book of Saint Cyprian* can be found at the oldest liquor store. My recipe book of magick is near a Southern drink recipe ingredient."

"Which ingredient?"

He faded and disappeared without answering.

UNLIKE SOUTH FLORIDA, which seemed to have more New Yorkers and Latin Americans than Floridians, North Florida was part of the Deep South. And, in Missy's experience, the Deep South was the only place she'd seen drive-through liquor stores. Being handed booze without having to leave your running car had led to many a Florida Man misadventure.

A waitress at the diner next to the motel told Missy that the oldest liquor store in San Marcos, hands down, was Gomer's, located in the neighborhood just outside of the tourist district. Gomer's Liquors was a family-run chain of liquor stores in and around the city and had been operating continuously since the 1930s after Prohibition had been repealed. Each store had a drive-through window on the side which was highly useful for parents with young kids strapped in the backseat or customers who couldn't get out of the car without falling down.

There was also an entrance in the front for those who were capable of walking and wished to browse. Missy and her vampire posse entered this door shortly before the store's closing time at 2:00 a.m. The clerk was a heavyset fellow with a beard like a Civil War Confederate general.

"Can I help y'all find—"

That's all he could say before Agnes mesmerized him. He sat back down on his stool behind the counter with his eyes rolled up in his head.

"How the heck are we supposed to find this book?" Sol asked. "There could be a million secret compartments anywhere in here."

"Even if it's hidden under the floor or something like that, the ghost gave me a riddle to solve," Missy said. "That should help us."

"I would never trust a ghost. They have a lot of baggage," Oleg said.

Missy wandered through the aisles of liquors and wines. It was quickly apparent that this was not the kind of place to find fine wines. The refrigerator cases in the back did seem to have a decent selection of beer, however, and the aisles of liquor were fairly well-stocked. What kind of Southern drink recipe ingredient should she look for?

In the mixers section, there were bottles of vermouth, lime juice, and bitters. There were Bloody Mary, daiquiri, and margarita mixes. Bottles with olives, maraschino cherries, and pearl onions were plentiful. So which was uniquely Southern?

Strolling down the liquor aisles it occurred to her that American whiskeys might just be the ticket. Not rye, but bourbon. What went into a mint julep? Bourbon. From Tennessee to Kentucky, the South was the homeland of bourbon.

The problem was, you couldn't simply hide a grimoire on a shelf behind bottles of bourbon. Workers stocking shelves would find it. Or the customer yanking out the very last bottle of Jim Beam would see the book sitting there among the dust bunnies in the very back of the shelf.

With Agnes looking on and Sol and Oleg standing guard at the entrances, Missy slowly walked past the major bourbon brands, the higher shelves holding the more expensive offerings. She'd always thought the concept of "top-shelf" quality discriminated against short people, but if you were wealthy enough to afford the overpriced liquor, you could command someone to pluck it off the shelf for you. The grimoire, however, would not be in such an exposed place. It would probably be hidden behind the rotgut on the bottom shelves.

A bell rang. Everyone looked up with alarm. The heavy chugging of a truck engine came from outside the drive-through window behind the counter.

Sol opened it. "Welcome to Gomer's. I'm Sol. Whaddya want?"

"Where's Earl?" asked a deep voice with a Southern accent coming from the truck cab.

"Earl's taking a dump. Whaddya want?"

"My usual bottle of Old Comfort and a pack of generic

menthols. You sure look pale, Mister Pointy Ears. Is your health okay?"

"Never felt better. Where would Old Comfort be?"

"Near the whiskeys and the brandies, I reckon."

Sol wandered uncertainly into Missy's aisle. She found the Old Comfort and handed it to him. It came in a plastic bottle, which probably prevented many drunken injuries. Sol handed it out the window to the man without asking him to pay and then tried to find the cigarettes.

"You know, if I was the suspicious type," the man said, "I'd wonder if you really worked in this store."

Sol rushed over to the window and stared into the driver's eyes for a moment.

"You no longer want cigarettes," Sol intoned. "You will drive away now and have no memory of what happened here."

The truck's engine revved and it rumbled past the window, disappearing into the night.

"That was uncomfortable," Sol said.

Missy was nearing the end of the aisle and hadn't seen any clues. Here were some craft bourbons she'd never heard of. She was surprised to see one brand named after San Marcos on a middle shelf. Was it actually distilled in the city? She picked up a bottle and examined the label for information. Yes, was made in a distillery just a few blocks away. Nothing was hidden behind the bottles.

"I'm taking a look in the storeroom," Missy announced to her colleagues.

"Please hurry," Agnes said.

You almost never find basements in Florida due to the high water table, so the storeroom was located on the main floor behind the beer coolers. Missy turned on the lights and regarded the heavy wooden shelves along the walls and piles of cardboard boxes on the shelves and floors. She wandered randomly through the obstacle course of boxes until she found what she was looking for.

Eight boxes of San Marcos Craft Bourbon were stacked on the floor in the very far corner of the room. One by one she moved them out of the way. Not until she picked up the very last box did she see the electrical switch-plate cover. Only a single screw held it in place, so she rotated the cover revealing a box inset in the wall. Inside the box was a single toggle switch. She flipped it.

A square of drywall pushed out slightly from the wall. Using her fingertips, she pried it open and removed it. In the space between two studs and backed by the drywall on the other side, was a canvas sack the size of a pillow. She grabbed it.

Inside the sack was a book that she partially withdrew. It had a leather-bound cover with the title, *The Book of Saint Cyprian.*

A shock like an electrical jolt ran from her hand, up her arm, through her heart, and into her head.

A brief image of a smiling, handsome man flashed in her eyes. It was her father, the man she had only known through a few photos. He smiled at her. The image faded, but she remained flooded with excitement, with energy.

And with a feeling of power and potential she had never felt before.

"Um, I think I found the book," she called out toward the other room.

THE BOOK WAS DEFINITELY the correct version. It had several unprinted leaves at the back filled with hard-to-decipher handwriting and drawings in ink. The signature of Don Mateo de Grenada was found on the overleaf of the first page of the book and in several places in the addendum. But Missy didn't want to study the book too much right now, because she was afraid that it would create energies that would be noticed by magicians in town.

Sure enough, when she got out of the car at the motel, clutching the canvas sack holding the book, a gray parrot took flight from a perch near the front door. The bird flew away to the east.

"We have to get out of here now!" she blurted to the vampires.

Afraid to let go of the grimoire, she brought it with her to her room where she frantically threw her clothes and toiletries into her suitcase. She left the room and dropped her suitcase into the rental car's trunk.

The problem, though, was the vampires. Yes, they were supernatural creatures with super-human strengths and abilities. They could move at times faster than the eye could register. But they were still old people. Have you ever gotten old people to organize and pack all their things and vacate a motel room in mere seconds? No, you haven't because it can't be done in under twenty minutes.

Missy finally got them all checked out and into the car, grumbling all the way.

"We haven't eaten yet," Sol complained.

"There's still blood in the cooler," Missy said.

"We could have had fresh, if you didn't rush us so much," Oleg said.

It was when they had just cleared the San Marcos city limits, but had to stop for gas, that they were caught. Missy was rolling up to one of the pumps when Bob's jeep and a black SUV pulled into the gas station with squealing tires and boxed in the rental car.

A huge African-American man exited the SUV and stood at the ready. Bob jumped out of his jeep and walked up to Missy's window. She lowered it.

"So you've had me under surveillance, hoping I'd lead you to the book?" Missy asked.

"Nope. I knew where it was because I'm the one who put it there. I was watching you because I was afraid you came to town to look for my book. I was making sure you didn't steal it."

He bent down until he was eye-level with Missy. He stared at her intently and suddenly she felt under magical assault. Her head flared with pain, as if twin drill bits were piercing her brain behind her eyes. She tried to pull up a basic protection spell but felt her power draining from her. Bob was incapacitating her. She barely had the strength to push the button to raise the window.

Shadows darted at the periphery of her vision and Bob screamed.

Agnes had jumped upon his back like a monkey and sank her teeth into his jugular vein. The African-American man tried to shake off the two vampires draining him. Sol was on the man's back, his jaws locked on the muscular neck. Oleg, who was as tall but not as big as the man, punched him hard in the jaw and held his head in place with two hands. While Sol feasted at the man's neck, Oleg bit the arm that tried to push Sol away. Oleg found a productive vein and fed readily.

At the next pump over, an older African-American woman finished pumping her gas and watched the vampire attack with disgust.

"Damn snowbird geezers," she said, shaking her head.

"Come down here every winter and bleed us dry. Literally. And too cheap to ever leave a decent tip."

Agnes, meanwhile, was seriously weakening Bob. His incapacitating spell had faded, and Missy felt her strength return. Missy didn't believe in using her magick to harm others, so she didn't have a large arsenal of spells for attacking. The one she had used to knock Omar Johnson off her porch wouldn't be appropriate here. But she did know a good sleeping spell. She closed her eyes, grasped the power charm in her pocket, and recited the invocation.

Bob's knees buckled and he dropped to the gas-stained concrete. The large African-American man required extra power but he, too, collapsed to the ground.

"Let's go, folks," Missy called to the vampires. "The attendant in the store may have called the cops."

All three were inside the car in a second.

"There," Sol said. "A long drive is always better after a hot meal."

"Glad it worked out for you," Missy said. "And thanks for saving me."

"I'm surprised the wizard and his thug weren't prepared for us to attack," Oleg said.

"I think their first concern was to neutralize my magic."

"And humans underestimate seniors," Agnes said. "They had no idea senior vampires could kick their butts."

The vampires snickered.

"It will take a couple of days for those suckers to recover from their blood loss," Sol said.

"Remember, Bob is not dead," Agnes said to Missy. "You need to expect him to come after you again."

Missy was sobered by the thought. "I know. Hopefully next time I'll be more ready."

She drove from the gas station toward the interstate. After she merged into the southbound traffic, she cast a simple spell to extend the longevity of the little bit of gas left in the tank. She wanted to get as far from San Marcos as she could before she stopped again to fill up.

19

EMBALMED OUT

It was a desperate plan. Matt decided to go undercover in a funeral home and hope to lure Omar Johnson into contacting him for corpses. He convinced his editor to give him a couple of weeks off, explaining he had the beginnings of an explosive story about body snatching and the biotech industry.

Not having any training in the funeral industry, which is the case for most of us, Matt hoped to sweet talk his way into a job as a sales rep or maintenance guy. But he didn't see any such job listings online. There was only one open job advertised at a funeral home or crematory in Jellyfish Beach.

Dean's Discount Undertakers was looking for an embalmer. Apparently, Jack, the embalmer Missy and he had interviewed, had flown the coop. No wonder, after Missy had warned him about Omar Johnson.

But Matt didn't know anything about embalming. How could he talk himself into a job like that? There were two steps:

lying about his qualifications to get an interview, and Wikipedia. Doesn't Wikipedia know everything?

Assuming the discount chain would be too cheap to do a background check, he crafted a fictitious resume and filled out the online job application with a fake last name. He kept his real first name so he wouldn't accidentally get tripped up. Henceforth, he would be known as Matthew Whipple.

Dean Mercer was the entrepreneur who started his chain of funeral homes. He was a tall, bony man in his sixties with a freakishly obvious black toupee. His office in a bank building in Jellyfish Beach was the headquarters of his other business, a direct-from-lease car dealership.

"I had no experience in the funeral business when I started Dean's Discount Undertakers," he bragged to Matt in his cluttered office.

"I can relate," Matt said.

"But I took it to a forty-million-dollar operation in just a few years. I have franchises all over Florida," he peered over his thick glasses at Matt. "Interested in a franchise?"

"Not yet," Matt said. "I need to save a little more money."

"You do that. My goal is to sell the company to one of the mortuary conglomerates. They haven't been interested because they think I'm too low-end. But low-end is the future of funerals, I'm sure of it. Most working folks can't afford to bury their loved ones anymore."

"I think it's a wonderful cause, bringing affordable funerals to the masses."

Dean smiled with pride. "It has become my purpose." He cleared his throat and looked on his messy desk for Matt's fake resume. "I see you studied funeral sciences with a concentration on embalming and restoration at Acme University. That's one of those online schools?"

Matt nodded. "They also have lab training down in Fort Lauderdale." Reading about the school was as far as his education went.

"Looks like this would be your first job as an embalmer. What else have you been doing? You look a little old to be just starting out."

Matt realized he should have put a bit more effort into his fake resume. "It's not on my resume, but I was a cowboy for many years," Matt lied with the first dumb thing that popped into his head. But anything would be better than admitting he was a reporter.

"Cowboy? Not exactly the right skillset. Normally, I'd prefer you to get some experience under a more senior embalmer," Dean said with concern.

Matt held his breath.

"But there's no time for such niceties. My embalmer in the Jellyfish Beach store quit without giving notice and left us with our pants down. You did receive your license, right?"

Matt nodded, feeling guiltier as his house of lies grew taller.

"You're the only respondent to my ad so far who isn't an ex-felon or ex-clergyman. When can you start?"

"Um. . ."

"How about today? You're not herding any cattle today, are you? No, of course not. You can fill out all the paperwork later, but there's a stiff at the county morgue that needs to be picked up tonight. A client's father named Wally Weesil. Boy, it took forever for the client to get his siblings to chip in for the down payment and this is our cheapest plan. Anyway, the viewing is Thursday, so you'll have to dive right in. Here's the keys to the hearse and the funeral home."

Matt caught the keys that Dean tossed to him. They were on a bottle-opener keychain.

"If you have any questions about the gear in the lab, no one's there now, but Mary Lou, the receptionist, will show up in the morning. If she can't help you, then just Google it." Dean shook Matt's hand. "It's great to have you on board. Gotta run."

Dean rushed out of the office. Matt stared at the keys in his hand and wondered why he had gotten himself into this nightmare.

MATT DROVE to the local franchise of Dean's Discount Undertakers, the same former fast-food restaurant he had visited with Missy. They must have already hired a new funeral director to replace the woman they had spoken to, since the viewing of the body Matt was picking up was scheduled for Thursday. But no one was there when he parked behind the funeral home.

Two hearses were in the rear of the lot, one new and shiny and the other much older. He clicked the key fob and the lights of the older one blinked. It made sense that this one would do the work while the newer one was saved for funerals.

He slipped into the front seat. The car reeked of cigarettes, decomposing bodies, and the ineffective pine-scented air freshener hanging from the rearview mirror. When he started the engine, hip hop music blasted from the speakers. He shut off the radio and grimly drove to the morgue.

When he got there, he wondered how one was supposed to pick up a body. He would have to ask someone. There was a main entrance, but a sign said pickups and deliveries were in the rear. He drove around the building until he found a loading dock and a double door beside it.

He parked the hearse nearby and went inside. The hallway was clearly not meant for the public, with exposed pipe and electrical conduits as well as stacked boxes. He saw a worker in coveralls walking by.

"Excuse me," Matt said. "Do you know where I'm supposed to pick up a, er, client?"

The man looked Matt up and down. Matt wasn't dressed as a body transporter. He dressed like a reporter who didn't make much money.

The man pointed down the hall. "Head this way and take a left at the next hallway. Claims are right down there."

Matt thanked him. He took a left where instructed and saw the Claims sign over a door with a frosted glass window. He just now realized he didn't have any paperwork that entitled him to take possession of a body. He'd just have to talk his way through this and see what happened.

He opened the door and entered a small waiting room with about a dozen chairs and a TV playing the HGTV network. There was a reception desk, but the window was closed. He tapped on it.

"Hi. Anyone home?"

A few minutes later, the window slid open. A middle-age African-American man looked at him suspiciously.

"I'm here to pick up Wally Weesil. I mean, his body," Matt said.

"You're with the funeral home?"

"Yeah. Dean's Discount Undertakers."

"Dean's." The morgue worker had a look of disgust like he had uttered a perversion. "I assume you don't have the proper paperwork?"

"You assume correctly," Matt said.

"Well, I'm not going to give you a hard time. Mr. Weesil is growing quite ripe, and we can't wait to get rid of him. Where's your gurney?"

"I'm supposed to bring my own gurney?"

"Hell, yes! We don't just give ours away. And you'll have to get him out of your van and into your funeral home. You need your own damn gurney."

"Okay. I'll be right back," Matt said.

He rushed outside and unlocked the hearse. It took a little while to figure out how to open the rear door. It swung to the side, rather than opening upwards like SUVs. He looked in the back where the coffins would go. There wasn't a gurney. But there had to be. He ran his hands on the coffin platform and found a latch to open a storage compartment. Stowed inside was a folded gurney. Pretty cool!

He unfolded and assembled it more easily than he had expected, then rolled it into the morgue. The gurney was a much lighter version of those used in an ambulance. Probably because it didn't need to have IV bags and oxygen tanks attached to it. As he pushed it down the hallway he wondered if he was beginning to get the hang of this undertaking business.

The attendant was waiting for him in an open door next to the one that led to the morgue waiting room. Matt followed him into a chilly room with refrigerated stainless-steel compartments to store the corpses.

"How am I sure you're giving me the right body?" Matt asked.

The attendant rolled his eyes at the unprofessionalism of Dean's Discount Undertakers. "My condolences to Mr. Weesil's family for choosing you guys."

"Everyone appreciates low prices," Matt said. "Especially grieving families."

"We'll see about that," the attendant muttered as he pulled out a giant drawer. Wally Weesil, presumably, lay there in a white body bag. The attendant zipped open the lower half to check the name on the plastic bracelet around the ankle. Then he signaled for Matt to help him lift the body and place it on the gurney.

"You good at restoration work?" the attendant asked.

"Um, not really." Matt wasn't sure what the man meant, but he had an idea and it wasn't pleasant.

"Wally here is our most famous guest at the moment. Remember that nor'easter we had a few weeks back? Well, Wally had a tall pine tree in his yard that was bent over by the wind and the top of it got wedged under the eaves of his house. Wally didn't have a chainsaw. He had to saw off the top of the tree by hand. He tried doing it from his roof, but that was awkward. So he climbed up the tree and sawed from up there."

Matt saw where this was going.

"When he finally sawed off the top, the tree sprang upright and catapulted Wally like a human missile. They found him six blocks away."

Matt made a mental note to add this to his file of Florida Man stories.

"I see why he needs restoration work," Matt said. "He also smells a little funny," Matt said.

"We've been storing him for weeks," the attendant said. "Maybe his family had to scrape together the money to pay your discount prices."

Matt smiled weakly and signed a form the attendant handed him. Then he and Wally were on their way down the hall and outside into the Florida sunshine.

"You couldn't have asked for better weather, Wally," Matt said.

It took him a few minutes to figure out how to get Wally into the back of the hearse. These gurneys were supposed to fold up as you pushed them into a vehicle, but he tried it several times, almost knocking Wally onto the asphalt, before he got the gurney inside.

As he started the engine, Matt realized how bad a fix he was in. He had been so focused on conning his way into the embalmer job that he had no idea what to do now. He had expected Omar Johnson would contact him and Matt would interview and perhaps trail him afterwards. Then Matt would simply quit. He hadn't planned on actually having to embalm anyone.

What if Omar didn't show up before Wally's viewing on Thursday? Matt had no idea. Wally's family might have a very yucky viewing.

How could he summon a ghoul? Who could he even ask? Even Missy wouldn't know, since Omar had shown up at her house without an invitation. Matt drove the hearse by the water treatment plant where the bodies were allegedly delivered. He circled the block a few times.

Omar, if you're in there, flag me down. Wally's really starting to smell.

No Omar. Matt pulled up to a closed gate behind the facility. He idled there for several minutes until a security guard shooed him away. There was nothing to do but return to the funeral home.

Now that he was familiar with the gurney, Matt had a fairly easy time getting Wally into the building and inside the former fast-food refrigerator, although his client had to be propped up in a vertical position to fit inside.

Matt looked with dread at the steel table and its drain. A large metal tank with a pump attached sat nearby. That must be for the embalming fluid. Matt shuddered at the thought of using it.

He noticed a laptop on the counter. Perhaps Omar Johnson

corresponded via email with the embalmer here like he had with Izzy Perez at the Jellyfish Beach Memorial Funeral Home. If only Matt could hack into the email account of the embalmer here. But how likely was that?

When he opened the laptop, he was surprised it wasn't password protected. It was asleep, but punching a single key brought it to life. A few applications were already running, one of which was email. He searched for Omar's name and was thrilled when several emails showed up in the Inbox and Sent folders.

Wow, this is almost too good to be true, he thought.

He read the emails. They were terse and business-like, similar to the ones he'd found in Joe Molloi's trousers but from a different email account. The most recent one was a month ago. That wasn't good. It indicated that Omar wasn't a regular buyer from this funeral home.

Matt responded to the email, telling Omar that he was the new guy here and wanted to renew the business arrangement. He requested that Omar contact him as soon as possible.

He hit "send." It didn't bounce. So there was nothing left to do but wait.

And wait. Matt sat in the funeral home until being there freaked him out too much. He took the laptop with him and went home for the night.

"SORRY I WASN'T THERE for your interview. I'm Moe Littleton, the funeral director here. I'm just starting here myself."

Moe shook Matt's hand a little too long with his big, calloused mitts. Maybe he was practicing how to deal with the bereaved. He was bald, short, and stocky. He looked more like a manual laborer than a funeral director.

"Where did you work before this?" Matt asked.

"I'm new at the funeral business, but I used to work in events, so Dean thought I'd be great for this job."

"You were an event planner?"

"Not exactly. I set up the tents, chairs, and tables at the events," Moe replied.

"I see. Well, I'm new at this, too. First embalming job."

"So Mr. Weesil's funeral will a first for both of us. I'm a little nervous."

"Same here," Matt said, but what he really meant was, *I'm completely freaking out.*

"Have you finished preparing the body yet?"

"I just brought him from the hospital yesterday."

"Well, you better get started," Moe said. "When you're new, everything takes longer than you think it will. Mr. Weesil has to present perfectly tomorrow at the viewing."

"Gotcha," Matt said before retreating to the lab to hide. He checked the laptop's email. Nothing from Omar Johnson, but there was spam offering a great deal on restorative tissue putty.

Matt killed time in the former fast-food kitchen, waiting for Omar to email him, until Moe popped his head in. He looked around the room.

"Where's Mr. Weesil? You still haven't started?"

"Don't worry," Matt said. "I'm doing prep work."

"It doesn't look like it." Moe's genial facade disappeared. "Don't leave me in the lurch, man. I can't afford for my first funeral to be a flop. Do I need to call in a temp embalmer to replace you?"

"No, no, not at all. Chill out, Moe. I'll have Wally looking beautiful in no time."

After Moe left, Matt sank his head into his hands. Maybe he should just steal the laptop and run away.

Moe opened the door again. "Dean says to ask the receptionist if you have any questions. Or just Google them." He closed the door.

About twenty minutes of Googling later, Matt felt like an expert in the field. This wouldn't be so hard after all. First, he had to clean and disinfect Wally's exterior. Then he had to pump in the embalming fluid, which would push the natural fluids out. Then he had to do some gross things to the abdomen which he didn't remember but he'd look them up again on the internet.

What could go wrong?

He opened the refrigerator, grabbed the edges of the body bag, and lowered the upright corpse back onto the gurney. He wheeled it to the table, found the gears for raising it to the table's height, and then slid the bag onto the table, making sure the head was on the little platform he assumed was for the head.

But now he had to get over a small hurdle: He had never touched a dead human before. Sure, he had moved Wally on and off the gurney, and onto the table. But Matt had merely grasped the body bag that held Wally, not the corpse itself. And now he to remove the bag and handle the body. Very intimately.

He didn't care how many layers of latex gloves he put on, he still didn't want to touch the dead guy.

He zipped open the bag enough to see Wally's face. Wally looked dead. Very dead. He had the gray, wilted look of food that had been in the fridge way too long. Plus, he looked like he had been catapulted six blocks and landed headfirst. How was Matt going to make him look like he was sleeping, let alone presentable?

Time to consult Dr. Google. As he opened the laptop, he received a notification of a new email.

It was from Omar Johnson.

"Thank you for your offer," the email read. "First, I must verify that you are legitimate and are not entrapping me. Then we will discuss this."

How long was that going to take? Matt panicked. He wanted to quit Dean's Discount Undertakers *now*. Like, right this minute.

Matt researched his embalming tasks on the internet. The more he read, his confidence plummeted. As the afternoon waned and the shadows in the room lengthened, he sensed a presence.

A tall man was standing in the darkness between the refrigerator and piles of boxes.

"Mr. Johnson?" Matt asked.

"I sense that you don't know what you're doing," the shadowy figure said.

"I'm just brushing up on the details. It's been a while since I got out of school." Matt had to avoid disclosing that he was a reporter. He didn't want to end up dead like the funeral-home employees who had spoken to him.

"I will pay five hundred for each body, given that they are not deceased for longer than seven days," Omar said.

Matt had a brief glimpse, when the man shifted into some light, of a huge mustache.

"Wally here has been dead for only few days," Matt lied, "and he's been in the fridge the whole time."

"How many bodies can you provide on an ongoing basis?"

"I don't know. I just started here, and as you can tell, this franchise is not a large operation."

"Are you willing to send me more than the bodies destined

for cremation? Are you willing to employ trickery to ensure families they are burying their relatives when you send them to me instead?"

"Sure," Matt said. Omar was giving him the creeps. But he nevertheless asked, "What do you want them for?"

Dark, angry energy drifted from the shadows.

"The biotech industry," Omar said. "These bodies will help living people survive illnesses and injuries."

In order to get Omar to open up, Matt decided to take a huge risk and feign sympathy with the ghoul's cause.

He said, "I was told by the previous embalmer that you're doing a noble thing, keeping your community from starving."

"What do you know about my community?"

"Almost nothing," Matt replied. "But every living creature deserves what it needs to survive. Starvation is a horrible way to die."

Uh-oh, he just went and admitted he knew the ghouls were eating the corpses.

"I'm happy to help you," Matt added. He was totally winging it now. "The dead don't need their bodies anymore and their relatives bury or burn them anyway. The way I look at it, this is no different than donating organs to save lives."

"Where have you gotten your information?" Omar asked.

"From the embalmer I replaced."

"I did not tell him these things."

"Some of them I guessed," Matt said. "I have a vivid imagination."

"Who are you, really?"

"Matt Whipple, first-year embalmer. Did you know I used to be a cowboy?"

"Would you be willing to recruit embalmers from the other franchises of this company?"

Clearly, ghouls were not used to dealing with human nonsense.

"Yes. I told you I want to help," Matt said, sounding as sincere as he could fake.

"Also, there are greener embalming methods that use natural ingredients instead of formaldehyde."

"I'll look into that and make a proposal to management," Matt said. Sensing that Omar was lowering his inhibitions, he asked, "How many are there in your community?"

"There are thousands of us in this area alone. Too many to feed. More keep coming to Florida. Ghouls need a place to retire, too, you know. And they think all the elderly humans moving here will be easy pickings. But then the elderly humans complain about how crowded Florida is, so they move to North Carolina."

Omar was getting worked up. He had gradually moved out of the shadows, so he was visible in a dark-gray suit and gold tie. His bold, white mustache stood in contrast against a face with pale flesh that didn't quite seem natural.

"And as Florida grows more crowded, it's harder for my people to hide, harder to find recently deceased people to snatch, and harder to lure victims to remote places to kill them. It has become so difficult for us to remain undetected, but we must. Our survival depends on it. Humans will try to wipe us out if they know we exist."

Yes, we would, Matt thought. That's the game plan.

"But more and more of us move down here. They sneak onto freight trains or container ships, or sit in the back seats of buses. Some even stoop to flying discount airlines. Many simply walk here. But those are all more hungry mouths to feed. And let me tell you, they're always hungry. It's like they have eating disorders."

"Can the bodies I send you help much?" Matt asked.

"I have been arranging this form of procurement for years now after I tapped into a deceased human's trust fund. Buying bodies used to suffice to supplement our food supply, but no longer. That's why I asked you to recruit others. But still, we are reaching a tipping point. An existential crisis for my species. We are facing mass starvation!"

Matt had to admit that even though he thought the ghouls were repugnant and evil, he did feel a little badly for them when Omar put it that way.

Omar was gesticulating wildly. His face was apparently unable to turn red like the face of a real human having a conniption.

"My clan who live with me in this city have become so desperate that we have burrowed into the recently buried coffins and eaten the dead. Do you realize how nasty those bodies taste after they've been embalmed?"

"No, but that does sound really nasty," Matt said. He lost whatever sympathy he had been feeling for the ghouls.

"You live humans should all be worried," Omar shouted. "We will be coming for you. I can't stop my people from rising up and going on the attack. In time, you will all be eaten!"

Omar's conjured human disguise vanished and standing before Matt was a full-on ghoul. Angular and bony, pale gray and slimy, naked and long-clawed, the creature looked at Matt with hungry yellow eyes. Its nose was two slits and below them distended jaws opened, revealing a giant mouth with long, pointy yellow teeth.

It moved toward Matt.

And he bolted from the room. He ran through the coffin showroom and out the front door.

"Are you finished yet with Mr. Weesil?" Moe called out after him.

Matt hopped in his car and floored it as he exited the parking lot. He'd worked a full day and wouldn't get paid for it. He never even took a lunch break. Maybe that's because he had been on the verge of throwing up for hours.

Moe was worrying about getting Wally prepared for the funeral, but right now the ghoul was probably picking its teeth with Wally's bones.

WELCOMING COMMITTEE

When Missy returned home from San Marcos, her two gray tabbies were waiting at the front door. They greeted her warmly as she rolled in her suitcase and carefully carried the grimoire in its sack. This, she slipped into her underwear drawer until she could think of a safer place to hide it. The cats' warmth continued as she fed them with their favorite wet food.

After they finished eating, the warmth disappeared. Brenda and Bubba made one thing clear: They were pissed off. What did she think she was doing leaving them alone for two days?

On the very rare occasions that Missy was away from home overnight, she had a neighbor come by twice a day to feed the cats. Missy gave Fran the key and the alarm code and that was that.

But since she'd been under magick attack, she'd been using a protection spell on the house on top of the burglar alarm to ward off intrusions of humans, monsters, demons, or antagonistic spells. Try teaching a normal human neighbor how to disable a protection spell and then turn it on again. Nope, wasn't going to happen. No more long trips for Missy.

So, for the short trip to San Marcos, which was really unavoidable, Missy left the cats alone. Go ahead, call her a bad cat mom. Go ahead, she was ready for the moral lashing. She set the cats up with an automatic dry-food dispenser and a water dispenser. She left the TV running on the animal channel which normally occupied them for hours.

She even created a new spell that gave them the sensation of being petted by a human hand when they triggered it by approaching her reading chair. Okay, the spell did freak them out the first couple of times when she tested it before she left, but they soon began to enjoy it. This spell was working the entire time she was gone.

So call her a bad cat mom. She'll take her lumps and move on.

The cats weren't as mad as they let on, but she spent the next half hour apologizing to them with belly rubs and plenty of treats. In minutes, they were purring like buzz saws.

Until the noise came from her bedroom.

The cats scattered to points unknown.

The noise came again. What was it?

It was . . . giggling.

Giggling? Yes, a male voice affecting a higher pitch as it murmured and giggled.

She grabbed her pepper spray from her purse, cast a quick protection spell around herself, and tiptoed toward the bedroom. She entered the hallway that connected the master and guest bedrooms and glanced into the open doorway of the master. No sign of anyone from this angle. She crept to the doorway and peeked inside.

There, in front of her dresser, Don Mateo of Grenada was trying on her bras.

Fortunately, he wore a linen undershirt, so a horrible image was not seared into her memory forever. But this was clearly unacceptable behavior, even for a ghost.

She cleared her throat.

Don Mateo looked at her. "Oops," he said.

"Yeah, oops. Don't touch my bras, panties, or any underwear. Don't touch any of my clothes at all."

"I was not snooping," the seventeenth-century ghost said. "You placed the grimoire in the drawer with these lady items and that is where I appeared. Remember, I am magically bound to the grimoire."

"Nothing compelled you to try my bras on."

He giggled. "A sense of adventure compelled me. When I was alive, I was not exactly familiar with lady undergarments. I was too dedicated to the study of magic and alchemy. I did not have time to pursue wenching and other such pastimes. Or to pursue marriage, either, sadly. But as a ghost I feel so liberated!"

Missy rolled her eyes. The ghost disappeared and her bra seemed to move by itself back to the drawer which then closed.

As she turned to leave the room, Missy found Don Mateo materialized again. Now, he was fully dressed in a blue sorcerer's robe and gold turban.

"I hope we get along," he said, "because you will be seeing a lot of me now that you have the grimoire. Please remember that I can help you in matters pertaining to your magick, magic in general, and demonology."

"But please not in matters of lingerie."

"Point taken."

Growling and hissing came from just beyond the doorway.

Bubba stared at the ghost, his ears flattened back, his tail puffy and twitching back and forth.

"I had no problem with cats when I was alive," Don Mateo said. "I do not understand why this one is so hostile."

"Maybe because you're dead?"

"That was hurtful."

"Bubba can sense your energy, but he can't smell you, and he senses you aren't a physical being. It's confusing for him. He hasn't seen a ghost before."

"Then maybe he just needs to get to know me." The ghost said as he crouched and reached out his hand toward Bubba.

Bubba backed up and hissed more loudly.

Don Mateo said something in Spanish in a low, comforting voice. And Bubba visibly relaxed. His ears went to their normal positions and his tail de-puffed. He moved toward the ghost and sniffed his spectral fingers. When he didn't find a scent, he looked up at the ghost with a confused expression. But at least it wasn't a hostile expression.

"I believe we are making progress," Don Mateo said.

"Your lack of scent might be a problem," Missy said.

"Oh, I can operate with scent, but that might cause an even a bigger problem."

Suddenly the scent of body odor, moldy clothing, and strange perfume hit Missy's nose.

"I see what you mean," she said, cringing from the stink.

Bubba didn't seem to mind. It was as if Don Mateo had been half-hidden and now emerged fully into view for the cat. He perked up and moved to the ghost, trying unsuccessfully to rub up against a leg that wasn't really there.

But the true problem soon became apparent when the ghost began sneezing.

"You're allergic to cats?" Missy asked.

"They did cause this reaction in me when I was alive. But do not worry. I will easily coexist with your felines."

His sneezes grew worse. He pulled a non-existent handkerchief from his non-existent breeches and blew his nose loudly and messily.

"I don't understand how a ghost can be allergic," Missy said. "I was assuming that the stench of you was just an olfactory illusion that you conjured to fool Bubba and me."

"'*Stench* of me'?"

"Odor. Sorry."

"It is not a conjuration," he explained. "It is a corporeal manifestation. As you know, I am a spirit, an untethered soul. I have energy and I exist with a will, but I have no physicality. I have strong memories and I can project those to living creatures. Some ghosts show people an image of them, some make noises, others move objects. We are using our energy to physically recreate what we remember from the physical world. Scent is just another thing we can recreate."

"You still didn't explain how it makes you sneeze."

"I am recreating how others smelled me when I was alive. In doing so, I activate my memories of how I smelled to myself. And how other things smelled to me. Including cat dander. I cannot help it; I respond to that like I used to."

He sneezed again several times. His handkerchief was getting soggy.

"Is that real snot in your handkerchief?" she asked.

"Ectoplasm. If only I could produce real snot."

Bubba continued trying to rub against his non-existent legs and Don Mateo continued sneezing.

"Farewell," he said. "I need a break from the kitties."

He dissolved before her eyes and was gone.

HER PHONE RANG. It was Matt.

"We've got a ghoul problem," he said.

"Yes, my trip to San Marcos went well, thanks for asking."

"We need to talk. Can you meet me tomorrow?"

"Sure. Talk about what?"

"There are too many ghouls to feed and they're getting more aggressive, going after living people as well. There's a good chance that hordes of them are going to come after us. But anyway, how was your trip?"

"'But anyway'? I didn't realize I was returning to a ghoul invasion," Missy said.

"Were the vampires fun traveling companions?"

"Better than small children, but that's not saying much. I did manage to find the grimoire."

"You did? I thought it would be like finding a needle in a haystack."

"It was, except I had help from a ghost."

"Every time I talk to you," Matt said, "it seems I have to come to terms with yet another supernatural entity actually existing."

"I'm not surprised ghosts exist. I am surprised this one has coherent conversations with me and has an allergy to cats."

"What? Who is this ghost?"

"Don Mateo of Grenada. He's the wizard who brought *The Book of Saint Cyprian* from Spain and added a bunch of Native American magic to it. I think I told you he was killed by an entity he conjured by accident. Now he's bound for some reason to the grimoire. Basically, I inherited him along with the book."

"Does the book have any spells for eradicating ghouls?" Matt asked.

"I don't know. I haven't studied it yet. I should mention that the head of the magic guild in San Marcos tried to steal the grimoire from me. He claims it belongs to him. The vampires saved me."

"It's good to hear your vampires are good for something other than complaining about their constipation."

WHEN MISSY HAD FIRST HEARD about *The Book of Saint Cyprian*, she had bought and studied a copy of the standard English translation. It reminded her of the books of King Solomon with their instructions for summoning spirits and creating amulets.

Now that she finally had Don Mateo's edition in hand, she went straight to the last section for his addendum.

A lot of it was indecipherable. Aside from a few notes in English, most of it was in antiquated Spanish. Several spells were apparently transcripts of the native Timucuan language. The book was printed on rich, heavy, vellum-like paper and each page of the addendum was packed with dense handwriting and drawings of magic symbols in brownish ink. Missy would need lots of help deciphering all of this. Maybe that's what Don Mateo's ghost was for.

Suddenly half the pages in the book flipped to the right, almost slapping her hand.

Wow. The grimoire itself was magical. Did it not want her to read the addendum?

The book now lay open to a chapter in the main book on the Red Dragon, with an illustration of an ornamental object with a vague dragon shape. She ignored it and returned the pages to the addendum.

The book snapped back to the Red Dragon chapter. Maybe it wanted her to read it. Too bad she wasn't up on her archaic Spanish.

"The Red Dragon talisman was a gift to Moses from the sorcerer who taught him his stuff. Such as the parting of the Red Sea."

Missy jumped in her chair. Don Mateo had appeared behind her. He was wearing his blue sorcerer's robe and gold turban.

"Look at the drawing more closely," he said.

She did, and felt the warmth of recognition spread through her.

"My birth father used it to mark the wax seal of the letter he left me," she said.

"That is correct. The Red Dragon later came into the possession of King Solomon. The talisman is said to amplify a magician's power a hundredfold. It also is supposed to allow you to summon dragons."

Missy had found a young, injured dragon in the Everglades not long ago. She'd also seen his mother and other dragons. Being able to summon dragons would be like calling in an airstrike from B-52s. It could come in handy someday, but probably not in downtown Jellyfish Beach.

"A letter from my father mentioned something about a dragon charm," she said. "It said it would be delivered when it was needed. What was that all about?"

A throaty engine roared down the street. A brown delivery van passed by the living room window and stopped briefly. An object thumped against the front door.

"Delivery!" Don Mateo said with a smile.

Missy got up from the table and opened the front door. A

nondescript cardboard box lay on her doormat. It was addressed in cursive handwriting to her on a small label without a sender listed.

"Are you merely going to stare at it?" Don Mateo asked.

She brought the box inside and placed it on the kitchen counter. The packing tape that sealed it was old and yellowed. The tape cracked open easily.

"Darn, no bubble wrap," Missy said. "I love to pop that."

Instead, the box was packed with shredded newspaper pages that were also yellowed with age. She started to reach into the box to find what as packed inside, but thought better of it. It could be a booby trap.

She upended the box and dumped the contents on her counter. Something metallic hit the surface. Clearing away the newspaper, she revealed the talisman. It was brass-colored, about two inches long and depicted its subject in the style of illustrations on early maps that were supposed to portray a dolphin, but looked more like a cross between a whale and a French bulldog. It barely resembled a dragon at all.

Power radiated from it. She'd never felt this much intensity from any charm, amulet, or talisman before. Nothing even close.

"This isn't the original, is it?" she asked. "It's not the same one that Moses and King Solomon had, right?"

Don Mateo laughed. "No. Copies were made of the original. Most are worthless, but there are a few out in the world that actually work. I do not know how your father acquired this or if he made it himself. The instructions in the grimoire for making one leave out a couple of steps deliberately."

"And this one definitely works. I can feel the power."

"Are you afraid to touch it?"

Missy gingerly reached out. Her hand tingled as it drew

closer to the talisman. When she picked it up, a jolt went through her arm to her heart.

She gasped.

"I feel so alive," she whispered.

"You must not hold it for too long," Don Mateo said. "It is best to do so only when casting a spell, summoning an entity, or commanding creatures to do your bidding."

She looked at him. "I command you to stay out of my lingerie drawer."

A shocked expression took over his face.

"I didn't believe you'd obey me when I told you the first time to stay out of the drawer," she explained. "Let's see if the talisman really works."

"I will certainly never touch your lingerie again."

"Good. I hope it also works on a larger scale, too," she said.

PAINFUL MEMORY

Missy had never visited anyone in jail before. She had been afraid that they'd have some new visitation system that was video only and that she wouldn't be in proximity of Harry Roarke. Her spell might not have worked via video. Fortunately, the county jail still used the old-school method she'd seen in the movies: sitting in a cubicle facing the inmate through thick plexiglass, speaking through telephone handsets.

"It's only a few days until the full moon. If I shift in here, I'm a dead man. They'll put me down like they did Chainsaw in his condo," Harry said, referring to the drug-dealing werewolf Affird had murdered.

"I know, Harry. Your lawyer is doing his best to get the video the man shot of the ghoul entered into evidence. He asked me to help you create an alibi."

"How?"

"I have a memory aide that hopefully will help you remember where you were on the night in question," she said, using a euphemism for the spell under the assumption their conversation was being recorded. "Maybe that will help us find a witness who can corroborate your story."

"If there was a witness, he or she saw me in shifted form," Harry said. "That's not exactly helpful."

"True. At the very least, we need a convincing story of how you got blood all over you. You don't happen to get nosebleeds, do you?"

"No. That would be too easy. Man, how I wish I didn't shower so thoroughly when I got home from the mall. We would have had DNA to prove it was different from that guy in the park. At least I hope it would be different."

"You still doubt yourself?" Missy asked, reading the worry and guilt in Harry's eyes.

"Yeah."

"Well, that's why I'm here." Missy glanced around to make sure the guard wasn't eavesdropping. "If this works, and the memories return, keep your voice down. You'll feel like you're experiencing the events all over again, so try to control yourself. And don't drop the phone."

"Are you hypnotizing me?"

"It's similar. You'll be in a trance of sorts. But afterwards you'll remember this exercise, and the memories from that night will remain fresh in your mind as if you never forgot them."

"Okay. I'm ready." He took a deep breath. "What do I have to do?"

"Just relax. Clear your mind. Think of a burning candle."

Harry opened his lips, about to ask something. But this was like putting a patient under anesthesia. Missy grasped the power charm in her pocket, chanted the short invocation, and summoned the energies she needed. Before Harry could speak, he was enchanted.

His eyes closed and his head dropped slightly, propped up by the arm that held the phone handset. His mouth opened and his jowls sagged. He moaned quietly. Then emitted a low growl.

Missy glanced around. The guard leaned against the wall by the door mesmerized by his smartphone. A lawyer and inmate were conversing loudly three cubicles down.

Harry twitched with pent-up energy. Fortunately, he still held the phone, allowing them to talk.

"What is happening?" she asked.

"I shifted. The others want me to surf with them. Cynthia is calling me. But I can't. I'm too restless. The moon is over the horizon, so large and bright tonight. It's driving me mad. I'm running down the beach and the urge to hunt is too strong. Now I'm running across the bridge over the Intracoastal. A car went by and didn't even notice me . . . I'm in town now, moving away from the lights and the noise and the people. I'm running down the railroad tracks. It's dark and quiet . . . I picked up a scent—a woman. A young one. She is alone. I'm trying to find her."

Oh no, Missy thought. I was hoping he had actually attacked an animal or something, not a human.

"Her scent is steady now. She's a few blocks away to the west. She's just past her time of the month. Sweat, faded cologne. She hasn't slept or bathed since yesterday. She's walking quickly. She's afraid."

Harry was silent for a moment. Then he growled.

"She feels threatened," he continued. "She's on a street just west of the tracks. Dark, hardly any streetlights. The homes are duplexes, low-rent apartment buildings. . ."

He growled more deeply. Missy looked around to make sure no one had heard.

"There's another predator stalking her," Harry said. "This is his territory, but he's not aware of me yet."

"Another werewolf?" Missy asked.

"No. A human. A bad one. He's high on some drug. He's following the prey. She hasn't seen him, but she knows she's being watched. He's circling around to cut her off. I have to drive him away from my prey. . . I've, I've. . ."

"What?" Missy whispered.

"I've lost my hunger for her now. My human conscience is getting in the way. She reminds me of my daughter when she was her age. I'm concerned now for this woman. I want to protect her from the human predator." He was quiet for a moment. "A car went past and I had to hide behind a bush. Now I'm moving again . . ."

He whimpered.

"The man is talking to the woman now. I smell her fear and his lust. I have to hurry . . . I'm racing down the street on all fours now, as fast as I can run . . . he's attacking her now! He pulled her behind a building. Trying to rape her, tearing at her clothing. She's screaming and trying to get away. He punched her . . . I'm there, I'm lunging at the man . . ."

Harry dropped the phone and thrashed in his chair. The guard looked over.

"It's okay," Missy said to the guard, beaming a big, fake smile. "He's just acting out."

Harry growled and snapped his jaws. He slowly relaxed and was quiet except for a small whimper. He shook his head and pawed at his face with the side of his hand. Then he slumped against the plexiglass between them, his face smeared against it.

Missy tapped on it. Harry opened one eye and then the

other and looked at her as if he didn't recognize her. His eyes focused with realization and he picked up the phone again.

"I stopped the predator. The woman got away safely. She's okay, except for a bruise where he punched her. I hope she gets help. I ran away. I ran and ran and somehow I ended up at the mall. When security was driving in my direction, I climbed up a drainpipe onto the roof."

"The spell is fading," Missy said. "What did you do to the rapist? Did you kill him?"

Harry shook his head. "He was alive, at least, when I left."

"You injured him?"

"I think I blotted out this memory because of disgust."

"What memory?"

"Of what I did. I could have torn off his head with a snap of my jaws. I could have disemboweled him with a slash of my claws. But I was so angry I gave him the punishment he deserved."

"What?"

"I snapped off his private parts."

"Oh my," Missy said.

"And I accidentally swallowed them. No wonder I woke up feeling like I'd had a bad meal."

"I see."

"He was bleeding like a pig. It got all over me. Could he die from that?"

"Possibly, if you severed an artery. Most likely, if he got prompt medical attention, he survived. With a lot of trauma."

"Yeah, lots of trauma. And I mean for me, not the rapist." He shuddered. "Is there something wrong with me psychologically?"

"It's not for me to judge. But at the time, you were delivering your version of justice."

"So what do we do now?"

"I'll contact your lawyer for you, and he'll take it from there."

After Missy left the jail, she called Paul Leclerc. He was pleased to hear about the breakthrough, and as a werewolf himself, he was not freaked out at all about the story.

"The rapist got what he deserved," he told her.

Missy believed the vigilante justice was too harsh, but was happy the rapist wasn't likely to assault any more women.

The next day, Leclerc told her that his investigators had canvassed the area hospitals and clinics. Due to HIPPA privacy rules, they couldn't divulge any patient information. But one ER did say they admitted a man for traumatic amputation wounds at 7:15 p.m. on the night of the full moon, which was shortly after the time Joseph Molloi was killed in Flounder Park on the other side of town.

Leclerc and his client agreed to embellish the story a bit and claim Harry did not have a weapon and removed the offending body parts with his bare hands. It was a weird alibi, but hopefully it would help get Harry Roarke out of jail.

MATT'S HANDS were shaking as he picked up his coffee cup, spilling half of it on the table. His face was death-white. If Missy hadn't known him, she would have assumed he was a vampire.

"Are you sure you need more coffee?" Missy asked. "You look like you've overdosed on caffeine already."

She had agreed to meet him at the cafe for a quick cup on her way to her evening patient appointments. He had sounded desperate when he called her.

"I met with Omar Johnson," Matt said.

"Really? That wasn't too bright. I told you about his visit to my house."

"I was undercover as an embalmer. He didn't know I'm a reporter. I had him believing we were setting up a business arrangement."

"Really? Good job."

"It was at Dean's Discount Undertaking."

"Are you saying the embalmer there has been killed?"

"No. He quit right after we talked to him. Dean was pretty desperate to hire a replacement."

"He must have been if he hired you."

"I'm good on job interviews, I guess. I learned I'm not cut out to be an embalmer, though."

"So what's the deal with Omar?" Missy asked.

"It's like you theorized. Ghouls are moving here along with everyone else, but their population is growing too much to sustain themselves. Omar is supplementing the food supply of the ghouls in our area by buying bodies. But his efforts can't keep up with demand."

"Why does everyone have to move to Florida?"

"The ghouls have gotten so desperate," Matt said, "that they've been tunneling into graves and eating the bodies. Who would want to eat a body filled with formaldehyde?"

"No bodies filled with formaldehyde for me, no way."

"But the most concerning thing is that Omar warned the ghouls will be coming after live humans. I've read that while they're known for eating corpses, some ghouls devour living people, like Omar did."

"Yeah, the ghouls that can shape shift lure them to their deaths," Missy said.

"We're talking thousands of ghouls here. It will be like a zombie invasion in Jellyfish Beach. We saw what Omar did to

Molloi and Perez, and that was to silence them. Imagine hungry ghouls doing that on a large scale."

Missy had witnessed a horde of ghouls escaping from the sinkhole in her yard. She knew how frightening it could be. Her solution at the time, luring them back into the hole with a scent, was only a temporary remedy. She needed to discover a more powerful weapon.

Missy filled Matt in on her trip to San Marcos, the grimoire she brought home with her, and the unexpected delivery of the talisman.

"Give me some time to study the book and the talisman," she said. "Maybe I can find a way to fight these ghouls."

"Not just fight. Destroy them. Or at least chase them out of Jellyfish Beach. To someplace like North Carolina."

22

DIETER: DEMON HUNTER

Dieter Dufusdunder received a whopping three hundred dollars from *The Jellyfish Beach Journal*. It was barely enough to pay his overdue utility bills. As far as he knew, the newspaper hadn't posted the video or written about it. Nevertheless, selling the video was a huge morale boost. It gave him an idea for a video series he could run on YouTube and possibly sell to a streaming provider.

It would be called *Dieter: Demon Hunter*. He would travel around capturing supernatural creatures on video. It wouldn't be like those lame ghost-hunter programs where they never really find a ghost. No, he would be more like a storm chaser, risking life and limb to get mind-blowing footage that millions of people would watch.

Once, about a year ago, he thought he saw a vampire attacking a woman on the beach at night. At first, he believed the couple was making out, so he didn't videotape them. But afterwards he got a glimpse of fangs and of some blood on the woman's neck. If he had been prepared, he could have gotten awesome footage.

And now he had the unbelievable video of the murder in the park. He was pretty sure the creature was a ghoul. So that makes two monsters in Jellyfish Beach in only a year and he hadn't even been hunting them.

Maybe he could really make a go of this. And ditch the pizza-delivery job.

Okay, first assignment: Track down that ghoul and get it on video again.

After his delivery shift was over, he hung out in and around Flounder Park for hours, hoping the ghoul would stop by. But the park was technically closed, so no people were around to attract the predator. When he got home, he did some more internet surfing on ghouls. A couple of sites mentioned that the monsters were said to frequent cemeteries.

So the next night, that's where he went.

The Jellyfish Beach Municipal Cemetery was on a main road across from the water treatment plant. At the sign by the gate he took a selfie wearing a big grin, because he never tired of selfies. His social media followers expected them from him wherever he went.

It was bright here from the streetlights, but after he hopped the fence and walked further into the boneyard, it became darker and quieter as he went. The lawn smelled recently mowed and the landscaping was meticulous. It was actually peaceful in there.

Dieter wandered toward the far end of the cemetery where the large public mausoleum stood behind a few small, private ones. He passed an open grave covered with an AstroTurf mat. A large party canopy spread above rows of folding chairs. A burial was probably taking place here in the morning. He grabbed a chair from the last row, turned it around to face out into the cemetery, and sat down.

Wait, first a clever selfie was called for. He pulled the Astro-Turf mat from the grave and stood at the edge of the grave with an exaggerated extension of his left leg sticking in the hole. A campy grimace of fear made the shots of himself just right. He replaced the mat over the grave and sat down, turning on his video camera.

He waited. And waited. There was almost no traffic on the distant street, and the only sounds were a couple of tree frogs and a gentle sifting of breeze.

Did ghouls really still spend time in graveyards? In the olden days it would have been easy to dig up a corpse for a meal, but nowadays the caskets were heavy duty and enclosed in concrete grave liners or vaults. It must be awfully hard to get through all those obstacles.

A thought crept into Dieter's head: A live human hanging out in a cemetery late at night would be a much easier meal than a corpse.

He brushed off the fear. Being a monster-hunter required taking risks. To get good footage he had to have his subject within the range of his lens. He had a good telephoto lens for his video camera, and a flash he could use at the right moment, but if he had to crop in a lot during postproduction, the imagery would be all grainy.

So he couldn't be too far away if a ghoul appeared. The viewer's perception that the cameraman was in danger ramped up the excitement a hundred-fold.

He glanced around. Hmm, even for an intrepid monster-hunter like himself, it might be safer to hide behind a grave-stone or one of the mausoleums. It would be like using a blind for wildlife photos. Yeah, maybe he should move, just in case.

A faint scratching came from nearby. It sounded like rats. The idea of rats foraging in a graveyard was pretty gross, but come to think about it, not as bad as the thought of ghouls doing so. He chuckled to himself as he stood up and started walking toward the nearest mausoleum.

The mausoleum was a small, one-story structure made of concrete with inset marble and unusual columns shaped like bamboo on either side of the metal door. It looked kind of like a tiki hut. The name Johnson was engraved in a marble slab above the door, with the names and dates of family members on a plaque to the right of the door. Dieter took a selfie in front of the mausoleum, with his hand on the door handle as if he were about to go inside.

The scratching grew louder. He tingled down in his lower regions from the pucker action going on. Goosebumps ran up his arms. Now, along with the scratching, came a whiny mewing that spoke of hunger and misery.

He ducked behind the mausoleum with only his head and camera sticking out.

The noises were coming from the open grave

Holy crap, it's showtime.

He readied his video camera and zoomed into the gravesite.

The AstroTurf mat was moving. It bulged upwards in places like the bubbling of boiling water. And then a bald head with sunken eye sockets popped up at the edge of the mat. Long, bony arms grasped the ground and pushed as the torso came into view. A bony leg swung out of the grave.

The ghoul squatted at the edge of the grave and sniffed the air through narrow nostril slits. The mat was pushed aside as more ghouls climbed out of the grave and joined their comrade, squatting on their haunches and surveying the scene.

Dieter had a hard time keeping the camera steady as his

entire body trembled. Despite his fear, he was thrilled to be getting this footage. It was going to rock the world!

The breeze shifted direction and the ghouls—there were now a half-dozen of them—rose in unison and loped across the lawn on all fours like primates. They headed for the mausoleum at the rear of the cemetery that loomed like a castle wall. The long structure was nearly two stories tall and was covered with rectangular plaques covering the openings of the crypts where caskets or urns were inserted. The occupied ones were engraved with the names of the residents. Bunches of flowers protruded from many of the niches on the plaques.

The ghouls reached the building and leaped up, trying to attack one particular crypt. Dieter figured it contained a fresh new neighbor. The crypt was above eye level and the ghouls needed to jump up to work on prying the cover off. Two of them managed to hook onto it with their hands and feet and dug at the cement with their claws. Their whiny mewing mixed with grunts and growls.

Finally, the lid popped off and dropped to the ground with a crash. The ghouls slid the casket out more carefully than Dieter expected. Attracted by the scent, more ghouls emerged from the open grave and rushed over to the mausoleum. There had to be nearly twenty of them now.

As soon as the casket rested upon the ground, the lid was flung open and the ghouls began their feeding frenzy. They growled and fought each other like wild dogs going after roadkill. Dieter captured all of it on video.

But he just had to get a video of himself against this grisly tableau. He stepped from behind the family mausoleum, knowing the ghouls were too engrossed in their feast to notice him. He pulled out his phone and composed the shot. Should he smile, or was that tacky? He decided to try it both smiling and somber-looking.

As he was taking the second video of himself, movement in the background of the shot caught his eye. It was the door opening on the mausoleum right behind him.

What the—

The crowd of ghouls poured out of the tomb and were upon him in an instant. He didn't even have time to scream.

THE GHOUL that called himself Omar Johnson when masquerading in human form, bashed the human's video camera and smartphone against the wall of the smaller mausoleum until they were shattered to pieces. Then he supervised the ghouls in returning the casket to its crypt in the main mausoleum and replacing the plate that covered the opening. It wasn't secure, but hopefully wouldn't fall off soon.

The videographer's carcass, what little of it there was, could remain on the ground. It would serve as a warning for humans not to prowl around in the cemetery at night.

Omar was larger and smarter than the other ghouls. He was the progeny of a demon and a ghoul, whereas most of the others were offspring of common ghouls. Possessing a greater intellect, as well as supernatural powers, cast Omar in his role as leader of the colony of ghouls in and around Jellyfish Beach. He didn't want this responsibility, but felt the obligation to accept it. Meanwhile, each week there were more ghouls joining the colony with more mouths to feed.

What was it about Florida? Why did everyone want to move here?

Matt's police scanner woke him at dawn.

"Code Five, Code Five. One victim. Jellyfish Beach Boulevard and Sixth Street. At the municipal cemetery."

Code Five meant a homicide. Matt imagined how many dead-person-found-in-cemetery jokes would be told this morning. But none of the cops who heard this call would expect, like Matt, that the homicide was committed by a ghoul. Or multiple ghouls, if Omar could be believed.

Matt made it to the cemetery quickly, just after the maintenance worker unlocked the gate so the first two police officers in their SUVs could drive in. Matt spotted the remains immediately. A passerby, probably an early-morning jogger, must have spotted them and called 911.

The carcass of the victim was draped atop a headstone near the fence. It was human and appeared to be male, and that was about all that was recognizable about it.

An officer Matt didn't recognize, a young guy not much more than a kid, vomited into a vase that held plastic flowers. The other cop, whom Matt had known since high school, greeted him with a nod but didn't say anything. He walked away, letting her stoically guard the scene until her supervisor and the medical examiner arrived.

An object deep in the cemetery caught his attention. He walked down an asphalt path toward the mausoleums and as he drew closer, he saw bloody clothing scattered about. Next to a small family mausoleum were the shattered pieces of a video camera and a phone.

Matt had a bad feeling.

He found the trousers of the victim behind the mausoleum. He was out of the view of the police officers and decided to violate a crime scene once again. The victim's wallet was in the rear pocket of the pants and Matt pulled it out with a pen. He saw the name on a credit card, then pushed the wallet back into the pocket.

The name on the card was Dieter Dufusdunder. The social media "influencer's" hunger for viral fame had taken a fatal turn. And Matt had lost a valuable source.

Dieter must have been there looking for ghouls but found more than he had bargained for. The smashed camera and phone were a sign that Dieter had shot some video of the ghouls and one of them was smart enough to destroy the evidence. That would probably be Omar Johnson, because the typical ghoul didn't seem very intelligent, based on Missy's description of the ones that came out of the sinkhole at her house.

Matt happened to glance at the plaque next to the door of the small mausoleum. It had the name of Omar Johnson and the years of his birth and death. Beside his name was that of Emelda Johnson, but the dates were blank. Three additional names, presumably their children, followed with blank dates.

This was Omar's burial place? Did his wife, Emelda, know that there was no Omar in here because a ghoul ate his body and went around looking like her dead husband?

The mausoleum seemed a bit odd, so Matt stepped back a few steps and studied it. Unlike the other small mausoleums, this one wasn't in a Classical style. This one looked like . . . a tiki hut? Yeah, the concrete roof was molded to look like a grass-thatch roof and the walls looked like bamboo poles.

Only in Florida would someone design their eternal resting place to look like a poolside party spot.

Just for the heck of it, Matt tried the door, two marble steps above the ground. It was metal and also molded in a bamboo pattern. The door was unlocked.

He *had* to take a look inside, but his recent encounter with Omar made him think twice. What if Omar was living in his mausoleum? Barging into his bedroom would leave Matt looking like what was left of Dufusdunder. His stomach curdled.

But he remembered that Omar only made appearances at night. Maybe he slept in here during the day like a vampire. Maybe he wasn't here at all. It would be a little too obvious for a monster to be living in a tomb with his name on it.

Matt glanced behind him to make sure no police were in sight and stepped inside. A small window in the door let in enough light to reveal a tiny foyer of sorts, with a marble bench for mourners. The bench faced a stone wall with six crypts behind it, three on the floor level and three above. Each was covered with a rectangular panel with a name plate. In the center of the top row, was the only one with a name engraved on it—Omar's.

The concrete panel of Omar's crypt wasn't as flush to the stone wall as the others. It was supported by a smaller inset panel that fit the crypt opening and he easily worked it loose.

The crypt was empty, of course. No urn or coffin filled its space. Instead, there was a large, rough hole in the bottom, toward the back, leading to the crypt below. Fighting his claustrophobia, Matt pulled himself headfirst into the empty crypt until he reached the hole. He shone his phone's flashlight downward to reveal the interior of the lower crypt, which also had a large opening in the bottom of it. Below that was complete darkness and the feeling of a large space. Moldy, earthy air drifted up from below.

This was the entrance to Ghoulville. Matt shuddered,

crawled out of the space, and slipped the panel back onto the crypt.

DETECTIVE AFFIRD HAD ARRIVED at the cemetery along with the forensics techs. Affird seemed exceptionally annoyed when he saw Matt sauntering down the path toward where the victim had been found.

"You're trespassing, Rosen," Affird said.

"No, I'm not." Matt gestured toward the front gates. "The cemetery is open."

"It's a crime scene. Get out of here."

"I think you're upset, detective, because the guy you think did the murder in the park has been in jail while two identical murders have taken place."

"Doesn't mean he didn't commit the first murder," Affird said. "There could be other . . . people like him doing this." He pointed to the lump beneath the yellow tarp draped over the gravestones.

Other werewolves, Affird most likely meant. Matt couldn't speak about werewolves and ghouls because no one would believe him. The exception was Affird, who couldn't mention the monsters because he didn't want anyone to know he believed in them.

"What about the video Roarke's attorney has?"

"It's the prosecutor's decision whether or not to drop the charges. It's not my call," Affird said, glaring at him from behind his dark shades. "What were you doing back there?"

"Just going for a stroll. You need to take a look near the first mausoleum. The victim's clothes are there and his video camera was smashed to pieces."

"Video camera?"

"Yeah," Matt said. "I think this might be the guy who took the video of the Flounder Park murder. The one he claimed he sent to you."

Affird shook his head. But his mood seemed to improve. He was the kind of cop who didn't approve of citizens with video cameras at inconvenient moments.

Affird and Omar had that in common.

23

MEN ARE PIGS

Missy answered her phone in the kitchen.

"We've got a problem," Matt said. He wasn't much for niceties.

"Worse than a ghoul problem?"

"It's the ghoul problem times ten. There's a big public event in Jellyfish Beach this weekend," Matt said. "I don't know how it could have escaped my notice until now. The Senior Pickleball Championship, topped off by the Papa Pickleball Exhibition."

"The Papa *what?*"

"Before the final match of the tournament, there are special matches with Hemingway lookalikes. The ones who competed in the lookalike contest down in Key West. It's a gimmick to drive more attendance at the pickleball tournament."

"I sure wouldn't want to miss that," Missy said with her best sarcasm.

"You're not understanding the danger. There will be hundreds more people in Jellyfish Beach for the tournament, and thousands of locals will turn out for the finals. All of them could be potential meals for ghouls."

"Oh my."

"Oh yes, and have you ever noticed what's next to the cemetery, just west of it on Jellyfish Beach Boulevard?"

"A city park."

"Yes," Matt said. "A park with several pickleball courts. That's where the tournament is being held."

"Oh my."

"Remember the videographer who had footage of the murder in Flounder Park? He was killed in the cemetery last night. By ghouls that live beneath the cemetery, I'm guessing. I would bet you that if any graves were exhumed, they'd find the corpses missing and ghouls sleeping there instead. They seem to have dug tunnels beneath the cemetery. I believe the tunnels connect with the water treatment plant across the street. That's why Omar had his suppliers drop off bodies from the funeral homes there. There are already tunnels below the plant for servicing the water mains."

"When we were there, I sensed some evil energy down below," Missy said. "With the ghouls coming out of the sinkhole at my house, they could be anywhere and everywhere beneath the town in the limestone fissures."

"I don't suppose there's anything in that spell book that can help?"

"It's going to take a while for me to make sense of Don Mateo's addendum, even with his ghost's help. But the talisman should give me extra power. Maybe enough that my repelling spell will drive the ghouls away from here."

"Okay. Let's do this," Matt said. "Can you meet me at the cemetery around midnight."

"I'll be there. Bring extra flashlights. And a sword."

"A sword?"

"Legend says ghouls can be killed with one sword blow. But if you hit them a second time, they'll be reanimated."

"I don't have a sword," Matt said.

"Then bring an ax."

"I live in an apartment in town. Why would I have an ax? Do *you* have an ax?"

"No. I don't chop wood. I do have an electric hedge trimmer. And a shovel. I'll bring the shovel," Missy said.

"The home-improvement stores are closed at this hour, so I can't buy an ax. I do have a baseball bat. I'll bring that," Matt said. "See you there."

Before she left, Missy searched her house for a better place to hide the grimoire. Not being a burglar, she didn't know which places were too obvious and should be avoided. Like the freezer. Or her lingerie drawer.

Brenda rubbed against her leg. And Missy got an idea. It was pretty gross, but that was exactly why it would lessen the chances of the book being found.

She sealed the book in a large Ziplock bag. Then, just in case, enclosed this in an even larger bag. Next, she scooped the day's waste from the two litter boxes the cats used. The one in the laundry room was more convenient for them and suffered the worst abuse, so she removed the clean litter and placed the liquid-proofed grimoire on the bottom underneath the plastic tray liner. Then she covered it with litter again.

Should she use a protection spell to guard it? No, hopefully the cat pee and poop would ward off intruders. Also, if Bob or another wizard came searching, they would immediately sense the spell. But she could use a grounding spell, a very simple bit of magick that grounds the charge of most searching spells and renders any object under the grounding invisible to the searching spell. The grounding spell, by its very nature, can't be detected.

She cast the spell, keeping it confined to the litter box. The smaller the area the less likely the lack of input would be noticed by the searcher. She realized she would have to move the grimoire to her bank's safe-deposit box as soon as she had the chance.

Next, she changed into old, dark-colored clothing, suitable for sweating and getting stained by ghoul goo. She stuffed the Red Dragon talisman into a tampon tube, to make it less likely to be found in case she was searched, and put it in her pocket. She also grabbed a few other charms and put a protection amulet around her neck. Just in case.

Grabbing a shovel from the garage, she went back inside, turned on the alarm and exited the front door. She locked it and headed for her rental car in the driveway.

Bob and his African-American friend were standing next to the car, barely illuminated by the front porch light. Bob's jeep was parked behind her rental.

"Dude! Good to see you," Bob said to her, grinning with malevolence.

His friend didn't say anything.

"Fancy meeting you here," Missy said.

"C'mon," Bob said, "you knew we would track you down."

"I guess. I just didn't expect it so soon."

"You stole my book."

"It's not yours. It belonged to my father. Is that why you killed him?"

Bob flinched. "I didn't kill him."

"I'm supposed to believe that?"

"I don't know who killed him. But he promised he would leave me the grimoire when he passed on."

"You're lying," Missy said. "He wrote me a letter saying the grimoire was stolen from him and he wanted me to find it."

"What is it the lawyers say, that possession is nine-tenths of the law? Well, the book was in my possession and you stole it."

"You're not very convincing, Bob. Do you mind leaving my property, or do I have to call the police?"

Missy pulled her phone from her back pocket. She unlocked the screen and then the phone promptly died. She couldn't get it to turn on, even though she was positive it was fully charged.

She looked at Bob and he nodded smugly.

"Sorry for frying your phone," he said. "Now will you let us in?"

She shook her head.

"Doug," Bob said in a low voice.

The large African-American man walked past Missy and tried the front door. It was locked, of course. So he simply yanked it open, destroying the door frame and popping the hinges. He leaned the door against the wall next to the gaping doorway.

"Bob has a strength-enhancing amulet around his neck," Bob said. "I use one, too, when I want to show off at the gym." As if the beer-bellied dude ever went to the gym.

The burglar alarm began its ear-splitting beeping.

"Turn off the alarm," Doug commanded Missy.

She shook her head.

Bob sighed, then waved his hand.

The alarm went silent. Doug went inside.

"Give me the grimoire now and save yourself a bunch of trouble," Bob said.

"It's not here," Missy replied with as much confidence as she could muster. "It's in my safe-deposit box at the bank."

"You're, like, the one who's totally unconvincing," Bob said.

He pushed her. "It takes hours of study to use that book, and you can't do that if it's locked up in the stupid bank. Now get inside."

"Don't touch me!"

He got behind her and pushed with both hands, forcing her up the front steps and into the foyer. Every single light had been turned on inside. Before she could do anything, her knees gave way and she landed on the tile, her arms barely having the strength to block her face from hitting the floor.

Her body went totally limp. She was paralyzed, lying on her stomach with her face to one side. What spell had Bob used on her?

Bob propped the broken front door in the doorway and stepped over her as if she were a discarded piece of clothing. He went into the living room where he looked around the furniture and closely studied the bookcase, reaching behind the books on each shelf. The hutch in the dining room, still damaged from the cyber-eel attack didn't take long to search. Then he disappeared into the kitchen.

The wooden scraping of drawers opening came from both the kitchen and her bedroom. The two men were searching manually for the grimoire. What a normal-human kind of approach. Pretty thuggish.

After almost an hour of hearing her home torn apart, Bob returned to the foyer.

"Okay, dude, where is it?"

"I told you it isn't here," she said, barely able to move her facial muscles to speak.

"And I told you I didn't believe you."

"Why aren't you using your magic to search for it?"

"I already did before we came into the house."

"You can't find it manually or magically. So why do you think it's here?"

"Because I know you're lying to me," he said in a dangerous tone of voice. "I have a good gut for detecting lies."

You have a big gut is what she wanted to say.

An unseen force lifted her from the floor. The sensation was like floating. Until her legs were violently yanked upwards and she was hanging upside down, suspended with her head about three feet above the tiles.

"I'm, like, not going to be a chill dude anymore," Bob said. He leaned against the wall where the living room met the foyer. His face was dark with anger. "I'm going to hurt you if you don't tell me where the book is."

Before she could answer, Bob's magic entered her head and she had the urge to blurt out the truth. It was a spell like the truth spell she used with men who didn't seem on the up-and-up during her rare dates. But this one seemed stronger. She tried to stop herself from saying something, but sheer willpower wasn't going to be enough.

To block his truth spell, she did a quick spell of her own that she'd developed to help her telekinesis—her innate ability to move objects with her mind. This spell empowered her mind to focus with a laser-like intensity and to blank out everything else that could distract it. She focused on defying Bob and remaining silent.

He didn't like the fact that she wasn't talking.

"No pain, no gain, I guess," he said, and waved his hand sideways, palm facing her.

Crippling pain flared in her fingers, like she had slammed them in a car door. She gasped and tears ran up her face and into her hair. Her head ached with the accumulation of blood from hanging upside down.

"I'm not really a bad dude. I'm not. C'mon, you can't blame me for wanting my book back. The book has tons of potential and I'm so close to unlocking its secrets. I'd be, like, totally stoked to use even a tiny bit of its power. Tell me where it is."

"At the bank." Her voice was a horrid croaking sound.

Her fingers continued to throb with pain that didn't lessen at all. When Bob waved his hand again she braced herself. What's he doing now?

The shriek slipped from her mouth. She couldn't stop it. Her feet exploded with agony as if steel nails were being driven into them one by one. The only way she could handle it was to change the focus of her concentration spell and use it to block the sharp stabbing in her feet and the excruciating aching of her fingers.

In doing so, she noticed that Bob's truth spell had faded. He was consumed now only with wrenching the information out of her with torture. Perhaps that gave her an opportunity.

The laundry room's door to the garage opened and Doug walked into the hallway. There was no expression on his face at all when he saw Missy hanging upside-down in the foyer. He walked into the kitchen and the symphony of drawers scraping and cabinets banging started again.

She had a desperate idea. But it required moving her concentration away from blocking the pain. She took a deep breath and focused on the kitchen, on the drawer at the far end of the counter, beneath the small library of recipe books.

The unblocked pain in her fingers and feet walloped her. She cried out.

Trying to use her mind to open the drawer, she whispered the spell that helped her focus and blanked out everything else. The pain was still there, but she ignored it as if it were merely a hard rain beating upon the windows. She drew a mental image of the drawer and imagined it opening, slowly and quietly. With every drop of will she had, she inched the drawer open.

Rummaging through her memory of the drawer's contents, she dug through the unpaid bills and take-out menus, random pens and rubber bands, until she found it.

The red, pocket-sized vinyl folder that held the key to her safe-deposit box. The mental image of it was so real and detailed, it was as if she actually felt it in her hand as she lifted it from the drawer and placed it atop the counter. She gave it a slight sparkle of energy to make it more noticeable.

A few minutes later, Doug left the kitchen and approached Bob with the key folder in his giant hand.

"Hey, man," Doug said. "You didn't see this in the kitchen?"

"No. What is it?"

"Safe-deposit key. Maybe she's not lying, and the book really is there."

"Dude, you're falling for her B.S.?"

"It can't hurt to check it out. Bring her to the bank and make her open the box. If she's lying, we'll kill her."

"If I don't get the book, she's gonna die for sure."

Missy's pain abruptly ended. She extended her arms downward just in time to keep her head from bashing onto the floor when Bob released the spell that had held her suspended in the air. She fell into an undignified heap on the tiles.

"I need a break," Bob said. "Why don't you go to Mickey D's and bring back some chow. We've got time to kill before the banks open."

"Yeah, no prob," Doug said, handing the key folder to Bob before moving the broken front door aside and replacing it behind him. The jeep rumbled to life outside and drove off.

"I still don't believe you," Bob said to Missy. "I still think the book is here. And I'm going to work on you some more after I eat."

He walked away and the guest bathroom door closed. Missy forced herself to her feet and decided to flee.

The broken front door, no longer attached to anything, wouldn't open.

She yanked and kicked it, but it wouldn't budge, as if it had been nailed to the doorframe. She ran to the sliding door to the porch, but that wouldn't open either. The back door in the kitchen was inoperable, too, as was the door to the garage.

Bob had trapped her inside with a spell of some sort. Her heart sank. She went to her bedroom and locked herself inside, knowing that Bob could easily get in with his magic. He was more powerful than her, no question about it. That's why he was the Arch-Mage of San Marcos.

Maybe someday, with the help of the grimoire and the Red Dragon talisman, she would attain greater power. She'd never cared about having greater power, and had no need for it. Until tonight. Yeah, being tortured and held captive makes anyone crave the power to overcome an abusive jerk of a man.

A man who would most likely kill her before the day was done.

Bubba and Brenda crawled out from under the bed and hopped on top of it. She sat next to the cats, petting them and scratching their cheeks. It was four hours since she was supposed to meet Matt. Why hadn't he come here to see if she was okay? Wouldn't he be concerned that she didn't show up and wasn't answering her phone? He acted like he was into her beyond their friendship, but this wasn't the way to show it.

She had another four hours to endure before her bank opened and her lie about the safe-deposit box would be revealed. Her only hope was to get a bank employee to call the police and save her.

She fought the urge to cry. The Red Dragon talisman was still in her pocket, hidden inside the tampon tube. She placed her hand on it and thought about Ronnie, the young dragon with a broken wing she had rescued from the Everglades and nursed to health in her garage. She'd had to fight many battles to save him from evil actors who wanted him dead.

Ronnie, can you hear me? she asked in her thoughts, hoping he'd reply telepathically like he was able to do. *Ronnie, I need your help. Please save me from these men who want to kill me.*

The talisman vibrated and a surge of power flowed into her hand and up her arm.

Wow, she thought, this thing has more power than I had imagined. If I could only figure out how to use it.

The rumble of the jeep returned to the driveway and soon the voices of the two men came from the kitchen.

"I hope you guys left some smelly poops in the litter box," she said to her feline friends. "That has to be the only place these pigs haven't searched."

Brenda meowed, as if to say, "Yes, I did." And then Missy waited for the mage to come and torture her more.

24

EYE IN THE SKY

The News 3 Eye in the Sky Chopper began its morning rush hour flight above I-95. It wasn't dawn yet, so all that was visible to pilot Quentin Brill were streams of headlights and the pools of arc sodium floodlights above the roadway. Even at this early hour, there was lots of traffic on I-95. There always was traffic on I-95. It was worse this time of year during the Season, but Quentin never understood why an influx of seniors and tourists would make the roads more crowded at 5:30 a.m. Why the heck were they awake at this hour and driving with all the commuters?

Quentin found this part of his job boring, and much preferred covering news events like hovering over police manhunts, shoppers stampeding on Black Friday, and roads blocked by alligators. That was the kind of stuff that local news was built for. But it wasn't frequent enough to justify the cost of him and the helicopter. The twice-daily rush hour traffic reports were his bread and butter. For as long as they didn't replace him with a drone. The only reason they hadn't was the publicity factor of a loud helicopter with a giant "News 3" painted on it.

His radar picked up a large aircraft in front of him. Channel 7 wasn't supposed to have their chopper in this area. It was reserved for him for safety reasons. Was it a police aircraft?

He radioed air traffic control.

"Negative," the controller said, "we have no I.D. on that craft. It's descending to two thousand feet. Maintain your present altitude."

It was odd, but Quentin continued his route. North then south. Then north. Then south. Hover over a wreck or traffic jam. End the flight with a swing over the ocean for some pretty footage they'd use during the weather report.

The collision alarm blared.

The radio crackled. "Chopper 3, turn west, turn west!"

He yanked the stick left just as the large aircraft came into view ahead of him.

But it wasn't a helicopter. It wasn't an airplane.

It was a dragon. Flying south over I-95 right at him.

Quentin didn't have the chance to shift the camera toward the creature. But time would never erase the image in his memory of making brief eye contact with the dragon as he was banking left to avoid the collision.

The dragon seemed to be smiling.

25

BANK WITHDRAWALS

Missy rode shotgun as Bob drove his Jeep to the bank, Doug sitting behind her ready to pop her head off like a dandelion should she try to escape. At least, that's what he said he'd do. It was strange driving through Jellyfish Beach early on a weekday morning among people heading to work and appointments while she was heading for her eventual death once it was clear that she had lied and the grimoire was not in her safe-deposit box. She was also hungry, since her captors hadn't offered her any of their fast food. Didn't her growling stomach realize that it was not long for this world?

At least she felt a little better knowing that Matt had not abandoned her after all. When they left the house a few minutes ago, she had heard a strange whimpering sound coming from above. There, attached to the ceiling of the front porch, was Matt. He was wrapped in a cocoon of silky strands.

"Oh my, what did you do to him?" she had asked.

"This hound dog came sniffing around not long after we got

here," Bob explained. "He would have been a problem. He'll be okay. For now."

Before long, the Jeep ended up stuck behind a school bus with its flapping stop sign sticking out on the left side. A long line of adolescents waited to board. They were deliberately taking their time, casually climbing into the bus while others sauntered down the sidewalk toward the line, walking as slowly as possible.

Bob smacked the steering wheel with impatience.

"Damn punks with attitudes," he muttered.

The last few students were going overboard with their feigned insouciance, dragging their feet as they moved slowly toward the bus and mugging for their friends already aboard.

"Enough is enough," Bob said, cursing under his breath.

Or maybe it wasn't swear words he was saying. He waved his hand, palm-out, toward the students.

And like the retractable cord of a vacuum cleaner, the remaining adolescents zipped forward and were sucked into the bus in an instant.

"I love magic," Bob said as the school bus finally lurched forward.

Soon the bus turned off into a side street and the Jeep was tooling along into a commercial district. The bank appeared, a one-story, freestanding structure that didn't look particularly bank-like. Bob parked away from the building, facing the street, as if he wanted to be ready for a quick getaway.

He turned toward his passengers. "Okay, I'm going inside with you, Missy. Doug, you stand by the back door in case she gets any stupid ideas."

"Won't it look suspicious that a hostile surfer-dude is looming over me?" Missy asked. "Like I'm being forced to hand over something? They probably won't let you into the vault with me unless I say you're my husband."

"I'm not going to be looming over you. I'm just going to hang out in the waiting area, close enough to hear you in case you try to say something stupid. I don't have to go into the vault with you."

She nodded and he followed her inside. She didn't know how she was going to get out of this unless she could whisper something to the employee who retrieved her box for her.

In the foyer outside the lobby, an elderly woman was using an ATM machine. Missy recognized her as a resident of Seaweed Manor where Missy had several home-heath patients. The woman was a werewolf, presently in human form. She looked a little disheveled and had a leaf and twigs in her hair. It look liked she'd shifted last night, even though it wasn't a full moon yet. The woman growled angrily when she saw her account balance on the receipt.

The bank was busy, with people already lined up at the teller windows and others sitting in front of the loan officers' desks. Missy gave her name to the receptionist and she and Bob sat in the waiting area. She glanced around, trying to figure out escape routes if it came to that. Bob fiddled with his smartphone.

A skinny salesman with a combover approached them.

"Are you being helped?" he asked unctuously.

"Yes," Bob said.

"Can you spare a moment so I can tell you about our special, low interest rates on home-equity loans?"

"No," Bob said.

"The rates have never been this low and won't last," the man insisted.

Bob's eyes seemed to grow dark and he waved his hand

toward the salesman. The poor man slid backwards across the faux-granite floor like an empty cardboard box in the wind. His face went pale and he quickly scurried away.

"I'm not taking out any loans," Bob said. "Took me years just to pay off my credit cards." He returned to studying a social-media app on his phone, which seemed, to Missy, a bit odd for the Arch-Mage of San Marcos to be so obsessed with.

Something outside caught Missy's eye through the glass front of the bank.

A giant shadow swept across the parking lot. Then a column of fire poured downwards and hit Bob's Jeep. The vehicle was engulfed in flames.

Bob was too engrossed in his phone to notice. The elderly werewolf was making another go at an ATM transaction and didn't see the inferno either.

But Doug noticed. The giant man appeared in the windows running around the building toward the burning Jeep. What he hoped to accomplish, Missy had no idea.

When he was halfway through the parking lot, two green-ish-brown reptilian legs appeared in the window from above. They were covered with large scales and the feet had lethal-looking talons. Before he could dodge them, they grabbed Doug and plucked him, legs dangling, up into the air and out of Missy's view. No one in the bank gave any sign they'd noticed.

It was Ronnie! And my, how he'd grown since she last saw him.

Get the mage to go outside and I've got this, Ronnie's voice said in her head.

"Um, Bob? Looks like you have some electrical issues with your Jeep."

He finally looked up from his phone. His eyes went wide.

Then he shot up from his chair and raced outside. Missy followed, but stayed close to the bank.

When they reached the parking lot, Missy looked for Ronnie but didn't see him. Finally, she realized what appeared to be a vulture or hawk circling overhead was actually Ronnie at a very high altitude to avoid being recognized as a dragon by normal humans. She wondered what had happened to Doug. She realized she didn't want to know.

Bob was frantically chanting in some unknown language, sounding like a livestock auctioneer who was about to wet his pants. He waved his hands toward the Jeep and the fire slowly went out. But it was too late. The vehicle was a charred husk.

Then Bob looked up into the sky. A lizard missile was sweeping down toward him.

Bob pulled from his pocket a cluster of short rods, with a cord running through their cores. He fitted them together, end-to-end, like a folding blind-person's cane. He now had a wand about three feet long that he aimed upwards.

Balls of fire shot from the end of the wand like a Roman candle. Ronnie had to weave sharply in his dive to avoid them.

Wow, I want one of those, Missy thought.

But one of the fireballs hit Ronnie's chest. He screeched and banked suddenly veering away from the parking lot. Doug still dangled from Ronnie's talons, which wasn't safe for either of them. So Ronnie dropped Bob's soldier into an open dumpster behind the neighboring fast-foot restaurant before climbing and circling the bank.

Bob's wand launched a couple more fireballs, and then a torrent of dragonfire engulfed him from above. He screamed and rolled on the asphalt parking lot, but somehow used a fire-extinguishing spell to make the flames disappear before he suffered serious burns.

Bob returned to his feet, his T-shirt and hair singed, but otherwise still able to fight.

Ronnie swooped in low and Bob ducked. Just as the dragon was passing above the mage, Ronnie swept his tail and knocked Bob into the air. The mage sailed across the parking lot and landed on a BMW, setting the alarm off.

Missy was becoming worried that this supernatural battle would attract attention from normal humans. Especially the wrong normal humans—the police. Fortunately, the car alarm finally ceased.

Bob pulled himself off the shattered rear window of the luxury car and searched the sky for his foe. He was bruised and bleeding but nowhere near being defeated. Ronnie must have realized the same thing and had ascended to a high altitude that was probably out of range of the fireballs. Missy could barely see his tiny shape circling above, and Bob seemed unable to locate him yet.

The elderly werewolf finally left the ATM, still growling over the experience. As she walked into the parking lot, she saw Missy.

"Hello," the woman said. "Aren't you the nurse who comes to Seaweed Manor?"

"Yes. I'm Missy."

"I think I have fleas again. Do you know of a good flea shampoo that won't hurt my skin when I'm in human form?"

"Yes, but you'd need a prescription," Missy said, keeping an eye on what Bob was up to. "My advice would be to get an over-the-counter flea and tick shampoo for dogs and use it when you shift into wolf form."

"Oh, never thought of that. I hate getting a bath when I'm a wolf."

"It's really the best way to get rid of the fleas."

A stream of dragonfire crashed into the parking lot behind the woman, just missing Bob.

"Thank you, Missy." The woman continued walking to her car. Fortunately, it wasn't the BMW with the Bob-damage.

Another customer left the bank, a hipster dude with a huge beard, shaved head, and tight, expensive jeans. He was so engrossed in the screen of his phone that he didn't notice Bob shooting his Roman-candle wand into the sky. He got into the damaged BMW, began backing out of his spot, then stopped suddenly. He leaped out of the car and inspected the damage.

"Anyone see what happened?" the hipster called out to Bob and Missy.

"You can blame the dragon," Bob said in a threatening tone and moved toward the hipster. In Florida, one needs to avoid upsetting deranged strangers, so the man got back into his car and quickly drove off. He looked like he could afford good car insurance.

Magic crackled in the air like electricity. Bob was now slowly waving his palms toward the sky, unleashing something more powerful than his fireballs. Ronnie was in danger. It was long past time for Missy to intervene.

Again, she regretted not knowing offensive spells for attacking, but that's not what her personal magick was about. It was more about protecting and healing. About doing good. Oh, and also about retrieving the tiny things she dropped that rolled under the refrigerator with all the toys her cats shoved under there. You know, tasks impossible for normal humans.

But now she had no choice but try to stop Bob.

She remembered the Red Dragon talisman, hidden in the tampon tube inside her pocket. In addition to summoning dragons, it was supposed to increase the power of her magick. Time to give it a whirl.

A binding spell shouldn't be too harmful. She went through the normal ritual she used when she was away from home and couldn't employ a magic circle. She began by clearing her mind and entering into a meditative state while concentrating on the spell's intended result. She drew energy from the air around her and the earth beneath her feet, as well as from within herself. Finally, instead of grasping the power charm she always carried with her, she took hold of the heavy artillery—the Red Dragon.

The surge of power entering her was frightening. She aimed it at Bob and released it, relieved to rid her body of its dangerous potency.

Bob became rigid, his arms frozen straight and glued to his sides. He appeared to be having a seizure, but soon the shaking stopped, and he remained standing as still as a statue. Her binding spell had worked, even on a powerful mage.

But for how long? She wasn't sure what to do now. She could flee, but he'd eventually come for her again. How could she neutralize him and keep him from being a threat?

Yes, she could kill him now while he was helpless. She had killed a vampire before, but didn't believe she was capable of murdering a human. At least not a helpless one.

But this was a moot point, she realized, as the horrible pain from before returned to her fingers and feet. Bob had been immobilized but not rendered powerless.

She quickly attempted a protection spell to block his attack, but she couldn't concentrate enough. In agony, she staggered backwards until her shoulder hit the wall of the bank.

A pickup truck drove through the lot on its way to the drive-through window. The immobilized Bob-statue stood in its way. The truck stopped, and when the driver realized Bob wasn't moving, he opened his window and shouted, "Hey, do you mind?"

No answer from Bob-statue.

A large shadow swept across the parking lot.

Uh-oh, Missy thought.

Finally, the truck backed up a short distance and then moved forward around Bob and went around the side of the bank.

The truck had moved just in time. Because Ronnie was right behind it, flying low at a slow speed. He hovered above Bob, blotting out the sun, giant wings flapping and sending litter and dead palm fronds scattering across the asphalt. It was the first time Bob's face had registered fear.

No, Ronnie, Missy called to him in her head. *Don't burn—*

Ronnie's hind legs with their long talons plucked the mage from the parking lot and carried him up into the sky, off toward the east. Missy watched as he grew smaller, resembling an owl carrying a rodent away for its dinner. Soon he was just a speck and finally disappeared.

What are you going to do with him? she asked telepathically.

I haven't—OUCH!—decided. But if he keeps up these painful magic attacks on me, it won't be good for him.

Oh my, Missy thought.

There was nothing she could do for Bob. He deserved whatever fate befell him. In the meantime, she needed to get home and rescue Matt who was stuck to her front porch ceiling. She knew he had the hots for her, but it would be cruel to leave him hanging.

FOR WHOM THE GHOUL TOLLS

The night air was redolent of popcorn, hotdogs, and Bengay. The finals of the Senior Pickleball Championship drew about 5,000 spectators, which was huge for Jellyfish Beach. The city's annual Velvet-Art Fair, the Sea Turtle Soup Festival, and the Mobility Scooter Races paled in comparison. Tonight, the crowds thronged the municipal park next to the graveyard, filling the regular and temporary stands and spilling out into the softball field.

Missy and Matt watched the action from a shadowy area on Jellyfish Beach Boulevard, where the park met the cemetery. They worried they might look out of place with Missy carrying a crowbar and Matt an ax, but so far no one noticed them.

The Papa Pickleball Exhibition was underway. Its purpose was pre-event publicity and to warm up the crowd before the final match of the tournament. Three doubles matches were played simultaneously on adjacent courts, with twelve portly, out-of-shape Hemingway lookalikes flailing away desperately with their paddles, white beards dripping with sweat. They all wore white tennis shorts and a variety of shirts indicative of Ernest Hemingway, from fishing shirts, to safari vests, to Cuban guayaberas.

"They're not very good, these Hemingways," Missy said.

"I think they'd do better if this was a running of the bulls," Matt said. "Alas, there are no bulls in Jellyfish Beach."

"No. There might be a minotaur or two, though."

Matt looked at her to see if she was serious. She was half-serious. Her employer, Acceptance Home Care, handled many kinds of supernatural and legendary creatures as clients, so she wouldn't be surprised if she learned that half-man, half-bull seniors citizens had retired to Florida. Really, why not? Everyone and everything retired here. Including ghouls, apparently.

"I can't believe we've had no ghoul incidents so far," Matt said. "I was worried that not raiding them last night would mean some tournament-goers would get eaten."

"We still have to get through tonight," Missy said. "We should go down there soon." The thought of creeping through tunnels made her shiver.

"You know, I was thinking about that. What if us going down there made things worse? What if it flushed them out into the cemetery and the park? You know, like disturbing a beehive."

"Sounds like you're looking for an excuse to procrastinate."

"Well, we've sort of rushed into this without planning as much as we should," he said.

"You're the one who was in such a hurry to confront the problem. You're the one who was freaked out because of the tournament. And as far as planning, you're the one who expects my magick to solve this problem. I'm the one who had to plan how my magick can do this."

"Let's not bicker," Matt said. "Man, those hotdogs smell good. Want me to grab a couple? They'll give us strength before we go down there. If we decide to go down there after all."

"*If?* You mean you're chickening out?"

"No, I'm just saying there might be a more practical solution. If we took the time to plan carefully."

"I'm not in the mood for a hotdog," Missy said with a tone that ended the subject.

The first of the Hemingway lookalike matches ended with the two victorious partners doing a victory lap around the courts, clowning it up to the cheering crowds in the stands. One Papa took a detour and exited the park. He stopped on the sidewalk not far from Missy and Matt where he pulled out a cigarette and lit it.

"That guy should definitely not be smoking," Missy said. "He's older and overweight and that's just a horrible idea."

Indeed, this was one of the heaviest of the Hemingways. He was sweating profusely as he puffed on his cigarette. It didn't help that he wore a replica of the author's Basque fisherman's turtleneck. Not an appropriate garment for a warm night in Florida.

"Should I say something to him?" Missy asked. "As a nurse, I think I have—"

Something was wrong with the Hemingway. He struggled to remain standing. His foot appeared to be caught in a storm drain.

Just as Missy and Matt moved toward the man, a pair of ghoul arms reached up through the drain's opening and grabbed the Hemingway by both ankles. The Hemingway fell to the sidewalk and before Missy could blink, he disappeared into the drain.

"Okay, so much for planning," Missy said. "We've got to go

down there now before any more Hemingways or—God forbid
— kids get taken. Where's this entrance you were talking
about?"

"In the cemetery. You won't like it, but it definitely connects
with the ghouls' tunnels. This way."

Matt turned away from the park and jogged down the sidewalk alongside the cemetery fence. Missy followed, hoping no
police car drove by to see them on the run with an ax and
crowbar. Matt turned the corner and climbed over the gate. He
offered Missy a hand, but she didn't need it. They jogged down
a central path between rows of gravestones and markers until
they came to a group of small mausoleums.

"A mausoleum designed like a tiki hut? That's gross," Missy
said.

"It's the Florida style of death. Come on, we're going
inside."

"Are you serious?"

"The decor is more tasteful in there. Notice whose place
this is?"

He pointed to the name engraved above the door and on the
plaque beside it.

"Omar Johnson," Missy said with astonishment.

"Yeah, the real one was supposed to be laid to rest here
before he was eaten by the ghoul that took his name and
appearance."

He opened the door and closed it once they were both
inside. He turned on his headlamp, the small, flat flashlight
strapped to his forehead that allowed his hands to be free.
Missy turned on hers. It was creepy inside. Definitely no tiki
vibe in here.

There were six crypts and Matt removed the panel covering
the upper-middle one.

"I think a ghoul came out of here the night the photographer was killed," he said. "I found his camera and stuff right outside."

"We're going in there? What if we bump into the ghoul on his way out?"

He held up his ax. "Remember, one good whack."

"But not two, because that would bring them back to life."

"Exactly."

Matt peered into the open crypt, shining his headlamp downward. He stepped back.

"Ladies first," he said with a smile.

"No way, buddy. You're the tour guide."

Matt hesitated, then grabbed the upper ledge of the crypt, pulled himself up, and swung his legs inside. Missy moved to the opening and shone her light toward the far end of the crypt, to the hole on the bottom, to assist Matt.

He rolled onto his stomach and slid backwards, arching his back until his legs found the hole, and slipped in below the waist.

"It was nice knowing you," he said. "I wish we were able to spend more time together."

"Okay, knock it off," Missy said. "I'll be right behind you."

"My feet are on the floor of the lower crypt and I'm now stepping into the hole in the bottom of that one."

He slipped into the opening until he was suspended only by his elbows.

"There's nothing to support my feet," he said. "I don't know how deep the drop is."

He inched lower into the hole, holding himself up with his forearms and palms with only his head showing.

"I think I feel—"

He disappeared. A distant grunt rose from the hole.

"Are you okay?" she asked.

"I think so. Except for my ankle. Come on down, it's nice and cool in here."

Missy grasped the ledge atop the crypt and swung herself inside like Matt did, mimicking how he had positioned and lowered himself into the hole. She stood on the bottom of the lower crypt and then pushed past her fear to step into the hole and lower herself into the unknown.

Something grabbed her ankles and she gasped.

"It's me," Matt said from below. "Drop a little lower so you can stand on my shoulders and I'll help you down."

Once her feet were firmly on his shoulders, she felt more confident. He squatted and lowered her. She released her hold on the upper crypt and then rested her arms on the floor of the lower crypt.

"You're almost done," Matt said. "Hang on while I get up and help you to the ground."

"Aren't we already under the ground?"

"Whatever. Okay, I've got you."

He was hugging her hips. It wasn't entirely unpleasant. But this wasn't the time for thoughts like that.

He lowered her the rest of the way to the floor of whatever space they were in. Their headlamps revealed that it was a very small cavern of sorts. It was mostly earthen, with patches of rough-textured limestone showing through. Low openings of tunnels about five feet high were on opposite sides.

Matt was right, it was cooler down here. There was a rich odor of earth, but also a stale mustiness. She also caught a faint whiff of decaying flesh.

"I'm getting really claustrophobic," Matt said. "What's our plan?"

"We don't really have one."

"Good to know, good to know."

"Back to what we discussed after I peeled you off my front-porch roof, the talisman will magnify the power of my spells. I was planning on using a warding spell to repel the ghouls from this area."

"But why did we have to come down here" Matt asked, an edge to his voice.

"The spell wouldn't be as effective if I was above ground and didn't know where the ghouls were. I was hoping to find where they were concentrated. I thought I explained that."

Noises came from the tunnel that extended in what Missy assumed was a westward direction. Missy's heart stopped. Grunting, heavy breathing, scuffling upon dirt and rock. It was getting closer.

Missy recited a protection spell and clutched her normal power charm. She didn't need to risk using the talisman just yet with a spell that she was already adept at.

Matt hefted his ax. "Turn off your headlamp," he whispered. "Turn it back on when the ghoul comes in here."

Missy hoped the protection spell would prevent the monster from entering at all, but if he did, she and Matt should be safe. Hopefully.

The creature sounded large and not agile at all like the ghouls Missy had seen. She readied her crowbar.

The thing was here. It tried to enter the cave, but bounced off her invisible barrier.

"Dang," it said.

Missy and Matt clicked their headlamps on at the same instant.

The creature wasn't a ghoul. It was a Hemingway.

This wasn't the smoker Hemingway who was pulled into the storm drain. This Hemingway wore a tan fishing shirt and was a little less fat, with a ruddy complexion and larger white beard. He looked more like Santa Claus than Hemingway.

"Where am I?" he asked. "Who are you?"

"We're beneath the cemetery," Matt said. "How did you get down here?"

"I fell," the Hemingway said. "We finished our match and I was going to get a hotdog and the ground just gave way beneath me. I fell down a hole and some large animal ran over me."

"Oh no," Missy said. "The ghouls are going to be attacking the crowd in the park. We need to go up the tunnel Papa used."

"Actually, my name is Ralph."

Missy crouched, closed her eyes, and concentrated on the protection spell, murmuring adjustments to it.

"Okay, Ralph can come in here now," she said. "I narrowed my spell so that it is centered around us only."

"What are you talking about?" the Hemingway named Ralph asked.

"Never mind. You can stay here or hoist yourself up there, if you can." She pointed to the opening above them to the mausoleum.

Ralph looked at the opening dubiously. There was no way he was in enough shape to pull himself up there.

"I don't want to stay down here. I'll follow you," he said. "No one should be alone in their old age."

"Was that last part a Hemingway quote?" Matt asked.

"Yes," Ralph said proudly.

"Well, knock it off."

Ralph entered the cave and made room for Matt and Missy to enter the tunnel. She let Matt go first, because he had the ax. The Hemingway followed behind her.

"Wait one sec," Missy said. "I want to include Ralph in the protection spell."

They had to stoop uncomfortably to pass through the tunnel. Missy's head kept hitting protruding rocks.

Illuminated by Matt's headlamp, the tunnel made crazy twists and turns as it followed the natural pockets in the limestone stratus. The sound of three of them shuffling along the uneven dirt and rock floor echoed loudly. Even their breathing was loud and labored. The sound of dripping water followed them the entire way.

Matt stopped suddenly. "Listen," he whispered.

From ahead of them, around a bend in the tunnel, came strange vocalizations—a chittering mixed with high-pitched mewing. There were also grunts and growls of some sort of animals feeding. Something snapped. Was it a bone?

Rapid footsteps raced toward them and Missy braced, making sure her spell was at full power.

A ghoul rounded the tunnel bend, running on four limbs like an ape. Its eyes were savage and yellow, its mouth hung open at an impossible angle, baring long, needle-like teeth, wet and gleaming.

It hit their invisible protective bubble and staggered backwards. Matt stepped forward and swung his ax, cleaving the creature's shoulder and half its chest. It fell to the tunnel floor, twitched once, then went limp.

Missy's protection spell formed a membrane to keep danger out, but it was possible to break out of it from the inside, as Matt's ax had.

The stench of sulfur arose, filling the space, but quickly faded. The dead ghoul's body wilted, shrinking until it resembled the tiny desiccated carcass of a bird.

"Oh my," Missy said.

"Wow," Matt said.

"Dying is a very simple thing," said Ralph. "I've looked at death and really I know."

"No more Hemingway talk," Matt said.

"Let's keep moving," Missy said. "They're just ahead of us."

They rounded the bend and came upon another cavern with a hole in its roof.

Four ghouls were feeding on another Hemingway. The author lookalike must have fallen through the hole like Ralph did. The monsters were making quick work of the corpse, but it was still recognizable with its white beard and red, Pamplona-style beret.

The nearest ghoul looked up from its meal and saw the intruders. It charged at the group and, like before, bounced off the protective bubble before Matt dispatched it with his ax.

Its three comrades charged. Ralph let out a very un-Hemingway-like squeal.

The ghouls leaped in the air, each reaching for them with their four claw-tipped limbs. Max chopped one with his ax, Missy slammed her crowbar into the skull of the next one, and Matt yanked his ax free just in time to drive the ax handle into the forehead of the third. Their dead bodies decayed at unnatural speed.

"Okay, let's hope these were the only ones west of the cemetery, let's head back in the other direction," Missy said. She tried to hide her shaking hands from the others.

They headed back along the tunnel with Matt and his ax in front, Ralph behind him, and Missy guarding their rear with her crowbar.

She began preparing the warding spell to repel the ghouls en masse. She wished she had the luxury of not being on the move. Casting a major spell was so much easier when she was within a magick circle in a quiet room. Fortunately, following the others made it easier to pay less attention to the walking and more to the spell casting.

She wove together the threads of the spell, and drew the energy from inside herself, from the earth around her, and from the nearby ocean. To do so, she had to shift some power away from the protection spell. But once the warding spell was complete, they wouldn't need their bubble.

As they passed through the cavern below the mausoleum, Matt briefly glanced back at them, illuminating the group with his headlamp. Ralph moved like he was in a daze. Seeing the other Hemingway devoured must have been a great shock to him.

"Are you okay, Ralph?" Missy asked.

"All stories, if continued far enough, end in death," he said, moving into the eastward tunnel.

Matt groaned up ahead. "If I hear one more Hemingway—"

A current of displaced air poured from the tunnel, carrying the stench of sulfur and death. The sound of a stampede roared like a river.

And then the horde was upon them.

27

FLORIDA ALREADY HAS ENOUGH MONSTERS

The ghouls were so tightly packed in the tunnel that some crawled atop others making dirt from the roof rain down upon them. The creatures were chittering and yipping in excitement, their claws clicking and scratching upon the rock, and their sheer mass pushed the group of humans backwards. Matt frantically thrust his ax at them.

As Matt backed up, he pushed Ralph who stumbled and sent Missy falling onto her butt in the cavern.

"Missy!" Matt shouted, "stand next to me at the tunnel mouth. We can cut them down as they squeeze out."

The ghouls pushed ahead, fighting among each other, to get to the humans. Ralph fell to the floor and Missy stepped over him to position herself next to Matt. Only one ghoul at a time could exit the tunnel and Matt took each down with a single chop of the ax. When two ghouls attempted to squeeze out at once, Missy hit the one that Matt didn't.

But her blow with the crowbar didn't kill her ghoul. It dropped to the cavern floor, and then attempted to get up.

"Matt, get it! It's not dead," she yelled.

"But we can't strike it a second time."

"With the same weapon," she guessed. "Hit it with the ax!"

The ghoul went down, minus its head. Missy watched and waited. It didn't rise again.

"We can't do this all night," Matt said in between chopping ghouls. "Where's your magick?"

"Give me a moment to concentrate so I can finish the spell."

She stepped back from the mouth of the tunnel. She had to do this right or all three of them would be killed along with innocent people at the park and who knows how many more Hemingways. In the center of the cavern her headlamp showed a place where there was more dirt than limestone, so she quickly knelt and drew a circle around herself with the crowbar.

She closed her eyes and pictured the spell as she had woven it up to this point. She added to it and infused it with the power she had drawn from herself and the earth. Here, below ground, the earth energy was stronger. And she sensed a nearby ley line converging with a great amount of flowing water in a nearby water main from the treatment plant. That added even more energy.

The time had come. She recited the invocation, in this case lines of Latin verse. Then she grasped the Red Dragon talisman in her pocket.

Her mind exploded with light. The power surging through her flung her to her feet and she felt as if she were floating inches above the cavern floor.

"Go, you vile creatures!" she commanded in a booming voice that sounded like Darth Vader.

Matt looked at her wide-eyed, his mouth open in astonishment.

The next ghoul in line had the same expression as Matt, but its extra-large mouth made the effect more dramatic.

"Go! I banish all of you spawn of Hell from this place, from this city, from this state. Go forth from our lands!"

The ghouls disappeared into the tunnel.

The problem was, Ralph was gone, too. The monsters had taken the Hemingway with them.

"Follow me," Missy said to Matt. "And keep an eye out for Ralph."

"Heck yeah. Whatever you say. I'm not arguing with someone with a voice like that."

Missy plunged ahead into the tunnel. Her headlamp picked up the tuft of hair on the butt of the last ghoul scampering around a bend. She followed it, emboldened by her surging magick and righteous vengeance.

But after she rounded the bend, she stopped. The tunnel was wider now, and several smaller ones branched off from its sides, but also from its roof. The ones extending upward, she realized, must lead to graves.

The ghouls had been pillaging graves throughout the cemetery. Had they emptied the whole place of people who should have been resting in peace?

Matt, coming up behind her, said something about "greedy fiends," but she barely heard him. The power of the spell was making her ears buzz.

She realized she didn't need to clear every tunnel of the ghouls. The warding spell was powerful enough to repel them from a large radius around her. So she forged ahead down the main tunnel.

She wanted to find the ghoul's leader, the one who called himself Omar Johnson. He had to be defeated and banished forever. And she wanted to mess him up pretty badly in the process.

She continued along the tunnel in what she assumed was an eastward direction. Matt followed, peering into the side tunnels to watch out for ghouls and hopefully find Ralph. Soon the tunnel began narrowing and descending at a sharp angle. Her headlamp picked up something smooth and reddish.

It was a large pipe, most likely a water main. The tunnel ended at the pipe and merged into a cavity that extended alongside the pipe. This cavity appeared to be manmade and probably allowed workers access for repairs and maintenance. They were nearing the water treatment plant.

She checked to make sure Matt was still behind her, then stooped down to move through the constricted access cavity. Faint humming of machinery came from above. She passed beneath the opening of a vertical access shaft rising from the cavity that had ladder rungs on one side. As they moved along, it became warmer and the mechanical humming grew louder.

Then, a pool of light was visible up ahead. It came from a shaft like the one she had passed earlier. Its lid or manhole was open, allowing illumination from floodlights on the plant property to spill down here.

She stopped and waited for Matt to catch up.

"They had to have gone up there," she whispered. "And they could be waiting to ambush us."

"Can't you blast them with something?"

"My magick doesn't do stuff like that. But I do have something that will distract them enough so we can climb up there."

She worked at recreating the stink bomb spell she'd used on the ghouls at her house, the one that smelled like rotting meat. This time, she threw in some sulfur and added her memory of Ralph's body odor, thinking the fetid Hemingway stench would really excite the ghouls. After adding extra power to it from the talisman, she launched it upwards and out of the manhole toward the eastern edge of the water facility.

The clickety-snickety of hundreds of sets of claws running away across pavement arrived even before the odor of the stink bomb drifted down to her.

"Man, that's bad," Matt said, covering his nose. "How could a sweet person like you produce something as foul as that?"

"I never said I'm made of sugar and spice," Missy said, returning her focus to the warding spell. "Let's go up there."

Since the passage they were in had such a low ceiling, she easily reached the metal rungs of the vertical shaft and pulled herself up high enough to get her feet to the first rung. It only took about eight feet to reach the surface. She carefully poked her head out to eye level.

No ghouls were around. She was inside a large area surrounded by chain-link fencing covered with opaque plastic. There were several small outbuildings scattered around, clusters of pipes and valves, and lots of other equipment she couldn't identify. The area was paved in asphalt and illuminated by flood lights. The city's tall water tower stood in the distance bathed in streaks of yellow by spotlights pointed upwards.

The horde of ghouls flowed from around both sides of the base of the tower and rushed toward her.

They must have discovered the rotting meat was just an illusion and then smelled fresh, live humans nearby. There were more than she had imagined. Hundreds of them, maybe more than a thousand. How had so many of them existed beneath Jellyfish Beach without being discovered?

"Oh. My. God," Matt said with a quavering voice.

Missy's courage briefly waned as she watched the ghoul army loping toward her on all fours, giant mouths snapping in hunger. She considered calling Ronnie to her rescue. But even if he got here in time, the resulting fire and carnage would attract too much attention and go against her ethics. No, she would stick with her plan.

The ghouls were almost upon her, saliva flying from their mouths, their yellow eyes fixed upon her.

She bowed her head in concentration and recharged the warding spell with all the energy she could summon. Grasping the talisman in her pocket she felt the power singing throughout her body, tingling from her toes to her scalp. Again, she recited the Latin verse and then modern English words in her head:

I am the vessel. I am the compass. I am the lightning. I am the rod and scepter. I am the staff of righteousness.

She raised her fist with the talisman inside it.

The ghouls skidded to a halt only ten feet away.

"Go!" she shouted in the unnatural booming voice of a large, male opera baritone. "Leave this city now, I command you, by the power of the Red Dragon. You *must* obey me!"

It just so happened a freight train was approaching on the adjacent tracks of the Florida East Coast Railroad. She was often stuck in her car for several minutes at crossings while these seemingly endless trains passed.

As this one rumbled slowly northbound beside the water treatment plant, pulled by three locomotives, the ghouls swarmed it. They climbed into hopper cars filled with phosphorus from the mines south of Miami, onto flatcars carrying containers from the ports, and even into cars carrying automobiles from overseas. They clung to every available space on the train, much like migrants from Central America hitched rides north through Mexico on the trains they called "the Beast."

But these ghouls weren't fleeing poverty and violence. They

were fleeing Missy. And they were returning to where they had come from.

"I wonder where that train is going," Matt said. "I feel bad for the folks up there."

"Sorry, but Florida already has enough monsters. Let someone else take them."

Scuffling footsteps behind them made Missy's heart jump. She whipped her head around to find a middle-aged man in a yellow safety vest over a denim shirt approaching. Matt lowered his ax and tried unsuccessfully to hide it behind his back.

"You folks aren't allowed in here," the man said. "This area is restricted."

"We kind of stumbled in here by accident," Missy said with a very fake laugh.

The plant worker looked them up and down with piercing eyes.

"You need to come with me to fill out an incident report," he said.

"Why?" Matt asked.

"Because you're trespassing. If you give me a hard time, I'll call the cops. They'll want to know why you're carrying an ax. Let me have that."

He reached out and Matt allowed him to take it away.

"Follow me," the man said. He led them toward an office trailer near the fence.

Missy had been feeling relieved when the ghouls departed, but now was filled with uneasiness. It was like that time when she was a kid and she and a friend were caught by the janitor sneaking into the school when it was closed. She remembered dreading her parents and the principal coming down hard on her in retribution. What was tonight's trespassing on city property going to result in?

The worker stopped when they reached the trailer. He motioned for them to climb the three steps into the office.

That's when Missy saw the scar. The open collar of his button-down shirt revealed a glimpse of his chest. And in its center was the top of a massive incision running vertically down his chest and roughly stitched closed.

It wasn't the careful sutures after heart surgery. It was the crude closing of the body cavity after an autopsy, work that would be hidden beneath a funereal suit. It was the kind of scar found only on a dead person.

Or a ghoul who was adopting the appearance of the dead person he had eaten.

She didn't even think. Her hand instinctively yanked the Red Dragon talisman from her pocket and thrust it at the worker.

His eyes widened in horror and he moved away from her. She lunged and pushed the metal carving against his chest.

The Red Dragon glowed like metal pulled from a blacksmith's furnace. It didn't burn her hand but burrowed into the man's chest with a sizzling sound and wisps of smoke.

The man screamed in agony. Then, for an instant, she was looking at Omar Johnson's face, his mouth contorted by his pain.

Until he became his true self—a large, powerful, ancient ghoul. It grabbed her wrist with its claws. Yet she pushed harder and the energy surging through the talisman doubled. Her arm ached from its throbbing and her hair rose from her head.

"Get out of my town!" she shouted.

The ghoul didn't leave. Instead, it died. It went limp and

dropped like a rock to the asphalt. Quickly, it dried up and shrank like the other ghoul corpses had, leaving a mummy-like husk on the ground.

Matt kicked the husk and it skidded under the trailer.

"I don't know why I did that, but it felt good," he said. He glanced at her face. "Are you all right?"

The talisman had stopped glowing and its energy subsided. She returned it to her pocket and wondered why she felt so down. Was this the spent feeling after casting a difficult spell? Or did she feel badly about killing the ghoul?

"It was a monster that ate corpses and killed some living people in a very gruesome fashion," Matt said, as if reading her thoughts. "You shouldn't feel any regret at all."

"I'm a nurse," she said quietly.

"Not for creatures from Hell."

Something was clambering up the ladder of the shaft they had exited.

"Oh, my," Missy said. She didn't have any spell prepared since she had thought all the ghouls were gone.

Matt approached the manhole brandishing the ax.

A white-haired head popped out. It was the Hemingway, Ralph. His face was streaked with blood and his beard was missing. Missy and Matt helped pull him out onto the asphalt.

"I'm so happy you're alive," Missy said, checking him for injuries. She found some contusions and bite marks on his arms and legs. "We need to get you cleaned and full of antibiotics. Ghoul bites must be especially unsanitary."

"How did you escape?" Matt asked.

"The monsters were fighting over me as they dragged me through the tunnels. They became more frantic to escape what-ever magic your friend was making. So they dropped me and somehow I managed to crawl into an empty tunnel and hide. Where are they?"

"On their way to New Jersey," Matt said. "We won."

"Man is not made for defeat," the Hemingway quoted, looking each of them in the eyes. "A man can be destroyed but not defeated."

"Oh, jeez," Matt muttered.

28

BESTIAL EMBARRASSMENT

M issy arrived home exhausted. It was 3:30 a.m. and she was planning on taking a shower, having some tea and a light meal, and then sleeping for six days.

But when she pulled into her driveway, her headlights swung across something odd at the edge of her yard and the street. That was the spot where she normally put her recycling bins on Friday mornings and her yard waste on Tuesdays. Whatever it was, it had not been placed there by her.

She backed the car so the lights were shining on the spot.

It was the remains of several iguanas picked clean of their meat and placed in a neat pile.

It wasn't the right day for yard waste. And she hadn't killed and eaten the lizards. She knew of only one character who craved "chicken of the trees," as iguana meat is often called.

Ronnie. The dragon had feasted on the invasive lizards from her and her neighbors' yards when he had lived in her garage waiting for his broken wing to heal. He was definitely too big to crawl through her garage window anymore. So, where was he?

She found out after she went inside and opened the sliding glass door in the living room so the cats could go out onto the screened-in porch. They sprinted back inside after two seconds on the porch.

Probably because there was a dragon sitting in her backyard.

"Hi, Ronnie," she said. "Thanks for coming to my rescue yesterday."

"Anything for you, girl." He had a slight Southern accent, which used to throw her off because she would have expected an English accent for a dragon—and that was after getting over the fact that the dragon was speaking in the first place. But Ronnie didn't have an English accent because he wasn't from a Tolkien novel. He was from Florida.

"I'm afraid to hear your answer, but I have to ask what you did to the mage you defeated at the bank? Did you kill him?"

"I was going to. He was attacking me with magic that hurt like you-know-what. And when you called me for help last night, I knew you were in danger and in pain and he was hurting you. He deserved to be barbecued."

"Yeah, he did."

"But I also know you're squeamish about killing. So I dropped him in a pond. It looked like he survived the fall."

"That's good."

"But it wasn't exactly a pond," he said. "Well, sort of, but not a pond full of water."

"Okay?"

"When I decided I wasn't going to put up with him zapping me anymore, I happened to be flying over the county sewage treatment plant. I dropped him in a sewage pond. I had perfect aim, by the way. He landed right in the middle of it. You'd be impressed."

"I'm sure Bob wasn't impressed," Missy said. "He's going to come after me again."

"Then I'll be happy to kill the jerk."

"He's the Arch-Mage of San Marcos."

"Why should I care?"

"He's the head of a guild of wizards and witches. They'd all come after me if I had Bob killed. Even though he deserves it."

"You should talk to this guild and tell them what he did to you."

Ronnie was right. The guild had been formed to keep black magic out of San Marcos and even if Bob wasn't literally using black magic and demons, he was using magic for evil ends. The guild would presumably punish him for that. She should tell them for her own safety, at least.

And there was her suspicion that Bob murdered her father. She had no evidence, and Bob had denied it, of course. She resolved to find out more about how her father died.

"I'll follow your advice," she said. "And, again, I'm so grateful you saved me."

"Aw, you're embarrassing me. I'll always be in your debt for saving me from Moloch."

Moloch was the ancient, evil god that had tortured Missy before her magick, with the help of Ronnie's mother, had fought the god and sent him back to Hell.

"You are prophesied to be a savior of your species," Missy said. "It was the least I could do. Have you found out yet how, exactly, you're supposed to be a savior?"

Ronnie seemed chagrined. "Um, not yet. I've just been hunting and eating and growing larger. My mother said it's time to find a mate and be a responsible adult."

"Okay. Be sure to let me know when you find out."

"I will. And let me know when your mango tree has ripe fruit," Ronnie said. The dragon had an addiction for mangos that was not typical of his species. "I need to go now before the sun rises and your neighbors see me."

They said goodbye, and the dragon crouched then sprang into the air, beating his massive, leathery wings. Missy's palm trees thrashed in the displaced air as if they were going through a hurricane. Once Ronnie was above the trees and power lines, he turned to the west and soon became only a tiny speck passing across the stars.

Missy had a strong feeling she'd be seeing the dragon again someday, for a more consequential reason than sharing mangos.

HARRY DIALED Missy's number from a payphone using a prepaid card. She answered after three rings.

"It's Harry," he said.

"Harry! Have you been released? I was so worried about the full moon tonight."

"Yeah," he said. "So am I. It took them forever to do all the paperwork. Talk about cutting it close. Anyway, I need a ride home. Cynthia isn't answering her phone. She usually goes all spacey before moonrise. And there's no way I'm calling a cab tonight. I could shift at any moment now."

"Are you at the county jail?"

"No. They had a van drop me and some other released prisoners off in town, at the Greyhound bus station."

The bus station was located on the site of a rental-truck business not far from Doug's Discount Undertakers.

"I'll be there in about twenty minutes," she said.

"Okay," he said nervously. "When it's a full moon, our shifting is involuntary, you know. And we can't control the timing, either."

"Relax, I'll get there as soon as I can."

Harry hung up. The rental-truck office had a small room with chairs that doubled as the bus waiting area. Harry didn't want to hang out in here. A large African-American man covered in bandages sat in a plastic chair next to a middle-aged surfer dude who smelled like crap. Literally. He even had brown stains on his clothing. Harry was no neat freak, but this was ridiculous. He had to get out of the stinky room pronto.

With the sun setting, the air was cooler and pleasant. But Harry couldn't enjoy it. He paced back and forth in the parking lot where the trucks were kept. Man, he didn't want to be caught out in public when he shifted. All this trouble to get released would be a waste if he ended up in the mall naked again and got thrown back in jail.

Or, worse, he could be shot by the cops if they saw him in wolf form. A favorite conspiracy theory among the werewolves he knew was that a couple of Jellyfish Beach Police officers carried silver bullets that fit their service weapons. There was always someone who knew someone who knew a werewolf supposedly executed on the spot by the cops. That's why he kept to surfing when he shifted, or took his development's shuttle van to wooded property west of town where residents loped about in the wilderness without a worry in the world.

The darkness was more complete now. Where was Missy?

It would still be a while before the moon rose above the horizon, but the moon didn't have to be seen to exert its power over him.

Already, he was getting that twitchy feeling that meant the transformation was coming.

A chipper young woman approached him in the parking lot. She had closely cropped hair, a stud in her nose, and a red polo shirt with the rental-truck logo.

"Have you been helped, sir?" she asked.

"Just waiting for the bus," he lied.

"Well, have a nice trip. Are you planning on moving soon? We're having a special on all our van rentals."

"Nope, no plans."

"Now's a good time of year to clean out that garage and move the stuff you don't need that often to a storage space. All our customers get a discount at Hoarders' Storage."

"No thanks. I live in a condo."

"I'm just saying that our special is so good that if you have any friends who need help moving—"

"I don't have any friends." His twitching was getting really intense now. He was surprised she didn't notice.

"Oh, I'm sure that's not true," she said with a big smile. "Well, you have a nice night now."

He meant to say thanks, but only a growl came out.

A frown came over the young woman's face. "Are you okay, sir?"

He growled again, more loudly. He gave a friendly wave goodbye, but hair was sprouting across the back of his hand and his fingernails were growing into sharp, black claws. In fact, hair was sprouting all over his body and the grinding pain of his musculoskeletal transformation began, a feeling like having every joint get dislocated while every muscle burned.

The woman's frown turned into an open-mouthed silent scream.

Harry howled. Actually, it was more of a whine, but he

couldn't help it. This painful stage of the transformation always made him sound like a weak, little cub.

The woman was already a hundred feet away and sprinting at record speed. Harry couldn't stay out here in the open, but he couldn't hide, either, or Missy wouldn't be able to find him. And he had forgotten to ask her what car she drove.

The seams of his shirt were splitting open. And now his pants, too. Man, this was getting embarrassing.

The dude who bathed in crap stood up inside the waiting room and pointed at him through the plate-glass window. Right, like that dude had the right to gawk at someone else.

Harry trotted to the edge of the lot where the lighting wasn't as bright. He stood behind a rental truck, but he couldn't stay there because Missy wouldn't see him. While he was there, his transformation into wolf-man ran its course.

Just then, flashing police lights approached from far down the straight avenue.

The rental chick must have called the police, he realized. Oh, man, where was Missy?

After all those days in the county jail, his first instinct was to run in the opposite direction of the flashing lights. What else was he supposed to do? And when he shifted to wolf form, he wasn't very good at logical thinking. He could be cunning, but he was a slave to his impulses.

He loped on all fours out of the bus station/rental-truck property and cut through a fast-food restaurant parking lot, then behind a pawn shop. Next he came across a weird-looking funeral parlor. The building was built like a burger joint, but there was a hearse parked out front. The hearse's rear gate was open, and a worker was sliding a coffin from a cart into the back of the vehicle.

Harry raced toward the hearse. The worker saw him

coming, screamed, and disappeared into the building. The vehicle was already running, air conditioning streaming out when Harry yanked open the driver's door.

He hesitated for a moment. Driving a car seemed like an odd thing to do when he was in wolf form. He hadn't done it before, never having had the need or desire. But when he shifted, he was capable of being bipedal, and he retained his hand capabilities with opposable thumbs.

So why not?

He slipped into the seat. He also didn't grow a tail when he transformed, so nothing got in the way there. He slipped the hearse into drive and took off, back toward the bus station.

WHEN MISSY ARRIVED at the bus station, a bus was pulling out onto the main road, revealing a police car parked in front of the building.

Oh no, she thought. Did Harry shift already? Is he getting arrested? She knew that this would be exactly what Affird wanted and that Harry might not even make it to the jail alive.

She parked off to the side and scanned the property. There was no sign of Harry. Was he hiding among the parked trucks? She walked around the periphery of the lot, behind the row of trucks, behind the building. No Harry.

As she circled back around to the front, she passed a female employee speaking with a male cop writing on a pad.

"I'm asking you again," the cop pressed, "did this man threaten you?"

"No, but he was turning into a monster right in front of me."

"You told 911 he was trying to hurt you."

"He was going to," the woman said. "His hair was growing,

and his teeth were growing longer. Even his nails were growing."

"I see. And it was dark out at this point?"

"Look, there's plenty of light here at night."

"Uh-huh. I think I have everything I need."

"Aren't you going to do anything? He *growled* at me."

"I'm filing an incident report. Have a nice evening," the cop said, closing his pad.

Missy returned to her car and decided to drive up and down the street, on the slight chance she could spot Harry. She waited for a pause in traffic to pull out.

A hearse approached at high speed. She'd never seen a hearse driving more than forty miles an hour. As it passed, she noticed something odd about the driver.

It was a wolf.

The hearse hit a pothole and the open rear gate swung wide.

A coffin slipped out and hit the street. It bounced once, then flipped over, spilling its contents.

A corpse didn't fall out. Instead, dozens of coconuts poured out, bouncing all over the street.

Whoever was supposed to be in that coffin would eventually receive a proper burial, Missy reflected. There were no ghouls remaining in town to dine on this particular dearly departed.

She pulled out behind the hearse and floored it. Honking her horn, she waved her hand out the open window and hoped Harry saw her in the rearview window.

She also hoped the cop didn't see the speeding hearse.

Thankfully, the hearse stopped at the next red light. Even werewolves obey traffic laws. She stopped in the adjacent lane.

"Harry, Harry!" she shouted out the window.

The werewolf glanced over.

"Get in my car, quick," she said.

He jumped out of the hearse and got into her rental car. She'd never seen Harry up close in werewolf form before. She avoided her patients in Seaweed Manor during full moons and insisted they didn't voluntarily shift in her presence at other times. He was still recognizable despite his furry face and elongated jaws. His fur was graying, and his bushy white beard protruded from the surrounding fur.

"You're late," he growled.

"No, I'm not. You shifted too soon."

"I don't care anymore. I just want to get home. I'm so hungry I could eat a whole cow, bones and all."

She didn't doubt him one bit.

DESTINY'S MIDDLE-AGED CHILD

"My little flower, how thin you look! You must take home some of my sister's moussaka. We need to put some weight back on you. No man wants to take a wife who's a skeleton. To bear children you must have meat on your bones," Atropos said from behind the counter at Three Sisters Sewing and Alterations.

"I think I'm a little late in life to have children and I'm not looking for another husband just now." She placed a pair of black pants on the counter. "You're right, I've lost some weight and need these taken in a bit."

"Why are you not eating? Or are you ill?"

"I've been through a lot of stress lately. It's okay, I'll gain the weight back quickly, that's for sure. But until I do, these pants need to stop falling off."

"Lachesis, get out here," Atropos shouted in her gravelly, Greek-accented voice.

"I'm busy right now," came her sister's reply in a similar contralto.

"It's Missy. She needs some measurements. Don't make her wait."

"You can't rush a Fate," Lachesis grumbled, entering from a back room. She carried a tailor's tape measure and marking chalk. "Hello, sweetness. Come over here."

Missy walked past the counter and the dry-cleaning racks and handed her pants to Lachesis. She stepped on a small wooden platform while Lachesis measured her waist and thighs, then marked the pants with the chalk.

"I have a feeling this alteration will be portentous," the elderly goddess said. "Take a seat over there and I'll do the work while you wait."

"Oh, that's okay. I don't need to know my future right now."

"There's no time like the present to know your future. *Sit.*"

Missy obeyed and plopped down on an old wingback chair. Greek folk music with the tinny notes of a bouzouki poured from unseen speakers. She was nervous about what Lachesis would tell her. It wasn't as if the goddess were some roadside psychic about to give her vague platitudes. This was the real deal.

The minutes felt like hours until Lachesis finally emerged from the back room with Missy's pants.

She said, "You need to eat more, little one."

"That's my destiny? Eating more?"

"I can tell you your fate. It's predetermined and beyond your control. Your destiny can be shaped by your decisions."

"Okay, I understand."

"First, I see in the stitching that there will be more family in your future."

"What does that mean?" Missy asked. "I hope it doesn't mean I'm getting pregnant."

"You will know when you are meant to know."

Gee, thanks, Missy thought.

"That path to greatness we told you about before? You still have it," Lachesis continued. "But there are obstacles along that path. You will be tested more than once in days and years to come."

"Oh, my. More tests? You mean like the magick tests my father set up for me?"

"I mean challenges. You will have foes that will get in your way."

"And possibly cut short your path," Atropos made a dramatic snipping with her scissors. "Along with your life."

"Your decisions and effort will determine if your destiny is to overcome those obstacles," Lachesis said.

"I was hoping this conversation would be about happiness in my future."

"Ah, my little flower, for humans to be happy is entirely up to them, regardless of their fates," Atropos said. "Someone with a short life filled with misfortune could decide to be happy."

"And their life would then not seem so bad," her sister added.

Missy thanked the goddesses, gave them each a big hug, and took her new knowledge and altered pants with her.

AFTER MISSY LEFT THE FATES, she drove to Squid Tower for some patient visits, knowing she had a little time to kill before sunset.

"You're driving like a bat out of Hell! And I should know. I've seen Hell."

Missy jumped at least an inch off her seat. The ghost of Don Mateo was suddenly sitting in the passenger seat.

"What are you doing here? I thought you were bound to the grimoire."

"And to its owner," he said. "Meaning you."

"You're bound to me?"

"Yes. Wherever you go, I shall go."

"Even when I go to the bathroom?"

"My lady, I would never dishonor myself by appearing during private moments."

"You didn't have a problem appearing in my underwear."

"I have apologized for that already."

Missy stopped at a red light and glanced at the ghost. He looked a bit ridiculous in his wizard robe and turban. He also looked semi-transparent.

"You should wear your seatbelt," she said.

"My what?"

"Never mind. Dumb joke." She accelerated as the light turned green. "We need to talk about my father. I want to know how he died."

"I was wondering when you were going to ask me," he said.

"I've been rather busy since I got home from San Marcos. And you're not always available. You show up when you want to."

"If you call me, I shall come. I may be delayed, however. Sometimes I am . . . incapable of any thought or movement," he said sadly.

She understood. It was rare for a ghost to have as much consciousness as Don Mateo. Most are merely faint traces of energy.

"Can you tell me about my father's death?" she asked.

"Bob did not kill your father," Don Mateo said. "A demon did. Which one, I do not know. And I do not know if anyone conjured the demon or whether it acted on its own accord."

"A demon like the one that killed you?"

Don Mateo snorted. Or, rather, his ghost made a sound similar to a snort.

"I was killed by a low-level, worthless demon because I was careless. The demon that killed your father was one of the most powerful ones, a top lieutenant to Lucifer. That is all I know. But I will help you discover more."

"Do you know what happened to my birth mother?" she asked.

"Alas, I do not."

Missy stared ahead at the road feeling grim. Did she really need to know which demon killed her father? What good would that do? She was a nurse with patients that depended upon her. Why would she put her life at risk to pursue a super-powerful demon when she could make more of a difference helping others?

Even if the others were vampires, werewolves, and the like.

"I think I'll pass on tracking down the demon for now," she said. "First, I should search for my mother and see if she's still alive."

"You must follow your own destiny," Don Mateo said.

Boy, this ghost was smarter than he seemed.

THE END

AFTERWORD

GET A FREE E-BOOK

Sign up for my newsletter and get *Hangry as Hell*, a Freaky Florida novella, for free. It's available exclusively for members of my mailing list. If you join, you'll get news, fun articles, and lots of free book promotions, delivered only a couple of times a month. No spam at all, and you can unsubscribe at any time.

Sign up at wardparker.com

ENJOY THIS BOOK? PLEASE LEAVE A REVIEW

In the Amazon universe, the number of reviews readers leave can make or break a book. I would be very grateful if you could spend just a few minutes and write a fair and honest review. It can be as short or long as you wish. Just search for "Fate Is a Witch Ward Parker" on Amazon.com and click the link to leave a review. Thank you so much!

COMING NEXT IN FREAKY FLORIDA

Book 4: *Gnome Coming*

They're coming for you

Midlife witch Missy Mindle seriously bungled a spell. Now, garden gnomes throughout Jellyfish Beach, Florida, are becoming possessed by an evil force and are exacting retribution for the indignities they've suffered under humans. If you have a gnome, you'd better beware. Missy has to undo the fast-spreading spell and stop the surge of "accidental" human deaths. The problem is, her regular job is home-health nurse for elderly supernaturals, and she also has to solve the murder of one of her patients, a member of the Werewolf Women's Club. She has help from Matt, her reporter friend, but, like the gnomes, the werewolves are out for revenge.

And something is coming for her, too.

Get *Gnome Coming* at wardparker.com.

OTHER BOOKS IN FREAKY FLORIDA

Have you read Book 1, *Snowbirds of Prey*?

Retirement is deadly.

Centuries-old vampires who play pickleball. Aging werewolves who surf naked beneath the full moon. To survive, they must keep their identities secret, but all the dead humans popping up may spell their doom. Can Missy Mindle, midlife amateur witch, save them? Get *Snowbirds of Prey* at wardparker.com.

Or Book 2, *Invasive Species*?

Gators. Pythons. Iguanas.

Dragons?

Why not? It's Florida.

Missy, midlife amateur witch and nurse to elderly supernaturals, has two problems. First, she found a young, injured dragon in the Everglades with a price on its head. Second, her vampire patient Schwartz has disappeared after getting caught by Customs with werewolf blood. (It's like Viagra for vampires. Don't ask.) Order *Invasive Species* today at wardparker.com.

ABOUT THE AUTHOR

Ward is a Florida native and author of the Freaky Florida series, a romp through the Sunshine State with witches, vampires, werewolves, dragons, and other bizarre, mythical creatures such as #FloridaMan. He also pens the Zeke Adams Series of noir mysteries and The Teratologist Series of historical supernatural thrillers. Connect with him on social media with the links below. Twitter (@wardparker), Facebook (wardparker-author), Goodreads, or wardparker.com.

ALSO BY WARD PARKER

The Zeke Adams Florida-noir mystery series. You can buy *Pariah* at wardparker.com.

The Teratologist series of historical paranormal thrillers. Buy the first novel at wardparker.com.

"Gods and Reptiles," a Lovecraftian short story. Buy it at amazon.com.

"The Power Doctor," an historical witchcraft short story. Get it at amazon.com.

Made in the USA
Monee, IL
13 November 2020